Compromised Undercover

A Lexie Sarconi novel

G.K. Parks
and Elisa Archer

Copyright © 2015 Elisa Archer

Copyright © 2025 G.K. Parks

A Modus Operandi imprint

ISBN: 1942710496
ISBN-13: 978-1-942710-49-3

For my muse

ONE

Giving my badge a final glance, I stuck it in the drawer beside my gun. I was done for the night. Officer Lexie Sarconi was officially off duty. Detective Michael Riley was on his way to my place since I offered to make dinner for the two of us. He'd been preoccupied with work, so it was the least I could do.

He hadn't said much about whatever was going on, and since I'd been sent back to work patrol until the detective's exam results were posted, I had no insight into what was brewing with the gangs unit. Whatever it was was being kept under wraps. Rumors hadn't circulated, and my usual sources for station gossip, namely Officers Kemper and Hawking, didn't know about any major ops in play. As far as they knew, things were quiet with gangs, but I knew better. Unfortunately, I couldn't tell them that.

Whatever Michael was doing had to be intense. I'd barely seen him, and when I did, he didn't look or act like himself. The fun, talkative guy I knew had developed rough edges and a brooding demeanor.

As I scooped the last spoonful of mashed potatoes into the bowl, there was a knock at the door. I wiped my hands and answered, giving Michael a quizzical look. "Did you lose your key?"

"No, but knocking is more polite than barging in." His blue eyes bore holes through me. "Didn't you say we have boundary issues?"

"That's not what I meant."

He stepped inside, locking the door and checking the peephole before running a hand through his dark hair. He wore jeans, a black leather jacket, and a t-shirt. It was different from the usual attire he wore to work, but I wasn't complaining. However, I wasn't sure why he was acting like he was afraid he'd been followed. IAD wouldn't be that interested in flushing out our relationship. Half the department already knew, even if they pretended they didn't.

"Is everything okay?"

"Yeah." Michael smiled and gave me a kiss. "If you don't care when I let myself into your place, why did you say we have boundary issues?"

"Because you used my razor."

"I'll buy you a new one."

"It was meant as a joke. Jeez."

I tried to return to the kitchen, but he grabbed my arm and spun me around.

"I missed you," he rasped, kissing me harder.

His actions took my breath away, and I melted against him. One of his hands tangled in my hair while the other pressed against the small of my back. His mouth moved to my neck, but before he could move lower, the timer beeped. He jumped at the sound, his hand moving toward his holstered weapon.

"It's okay. The ding means dinner's ready." I'd never seen him so on edge before. "Are you sure you're all right?" I gave the front door an uneasy glance. "Is something going on I should know about?"

"Everything's fine. I'm just jumpy."

"Tough shift?"

"Not really." He forced a smile onto his face. "Give me a minute to get cleaned up. I'll meet you at the table." He headed for the bathroom.

"You better not touch my razor," I teased.

Despite what he said, something was wrong. However, if I pushed, we'd fight. And I didn't want that. Michael wanted separation of church and state or rather work and home. I'd never been particularly good at that, but right now, he needed a break from the job. So I'd give it to him. Or at least try.

Dinner was uneventful. Thankfully, Michael didn't shoot the steak or mashed potatoes when a second timer sounded. I tossed a few cautious looks in his direction, but he never met my eyes.

"Are you staying over tonight?" Taking the broiler pan to the sink, I turned on the water and began to scrub.

"I dunno."

"If you have something else to do, you don't have to stick around. I'll understand. You have a lot going on with work. I get it. It's fine."

"Lex, I want to be here."

"Are you sure about that? Maybe you should tell that to your face."

He reached around me and turned off the water. "What's wrong, honey?"

"I don't know. You tell me." I turned back to the dishes. *You said you weren't going to bring it up*, I reminded myself.

Michael's fingers brushed against my hair, but I shrugged away. He reached for my arm, grazing the scar that ran along my forearm. It wasn't fully healed and would continue to fade, but it was still a little sore and dark pink. I hated it, and so did Michael. It was a reminder of how quickly things could go south on a call. "Lexie, I can't."

Jerking away from his gentle touch, I went into the living room. "Why can't you? Don't you trust me?"

"Honey, I'm sorry, but I can't."

"Yeah, I know. You don't want to talk about work. But we're both cops. That's a huge part of our lives. We have to talk about it at some point, unless you expect us to always eat in silence. I know we haven't been dating that long, but I'd like to think we're still capable of conversation."

"We can have a conversation."

"Like what? How's the weather?" I hated it even as I said

it. I didn't want to fight with him. Yet, here we were again, even after I promised myself not to nag him about the job, but I'd been picking up on his anxiety and tension all night. I couldn't take it anymore.

He chuckled. "Have you seen any good movies lately?"

I sighed. "I don't know what's gotten into you." I gestured dramatically at his outfit. "But this isn't you. This isn't the Detective Michael Riley I know."

"Lex, it's not that I don't want to tell you. It's that I can't tell you."

I stopped what I was doing and dropped onto the couch, dumbfounded.

He sat on the coffee table, directly in front of me. "Listen, I've been assigned an undercover op, but it's very hush-hush. Only a handful of people know about it. I can't tell you anything else for everyone's safety."

"Don't you trust me?"

"Of course, I trust you. But I can't say anything. I have orders. Lives are on the line."

"I would never say anything to anyone. Do you think I'd do something that would jeopardize your safety?"

"No. Of course, you wouldn't." His gaze flicked to my scar again. "I swore after that happened that I would never do anything to endanger you. The less you know about my assignment, the safer you'll be."

"How does that make any sense?"

"It just does."

"So when you go on a shooting rampage the next time the kitchen timer dings, will you at least tell me to duck and cover first?"

"I'm a little jumpy. It happens, Lex. But your cooking isn't bad enough to warrant decimating the kitchen to avoid eating whatever you prepared."

"In that case, no dessert for you, and you can cook next time."

"But dessert's my favorite part." His eyes twinkled. "You do it so well."

"Too bad."

"Lex—"

"Forget it. I'm sorry I brought it up."

"Me too." He went back into the kitchen. A moment later, the sink turned on.

"You don't have to clean up. I got it. If you need to leave, you can. It's fine."

"I don't mind. You cooked. I clean. That's the rule, but the dessert discussion isn't over yet. And I hope you realize we aren't actually talking about dessert." He finished in the kitchen and returned, drying his hands on the towel. "I'm not going anywhere tonight, unless you don't want me here. But I'm done arguing." He pushed out his bottom lip and gave me big, sad puppy dog eyes, which looked ridiculously sexy on him. "Can we please make up now?"

A smile crept onto my face despite my best attempts to hold the scowl. "I don't know. I think you may have to work for it."

"That won't be a problem."

TWO

By the time I woke up the next morning, Michael was gone. Perhaps the honeymoon phase of our relationship was over. We'd been dating for over four months. Did that mean breakfast in bed and a goodbye kiss were no longer in the cards?

Grumbling to myself, I went into the bathroom and showered. As soon as I wiped the steam from the mirror, I was horrified and pissed. "I'm going to kill you." I stared at the hickey he'd left on my neck.

Michael had never marked me before. I cursed and huffed while digging through my makeup bag for concealer. Last night, after we'd made up and gone to sleep, he'd woken me around four a.m. Usually, he'd let me sleep, but there had been a frightening desperation to him. I thought maybe he had a nightmare, but he didn't want to talk. He just wanted me. Once we started kissing, he knew he had me. There was no need for a lasting reminder. That wasn't Michael, not the Michael I knew. Something was wrong.

I wasn't sure exactly what it was. But it had to do with work. For Michael to behave like this, I couldn't help but think he was afraid his next shift could be his last. Was he afraid we'd never see each other again?

Anxiety and dread filled me, but I pushed it aside. Michael said he'd been working undercover. That must have led to the personality shift and these new quirks. But our conversation about lives being at risk replayed through my mind. This was bad. And not knowing only made it worse.

After caking on the concealer and dressing for the day, I grabbed a travel mug and drove to the station. During roll call, I ignored the strange look my partner, Officer Kemper, kept giving me. Sure, I'd been out on sick leave for a while, but this was unnerving and a little rude.

I tugged on my collar, hoping to pull the uniform shirt higher on my neck, just in case. Dating other police officers wasn't exactly encouraged by the brass. Forms were required, and under most circumstances, the affected parties weren't allowed to be within the same chain of command. It was why Michael and I were keeping things quiet, even though everyone in gangs already knew. But as long as we didn't flaunt it in their faces, they had plausible deniability. Once I made detective, we'd disclose. That was the plan.

"Hear any good gossip?" I asked, hoping to derail Kemper's constant staring.

"Are you talking about the large-scale sting operation vice is planning?" he asked as we made our way to the front desk.

Today, we'd been assigned to answer phones and take statements. It was a calmer way to spend the day than patrolling. After our last big assignment, the brass had kept us indoors as much as possible. I wasn't sure if it was because we were waiting to hear about our potential promotions or if the powers that be thought it'd be best to avoid another incident.

"What sting operation?"

"Apparently, the mayor wants to shut down most of the city's sex trade. Vice has this huge multi-phase plan in the works. I was hoping you knew something about it."

"It's an election year. The mayor's platform is centered on cracking down on crime. It makes sense."

"That's not what I meant. You used to work vice. I figured you'd know what was going on, if they wanted help or were looking for volunteers. It'd be better than working a desk all week."

"You want to volunteer to assist vice?"

"Maybe. You used to work for that unit. It's gotta be more

fun than this, right?" He scrutinized me. "Did you volunteer? I bet you were the first person they asked."

"I didn't even know about it."

Kemper gave me a sideways look. "Are you yanking my chain?"

"No. This is the first I've heard about any of this. How did you even hear about it?"

"I heard Lieutenant Peterson talking to Sergeant Hunter. Vice needs extra officers to act as decoys. The other day, the sarge asked if the lieutenant could spare some people, but they never made an announcement or asked for volunteers. I figured they tapped whoever they wanted. Since you basically got to write your own ticket when you left vice, you'd be the first person they would ask. I was hoping you could put in a good word for me."

"Sorry, Kemper, but no one's said anything to me about it." I touched my scar. "Hopefully, this will be a nice deterrent from the brass asking if I'll go back to the skin squad." The last thing I wanted was to go undercover as a sex worker again. "If you want to do it that badly, why don't you ask Peterson about it? You have that college jock look. With enough hair gel and eyeliner, someone will want to tap that ass."

"Are you propositioning me? Because I'll give you the friends and family discount."

"Ugh," I cringed, "the family discount. What is wrong with you?" I nudged him in the ribs with my elbow, indicating I was poking fun. "That's sick, man."

"I didn't mean it like that." He reddened, realizing he'd shot his mouth off without thinking. "Ick. I don't want to think about it."

"Think about what?" Officer Hawking asked, joining us at the front desk.

"Kemper prostituting himself to friends and family," I said.

"I don't want to think about that either," Hawking agreed.

The next few hours flew by while we fielded phone calls. I'd been asked to frisk several female suspects and was forced to sit in on a couple of Detective Lightman's interrogations. Usually, Detective Samantha Preston was around to do that, which made me wonder if she was working with Michael. Were either of them at the station today?

"I heard you're interested in my offer," Lightman said once the room emptied. "The exam results should be posted later this week. Once they are, I'll have a desk cleared off for you."

"Is there anything I can do in the interim?" I asked.

"Sitting in on these interrogations is more than enough."

The questions he asked had to do with arms deals, but I didn't know who the players were that he had mentioned. He'd rambled through things so quickly, I didn't have time to take notes. When I tried, he told me not to. He didn't want me there to assist. He wanted me there to make the suspects feel more comfortable in the hopes that would convince them to talk. But they hadn't.

"I could—"

"No, Sarconi. You did plenty."

The sarcasm wasn't lost on me. No one he questioned had given up a name or a source. They played stupid, or they really didn't know.

Lightman didn't say anything else to me as we made our way down the corridor. Even though he invited me to join his team, we weren't particularly chummy. Most days, he barely tolerated me, so I didn't dare ask about Preston or Riley. Apparently, the entire unit was under a cone of silence.

When I returned to the front desk, Kemper was about to make a lunch run. After placing my order, I sat next to Hawking and watched as he filled out a form.

"Have you heard about any ongoing investigations with gangs?" I asked. "The suspects Lightman just questioned were being grilled about buyers and sources. Do we have any idea what that's about?"

"I don't know. I've seen Detective Devereaux scurrying in and out of the conference room all day. But you know gangs, they always play things close to the vest." He glanced at my scar. "Sometimes, too close."

"Agreed. I get there are security issues, but we're cops.

We're all on the same team. One of these calls or walk-ins could be relevant to whatever they're working on. It'd be nice if we got a heads-up."

"Most briefings are above our pay grade. Think about it for a second. There are only a handful of detectives and dozens of officers. Telling us about something secret would jeopardize the mission because it's more likely one of us would run our mouth since there are so many of us." He smiled. "Have you met your partner?"

"Kemper wouldn't blab on purpose."

"No, but get a few drinks in him and put some lovely lady within earshot and he'll spout out whatever comes to mind in order to impress her." He lowered his voice. "A lot of guys around here are like that."

"What about present company?"

"Some of us know better. But I can see with all these questions that you are more than ready to make detective. Have you heard anything yet?"

"Not yet. According to Lightman, the results are supposed to be posted sometime this week. He said he'd clear off a desk for me, but I doubt he has any insider knowledge on the rankings."

"Either way, let me know when I have to start calling you Detective Sarconi."

"Don't jinx me."

He grabbed a blank sheet of paper from the copier. "What kind of cake do you like?"

"Why?"

"It's a simple question."

"I like all cake."

"If you had to pick." He held the pen poised above the paper.

"Chocolate fudge."

"Okay." He jotted that down.

"Are you getting me a cake to celebrate?"

Hawking folded the paper and tucked it into his pocket. "Maybe I'll get you a cake if you bombed the exam and are stuck working patrol."

"Gee, thanks."

Before he could reply, the phone rang.

"Police," I answered. "How may I assist you?"

The caller had a few basic questions about procedure. Once that was settled, I took a break from the phones and ate my lunch. I was almost finished when Detective Preston came through the door. She looked stressed and overwhelmed, a little like the way Michael had looked last night. She glanced behind her a few times before shaking it off and making her way up the stairs. That wasn't good.

After lunch, I decided to throw caution to the wind and knocked on the open conference room door. Preston's eyes shot up, like a deer caught in headlights.

"What is it, Sarconi?"

"I wanted to see if you needed help with anything. Lightman had me sit in on a few interrogations earlier. It looks like you're a man short. Any idea where Riley is?"

She didn't say a word, but she knew exactly where Michael was and what he was doing. "Thanks, but we'll manage."

THREE

When I arrived home that night, I found a sticky note on my front door. *Forgive me.* I wasn't sure what to make of it. Obviously, Michael had dropped by to apologize. I wasn't even sure why he was apologizing. Granted, I had a mental list of possibilities, but he was too stubborn to admit to most of them. After going inside, I spotted a vase of red roses and a stuffed teddy bear.

"I used the key," Michael said from the kitchen. He stepped into the living room, wearing an apron tied around his waist and looking more like himself than he had in the last two weeks. "I figured I owed you dinner to make up for yesterday. I even have a few conversation topics picked out, but we should probably avoid politics and religion. We fought enough yesterday."

"You just want me to feel like an ass for all the names I called you."

"I don't remember you calling me names."

"You weren't here. You already left." I indicated my makeup covered neck. "Did you think that was funny?"

He wrapped his arms around me. "I got a little carried away." He kissed me gently. "If you want, you can mark me too. Then we'll be even."

"Just don't do it again." I pulled away so I could look him in the eye. "Why did you do it? You know how hard this would be to explain at work."

"I didn't mean to. I was in a weird headspace and needed to get lost in you for a while." He stepped away. "Honestly, I'm still in that headspace, but I wanted to see you. Sam said you were looking for me today."

"When did you see Preston? I was up and down the stairs all day. I don't remember seeing you. Were you even at the station today?"

"No. I was elsewhere."

"Where?"

"I was around. Checking on leads. Y'know, the usual. Come on, Lex. You know I can't talk about this. Why are you asking? Do you really want to go another round?" He returned to the kitchen and resumed stirring whatever was simmering on the stove. "Why don't you pour a glass of wine and relax? I heard the results of the detective's exam will be posted tomorrow. Are you nervous?"

"Tomorrow?"

"Yeah." He grinned. "You didn't know?"

"Lightman said they'd go up sometime this week. Not tomorrow." Butterflies took off in my stomach. "What if I didn't score high enough?"

"I'm sure you did great."

"Yeah, but what if I didn't? My brain got pretty scrambled. Maybe I botched it."

"You know you didn't. You had everything you needed to know memorized. You could recite the codes in your sleep. And you have the experience and instincts to back it. I bet your name's gonna be at the top of the list."

"What if it's not? What do we do? Do we disclose? Do we keep it a secret? Does it even matter? It won't be like we're working together, not with gangs keeping their ops so close to the vest."

He stroked my cheek. "Sweetheart, there's no point in worrying."

"Thanks." I ran my hand up his arm before returning to the living room. Despite the compliment, things were still awkward between us and now I had career anxieties to contend with too. "Are you sure you don't need help with dinner?"

"I'm positive."

"Are you saying that because you don't like my cooking?"

He laughed. "I don't believe there's a right answer to that question, so I'm pleading the fifth."

"We're not in court."

"Still taking the fifth. Go get changed. Dinner's almost ready."

When I returned, Michael was putting dinner on the table. He'd made chicken with mushrooms in a honey Dijon sauce over a bed of rice. It was fantastic.

"I thought you only knew how to make red sauce and pasta."

"Don't you mean gravy?" he asked, teasing me. Tonight, he was pulling out all the stops and making a real effort.

"You know that term is not appropriate under my roof." I winked, recalling our first date. I scooped more chicken onto my plate. "Seriously, where did you get this recipe?"

"It's something I came up with based on this thing my mom used to make at one of the restaurants where she worked. I could never get it to come out quite the same, but it's damn close."

"I'm guessing it's better."

The smile tugged at his lips. "I'm glad you like it." While he watched me eat, he asked about my day and did all he could to keep the conversation flowing. I wished he didn't have to try so hard. Things between us had never been this difficult, and I wondered if maybe the problem wasn't the job. Maybe it was us.

"I'll clean up," he said, scooping the plates off the table.

"Uh-uh. You know the rule."

"That only applies to when you cook." He settled behind the sink while I grabbed a towel to dry. "Assuming you aced the exam, these could be your last few shifts working with Kemper. I'm counting the hours until you're off the street and away from him. We should celebrate."

"Kemper's not that bad."

"You know how I feel about the guy."

"He learned from his mistakes."

"Has he? Really?"

Wanting to avoid a second argument in two days, I changed the subject. "Did you hear anything about vice having a large scale op in the works?"

"No, but I haven't been dialed into everything going on at the station."

"When's the last time you were even at the station?"

He gave me a look and handed me another plate to dry. That conversation was over. "Hey, do you want to watch a movie? We haven't had a movie night in weeks."

"You want to go out?"

Something flashed behind his eyes. "I thought we could stay in and stream something." He jerked his chin toward the living room. "See what you can find. Lady's choice."

Once I finished with the plate, I settled onto the couch and grabbed the remote. Nothing caught my eye. By the time Michael joined me, I'd stopped on the latest superhero movie. "Have you seen this?" I asked.

"No, but I wanted to."

"Should I make popcorn?"

"Only if you want it."

I shook my head. "I'm full."

He dimmed the lights and sat beside me. I snuggled against him and stared at the screen, but I wasn't focused on the movie. My concentration was shot, my brain twisting over whatever was going on between the two of us and the pending results of the detective's exam.

When the movie ended, Michael got up to stretch which made his t-shirt cling to his chest, accentuating his toned pecs and abdominals. I smiled. Michael Riley was one sexy beast.

"What are you looking at?" he asked.

"You."

"Did you change your mind about marking me as your territory?"

"Michael."

He shook his head. "I was joking. Maybe. Like I said earlier, weird headspace." For a moment, he looked sad. "I shouldn't have waited so long. This isn't fair to you."

"What are you talking about?" My stomach clenched. "Are you breaking up with me?"

"God, no." He held out his arms, beckoning me toward him for a hug. Once I was on my feet and safely in his arms, he gave me a tight squeeze. "Lex, I love you. None of what's going on has anything to do with you. It's all me."

"That sounds suspiciously like break-up lines. It's not you, it's me. Isn't that how it goes?" I pressed my lips against his shoulder. "You've been so different lately. If you've changed your mind. If—"

"No." He held me at arms' length so he could look into my eyes. "We are good. We're better than good. We're amazing. You are amazing."

"So what's the problem?"

"I can't talk about it, but working undercover these last couple of weeks has really screwed with me. My cover identity is a real asshole. Trust me when I say you wouldn't like him." He pulled me closer. "I've been trying not to bring that part home with me, but it's hard. When I'm alone at my place, it doesn't matter. I can stay in character, but around you, I'm not sure how well I've been succeeding. I would never hurt you, but if I was in my right mind, I wouldn't have left a love bite on your neck last night."

"Excuses, excuses." I wrapped my arms around him. At least we were finally talking.

Swallowing, he pulled away. "The reason I came over tonight is because I won't be around for a while. They're establishing a cover apartment for me. It should be a short-term assignment, but that means at least a few weeks, maybe more. I should have told you sooner the reason I came over tonight was to say goodbye."

"Okay." I struggled to appear indifferent, but I feared tears would fall. "How dangerous is it?"

"I'll be fine."

"That's not an answer."

He pressed his lips against mine. "I'll be back soon. I promise." He looked at the clock. "I have to go. Lightman wants to meet up tonight and go over everything before throwing me in the deep end."

"Be careful."

"You too. And when I get back, we'll celebrate your promotion the right way, Detective Sarconi."

FOUR

Hot tears stung my eyes. It was stupid. I was being stupid. Michael had an assignment. I needed to be understanding.

Wiping away the nonsensical, wayward tears, I gave the teddy bear he bought me a final hug and climbed out of bed. It was a new day. Time to pull it together.

On the nightstand was a velvet box I didn't remember seeing. Inside was a heart pendant. Blinking away a second round of pointless tears, I closed the box and put it back where it was.

"Damn you," I said to the empty room, a mix of emotions swirling through me.

Doing my best to ignore the voice in my head that said the trinket was a goodbye gift, I padded into the bathroom. After showering, I checked my phone to find a waiting voicemail message.

"I have to cut all communication, but before that happens, I want to tell you I love you, Lexie. Or rather, I guess I should say I love you, soon-to-be Detective Sarconi." He paused. "I'll see you soon, honey."

That was my Michael, not the undercover asshole he was pretending to be but the man that I had fallen for. A wave of relief washed over me. I smiled, spotting the flowers sitting on my kitchen table. At this rate, I'd need to find a therapist by the afternoon because I had turned into an emotional wreck. Pushing the feelings aside, I went to work.

"Hey, Lex, how are you?" Kemper asked when I emerged

from the locker room in uniform, ready to start my shift.

"Fine. Why?"

"You don't look right. Are you still experiencing symptoms from the concussion?"

I glared daggers at him. "I'm fine." I had heard his apology and excuses one too many times. He screwed up, and we were attacked. End of story.

"Are you sure? You're late. You're almost never late."

I looked at my watch. I had missed roll call. "Shit. Any idea what I'm doing this tour?"

"Ask Hawking. The lieutenant paired the two of you up today. I guess he figured you'd show eventually."

"What are you doing?"

"Foot patrol. I'll catch you later." He disappeared down the corridor.

I entered the squad room in search of my assigned partner and spotted Hawking clicking away at the keyboard. "Hey," I took a seat across from him, "what are we doing today?"

"Phones and walk-ins again." He looked annoyed. Fielding complaints and taking statements could get boring fast. It was a lot of paperwork for one day. "Have they posted the results yet?"

"I don't think so. I haven't looked, but I'm sure Kemper would have said something."

"I'm sure you passed. You drove us all crazy with your damn note cards." He assessed me carefully. "Is everything okay? It's not like you to miss roll call."

Was I really that punctual? "I had some things to deal with this morning."

"You should let the watch commander know you're here. I'll man the desk until you get back."

"Thanks."

"Sarconi," Lieutenant Peterson bellowed before I made it down the corridor, "come see me."

Obeying, I went into his office. "Sir?"

"How long did you work vice?"

I didn't like where this was going. "About two years, give or take."

"There's a shortage of personnel in their department

right now. Something happened with a raid. A lot of decoys were compromised. I don't know all the details, but since they have a big multi-department operation in the works, I'm sending my best uniforms over to help. Tomorrow, you'll report to them."

"Uniforms?" My heart sank. The lieutenant must have seen the results. He knew I hadn't ranked high enough to be promoted. What was I going to do now?

Peterson tried to hide his chuckle. "Is that a problem, Sarconi?"

"No, sir. I didn't realize I'd have to work vice again. After my transfer, I thought...I don't know."

"Are you refusing an assignment?"

"I guess not."

"It's only temporary. Give it a couple of days, and you'll be back here answering phones."

"Great."

"You don't want to answers phones either?"

I wanted to scream, possibly cry, but neither was appropriate for work. I'd already shed enough tears this morning. "Sir, have the results been posted?"

"Didn't you hear the announcement at roll call?"

"No, sir." Hawking hadn't mentioned an announcement. Neither had Kemper. So much for my friends having my back. "I missed roll call."

He rocked back in his chair and folded his hands over his stomach. He already knew I hadn't been at roll call. "You haven't gotten that detective's shield yet. Roll call isn't optional."

"No, sir."

He moved some things around on his desk. "The results will be posted at end of shift. It wouldn't be fair if I let you look at them early."

"No, sir, it wouldn't."

He winked at me. "Get back to work."

"Yes, sir."

Before I made it out the door, he said, "Sarconi, this temporary reassignment to vice won't last forever. It may even do you some good. You'll see."

Why did I want to be a cop? Today the universe had stuck

a cosmic kick me sign on my back. Michael was gone. It felt like my career was hanging by a thread, and to top it off, I had to go back to vice. If I didn't pass the exam, maybe I'd go into a different profession. I had some talent as a streetwalker, or at least that's what everyone around here thought. The pay wouldn't be bad. The work, well, that was another story.

Hawking took one look at me. "Uh-oh. What happened? Did you get written up?"

"Worse. I may have to become a sex worker."

"What?"

"The lieutenant said I have to report to vice tomorrow morning. Do you think I could ask Kemper to go in my place?"

He chuckled. "Maybe they need you to monitor the undercovers over the radio. Don't jump to conclusions. I know you think you're hot stuff, but there are other possibilities."

"With my luck, I doubt it."

"Well, let's hope you passed that exam because I don't think they send detectives to fill in as decoys." He jerked his chin toward Preston, who was making her way toward the door. "Why don't you ask if vice tried to recruit her too?"

"I'm sure she's too busy working on a gang bust to be bothered with anything else."

The phone rang, cutting off our conversation. Hawking answered while I watched Preston head out. She was pretty—tall, blonde, legs for miles, thin, and Michael's ex-girlfriend. Did that mean he thought I was prettier than her or she was prettier than me? Clearly, he didn't have a type since I was short with wavy brown hair. We were both thin, but somehow it looked more impressive on her. It was the tall factor. Tall always translated into sexy while short translated into cute. I must have been giving her the unintentional stink eye because she turned at the door, giving me a confused look. Quickly, I looked away as if I hadn't been assessing my rival.

She isn't your rival, I corrected. I liked to think of her as a role model, a kick-ass detective. Someone who didn't have to work for the skin squad. Why couldn't I be more like her and less like me? Maybe then, Michael and I wouldn't be having issues. Dammit, why was I having this insipid internal dialogue? They broke up for a reason. Their issues must have been worse than our issues, except I couldn't help but wonder if this was how it started, with strained conversation and kept secrets.

For the rest of the day, I fielded calls and walk-ins and tried not to think about the pending exam results, Michael, or what tomorrow would bring. Luckily, the work kept me busy until it didn't.

"Earth to Lexie," Hawking waved his hand in front of my face, "you still there? Or have you left orbit?"

"What?"

He pointed to his watch. "We have a half hour until shift ends. Did you finish that last report?"

"I'll get on it." I focused my attention on the computer screen.

As soon as I finished, I hit print, put the copy into a folder, and stuck it with the other pending casework. A woman had reported a diamond necklace missing from her hotel room. Hotel security hadn't bothered to investigate properly or call the police. She took matters into her own hands and reported it herself, so someone would have to perform a preliminary investigation and follow up. However, that person wouldn't be me.

After changing in the locker room, I checked to see if the results had been posted, but I didn't see them. Maybe it was better not to know, except not knowing would drive me crazy. I circled a few times, debating what I should do.

As I passed the roll call room, I noticed several fellow officers clustered together. I thought the results were going to be on the bulletin board out front, not in the roll call room. Of all the days to show up late.

"Hey, Lex," Kemper pointed, "good job."

He didn't say anything else as he brushed past me. For him to keep his mouth shut, I had to assume he hadn't gotten good news. Had he even taken the exam? I couldn't remember. He'd gone back and forth after the attack, wanting to take the blame, which he did. That alone would have screwed up his chances of scoring high enough on the performance portion.

The group clustered around the wall stepped aside, making a path for me. I scanned the list. My name and badge number were written beside number four. I wasn't at the top, but I was damn close. It wouldn't take long to get placed, especially since Detective Lightman had already tapped me for a spot in his unit.

A wave of dizziness hit me. I teetered backward until my butt bumped against one of the tables. Resting my hips there, I stared at the board, unsure about any of this. Today had been an emotional rollercoaster. I should have been elated. Instead, I was confused.

On autopilot, I drove home, entered my empty apartment, and looked around. The laundry had been piling up, so I dropped it into the washing machine, made dinner, put the clothes in the dryer, took out the trash, and flipped on the television. When the dryer buzzed, I folded the clothes and changed for bed, deciding to wear Michael's t-shirt. It was soft, oversized and, even freshly laundered, held the vaguest hint of his aftershave. More than anything I wanted to talk to him. I needed someone to help me make sense out of today.

Grabbing my cell phone, I called my best friend. "Hey, Amber."

She could detect my mood in one syllable. "What's wrong, Lexie? What happened?"

"I passed."

"You passed what?"

"The detective's exam. I mean it's not really pass or fail, but I scored high enough that I should be promoted soon."

"That's great." She paused. "Isn't that great? Why do you sound like that's not great?"

"Peterson reassigned me. I have to go back to vice tomorrow."

"But you were promoted."

"Yeah, but it doesn't go through automatically."

"That's stupid."

I snorted.

"Did you tell them that's stupid?" she asked.

"No. I want to keep my job."

"Do you?"

That was the million dollar question. "I love this job. At least, I used to."

"I know. I remember. That doesn't mean you can't change your mind."

"I want to be a detective, work investigations, and make a difference."

"It sounds like you'll be getting your wish soon. So what's the problem?"

I didn't want to say it, but Amber was one of the few people I could tell all my deep, dark secrets. "I'm scared. Last time, I got lucky. What if my luck runs out?"

"Have you talked to anyone about this?"

"I'm talking to you."

"No, Lex, I mean a professional."

"You're a hospital administrator. I'd consider you a professional."

She laughed. "Stop being a pain in the ass. You know what I mean."

"I spoke to the department shrink after the last incident. Ending up on a bad call is always a possibility. I've made my peace with that, I think." I tried to figure out exactly what the problem was. "That isn't what has me worried. I'm afraid someone will follow me home again, and vice occasionally runs up against some pretty scary offenders."

"You think a serial killer will follow you home?"

I stared at the ceiling. "Does that sound stupid?"

"If anyone else said it, I'd make fun of them, but it's you. So no, I don't think it sounds stupid. All I have to say is it better not happen."

"Agreed."

Amber sighed. "Where's Detective Ruggedly Handsome?"

"Away."

"Is that part of the reason we're riding around on the Lexie Sarconi anxiety train?"

I looked over at the teddy bear. "Maybe."

Amber laughed. "Do you remember when you swore off men and wanted to have nothing to do with any of them?"

"I should have stuck with that."

"Uh-oh. What did Riley do? I'll hunt the bastard down and kick his ass."

"He didn't do anything. He's working."

"You're worried about him too. Do you want to come over? We can watch movies and bitch about everything."

"I have an early morning."

"You could call in sick. I'll get you a doctor's note."

"I have to be there." More importantly, I couldn't let fear control my life. I'd been trained and battle tested. "I should get to bed. I'll need to be sharp tomorrow."

"Be careful. I love you."

"I love you too."

Snuggling under the covers, I went to sleep, dreading the next day. At five a.m., the sound of my own screams woke me. I flipped on the lights and reached into the nightstand for my Glock. The cold steel eased my fears. I took a few deep breaths, wiping the sweat off my face with the back of my hand.

The last time I worked vice, I'd been dressed as an escort. Skintight leather mini-dress, spike-heeled, thigh-high boots, and a collar. It was the fetish the serial killer had. It wasn't exactly original. Then again, neither was his method of killing. He liked to slice and dice in a manner similar to the notorious Jack the Ripper. Someone should have told him he was on the wrong side of the pond and lacked the proper accent.

A joint task force had been formed between homicide and vice. I volunteered since I fit the profile—petite brunette. The rest was makeup and props, but after a week and a half working the same few blocks, I convinced him to take the bait. I led him to the motel room we'd booked for the operation and listened to the radio chatter and instructions through my earpiece.

Before the officers could breach, he had snuck up behind me and thrown me onto the bed. He was on top of me, one hand fumbling beneath my dress while the blade slid down his sleeve. I had seen the light reflect off it. What ensued was a fight, followed by a quasi-negotiation between the homicide lieutenant and the killer. During the exchange, I'd used the distraction to put him in a Brazilian jujitsu hold until he was cuffed and taken away.

Unfortunately, my nightmare didn't have the same happy ending. My subconscious recreated the event without the added bonus of backup arriving. Instead, I was pinned to the bed, unable to move, knowing exactly what was about to happen.

Truth be told, after the ordeal with the serial killer, I'd lost my edge for vice. It's why I transferred and why I was having a hard time now. So how was I supposed to report to them in a few hours without losing my shit?

Hiding in my room wouldn't solve the problem, so I threw on some clothes, grabbed my gym bag, and headed for the station. After running a few miles and spending almost an hour taking out my frustration on the heavy bag and a fellow officer who wanted to spar, I showered and went to the firing range. After expelling a few magazines and decimating the target, I felt better. At least I did until I stepped out of the elevator.

FIVE

"Alessandra," Officer Jane Reeve called as soon as I set foot in vice, "where the hell have you been for the last few months?"

"Lexie," I growled. I hated it when people called me Alessandra, even if that's what was written on my birth certificate. "I've been around, working patrol mostly." I scanned the room. "Everything still looks the same."

"Everything is the same. At least you got out while you could. With the current shortage, no one's getting transferred to any other divisions."

"A lot of good it did since I'm back now." I rolled my eyes. "This better be temporary."

"Didn't I see your name near the top of the list?"

"Number four."

"Hey, that's my girl." Jane held up her hand for a high-five. "You didn't even tell me you planned to go the investigation route. Were you afraid I'd try to hitch my wagon to yours and outdo you?"

"Definitely." Jane had a few more years on the job than I did, but she'd been happy wearing the uniform and securing a permanent place with vice.

"In that case, they won't be able to keep you here, unless you get tapped and accept the offer."

"No way."

"What unit are you hoping to get assigned to?"

"Gangs."

"Really?" She cocked her head to the side. "I didn't see that one coming."

Sergeant Hunter stuck two fingers in his mouth and whistled, something he always did to get our attention. "People, let's get to it. We're burning daylight."

"I'll fill you in on everything later," I whispered to Jane.

A group of us non-vice fill-ins was ushered into a large conference room and asked to take a seat while the sergeant gave a briefing on the current operation he had in play. Vice hoped to execute a phased plan of attack to take down most of the gang-run prostitution rings, a few madams with their higher end escort services, and the lowlifes who traded sex for drugs or money, but the main objective was gaining intel on the newest player who had emerged on the scene.

"We don't know much about him," Sergeant Hunter said. "But we've been hearing whispers about the Shark. We suspect he may be deeply entrenched in human trafficking, but these are mostly rumors we've heard from informants and a few of the unlucky bastards we've busted. However, the rumors haven't stopped. The intel we've gathered suggests there could be some truth behind it, so while we institute this three-pronged assault to shut down the sex industry, we're also looking to learn as much as we can about the Shark."

"That's not much to go on," someone said.

"It sounds like we're chasing the boogeyman," someone else said. "Why do you need our help if you already have so many people working on this?"

"We performed a raid at a suspected brothel a couple of days ago," Hunter said. "We made plenty of arrests, but the reason we sent so many officers in was because our intel indicated the Shark would be there. He was not. When the raid became highly publicized, everyone was compromised."

I'd seen the social media posts and news coverage. The mayor used footage of the arrests, including the decoy officers and support teams who were present to announce his agenda to crack down on crime. For him, it was a win. For every compromised cop, it was a lose.

"That's why we're in the current bind and need additional manpower. The mayor wants to prove his plan has teeth, so we're getting pressured to make a show of pulling lowlifes off the street. Every department has something major in the works right now. Narcotics is busting suppliers and dragging in entry-level dealers, and we're collaring everyone we possibly can for solicitation. It's a numbers game. You," he scanned the room, "are going to be decoys for the first phase of our attack. As soon as you get the money, we'll have officers roll in and make the arrests. Do what you can to cultivate informants. Make friends with the sex workers and see what they can tell you about the Shark. See who you can turn. You've all been here long enough to know what threats to make and incentives to offer. We want the big fish, not the guppies, so the district attorney's office is willing to deal for promising information. Are there any questions?"

A few people asked about signaling to the officers or if we were using radio communication. It was the usual protocol. A couple of plainclothes officers were positioned close by. We'd signal and delay until the badges came knocking.

We were starting the first phase by busting johns and what I liked to call the non-unioned sex workers—the prostitutes pimping themselves out for cash or a fix. The second part of the operation would entail making more significant arrests of middle management. Lastly, if everything went smoothly, the sarge wanted to bring down the high-end escort services. Somewhere in that mix would be the intel we wanted on the Shark, assuming this unsub wasn't just another urban legend.

We had three weeks to crack down on the sex trade. The plan was to be executed in phases. If we were lucky, things would go well, and the larger prostitution rings would be shut down. However, if the op turned into a bust, we'd still make dozens of solicitation arrests. The mayor would look good either way. *Damn politicians*, I thought.

"Okay." The sergeant passed out assignments, making sure our groups consisted of five officers each, three decoys and two patrol officers per team. At least there was safety in numbers. "Go get undressed, and we'll put you on some corners."

"Just what I want to hear," I muttered.

"Sarconi, hang back a minute," Hunter said. When the

room cleared, he walked over to me and held out his hand. "It's good to see you. How have you been?"

"You should have asked me that yesterday, sir." I always liked Sgt. Hunter, even if I didn't like the job. "I never expected to be back here."

"Truthfully, you're the last person I expected to see walk through that door. I guess the timing was off. Congratulations on your upcoming promotion."

"Thank you, sir."

"Any chance you'd want to hang around here?"

"Not even if hell froze over."

He snorted. "This is only temporary. You know how we operate. Give me a few weeks, and we'll get you on your way." He smiled. "I heard you've been shaking things up with the gangs unit. You're such a troublemaker. We've missed that around here."

"It sounds like you've found enough trouble without me."

"I guess you rubbed off on the rest of us." He jerked his chin toward the door. "Your old partner insists you work together, so go get reacquainted with Reeve."

"Aye, sir."

Returning to the bullpen, I went to Jane's desk and took a seat in her chair. A few minutes later, she returned, sliding a manila folder toward me. Without a word, I picked it up and flipped through the pages. This was the intel vice had on the Shark.

So far, they didn't have much to go on. No identity or exactly how far his reach extended. But there was enough in the folder to indicate he wasn't a figment of someone's imagination or a scary story circulating on the streets.

"Has anyone checked with the FBI or the organized crime unit to make sure we aren't stumbling into something international or mafia related?" I asked.

"We've asked around. No one knows anything, and if they do, they're not telling us." Her sigh sounded more like a snarl. "I can't stand those know-it-alls with their suits and sunglasses. Pencil pushing morons are what they are." She grabbed the file out of my hands and pulled out a fax, placing it on the desk in front of me. "This was their suggestion for the Shark's profile."

I skimmed the page, seeing the rudimentary psychological and physical specifications. Profiles based on little more than conjecture were never accurate. I doubted this one was either. "Upper-middle class, Caucasian male with prior sexual offenses. That sounds like half the men in Congress."

Jane laughed. "Maybe we should start there."

"Well, they would have international contacts and connections with customs."

"Hey, you solved it already. Let's write our report and call it a day. We'll hit up the bar. My treat."

"If only it were that easy." I finished reading the file, but there wasn't much to go on. "Have the detectives made any progress?"

"Everything they know is in the file," Jane said. "That's why the entire unit's working on this, so we add whatever we discover as we go." She pointed to the whiteboard pinned to the wall. "That's everything we've learned from our contacts. Most of it hasn't been substantiated yet, but it's all we've got to go on."

I squinted at the whiteboard covered in notes and photos. "Do I have time to catch up before we hit the streets?"

"Absolutely. Go familiarize yourself with our current progress. I'll meet you in the locker room. I'll even pick out a nice outfit for you to wear tonight. I think I remember your size and style."

"No feather boas," I warned, "since they are a strangulation hazard, and I will use it to strangle you."

"Whatever you say, Lex. You know you missed me."

The board didn't provide as much valuable information as I would have liked. Everything had been covered by Sgt. Hunter in our briefing. Frankly, this was a department wide operation, designed to make everyone look good. However, it was doubtful an operation like this would have any lasting effect. Eventually, someone else would step in and fill the gap left by whatever arrests and crime rings we dismantled, but in the short term, it would do the city some good. Too bad there wasn't this level of trust and transparency in the gangs unit. Maybe then I'd have some idea where Michael was and what he was doing.

Brushing away my frustration, I met Jane in the locker room. She'd taken several outfits out of the vice wardrobe. Among the items were a hot pink miniskirt and matching bra with a see-through mesh tank and black stiletto heels. *Great.*

I stripped out of my police uniform, missing the annoyingly over-starched fabric as soon as I slipped into my new outfit. Most days, I hated the police uniform. Today, I would have paid money to keep it on.

"Terri Carver's going to decoy with us," Jane said, "and we have two plainclothes nearby to make the busts. We have a few rooms reserved at the usual fleabag motels, so that should help too. We're keeping as low of a profile as possible, so don't do anything to draw undue attention to yourself or the arresting officers."

"I know how this works."

"Well, you're probably rusty from responding to calls and flashing that shiny badge of yours. Don't do it this time. It'll get us all in trouble."

I dug through the makeup bag for concealer to cover my scar. "No matter what I do, I have a bad habit of finding trouble."

She stared at my scar while I applied the makeup. "Rough call?"

"Yeah." I glanced at her through the mirror's reflection. "Thanks for the get well balloons. I meant to say it sooner, but there was a lot going on."

"Don't worry about it. There's always a lot going on. We're cops. It comes with the territory. But that was the least I could do. I would have preferred to put a bullet in that bastard myself."

"Detective Riley took care of him." I met her eyes in the mirror. "I'm glad he showed up when he did." Before I could say anything else, Officer Terri Carver walked in. "Hey, Terri, nice dress. Don't you want to change into something from the vice closet?"

"Ha ha." She grinned. "Are you two finished primping? We're on the clock, and if we're the last team out, we'll get the worst location possible."

"You mean the best location possible," Jane and I said

simultaneously.

The worst location would have the fewest busts and the least amount of sleaze. We exchanged a look and laughed. It had been more than six months since we'd worked together, but it was like time had stood still. We were perfectly in sync, as usual. Perhaps there was one good thing about vice, and that was getting to work with Jane again.

Terri sighed. "Can we get this over with, please? Comments from the peanut gallery won't make this evening any more pleasant, and I bet Briggs we'd make more busts than his team. If we lose, I told him we'd fill out his reports for two weeks."

"Why in the world would you agree to that?" I asked.

"Because if I win, he and Jimenez promised they'd be the entertainment at my sister's bachelorette party," Terri said, earning a choked laugh from Jane.

"Fine," Jane said, "but I expect an invite to that party." Her gaze shifted to me momentarily. "Lex and I will be there in a sec." After Terri left, Jane scooted closer. "Are you okay working the corners?"

"Sure, I'm a cop. We do what we're told."

"Hey, you're talking to me. I know what happened, why you left vice to go back on patrol. If you can't hack it, let me know now. We have to have each other's backs out there."

"Have I ever lost my shit in the field?"

"No, but I remember you shaking like a leaf once that perp was cuffed. I was afraid you were going to go into shock or something."

"Since I'm such a liability, why'd you insist we work together?"

"Because you've always had my back. And you're good police. I'd take you in my corner any day, but I want to make sure you're up for this. If you're not, we'll talk to the sarge. You can work inside the van, coordinate, make the arrests, whatever."

"You sound like my boyfriend." I took a deep breath, burying my annoyance and anger. "I can handle it. I may not want to, but I can."

"Boyfriend? Since when?"

"What? I'm entitled to a life outside of work."

"Yeah, I guess." She gave me a sideways look. "How long has that been going on?"

"Not that long."

She studied me a while longer. "He's a doctor, isn't he? Amber finally set you up with someone."

"Hey, I didn't spend all that time in the hospital for nothing."

She snorted. "Good for you, Sarconi." But she grew serious after a moment. "Just know that you don't have to handle this if you don't want to. There's no reason why you have to torture yourself. If you get out there and want to pull the plug, say the word. I will go to Hunter and get you assigned to a support role if need be."

A part of me wanted to take her up on it. But I couldn't do that. I was a patrol officer, even if I was so close to getting my detective's shield I could practically touch it. But that didn't mean I deserved special treatment. It'd be okay. Jane had my back, even if I had just lied to her face. But that was for Michael's benefit as well as mine. That had nothing to do with our friendship or the assignment. Plus, it was a lie of omission, so it didn't completely count. Jane would forgive me for it.

"I'm fine. I'm sure no one wants to do this, so there's no reason why I should be exempt. Backup is a radio call away, and you and Terri are on the street with me. We're good to go." I went to the door and pushed against it. "Let's roll."

SIX

"Need a hand?" I purred as a forty-something guy who had been ogling me for the last ten minutes approached. He let out an uneasy chortle. His eyes swept over my spike heels, the super short hem of my miniskirt, and stopped on my present and perky cleavage that was hanging so far over my top I was afraid to bend over. "Maybe some head?"

His pupils dilated, and he reached into his pocket to fondle himself. *Perve.* He stared at me with dead eyes, studying every asset I had to offer before going back to the bus stop.

"Sicko's jerking himself off," Jane muttered. She was dressed in a similarly slinky outfit and was working the adjacent street. "I can't decide which is worse, the ones who are upfront about what they want or the ones looking for free samples to keep themselves warm."

"Ugh. It's no wonder I didn't date when I was working vice. The human race is depraved and disgusting."

"Think of it as a compliment. Someone's fantasizing about you." She shot a look at the bus stop. "I think he finished."

"Gag." I leaned against the wall and placed my right heel on the brick. Maybe it was sexy. Maybe it wasn't. I didn't care. I just wanted to go home and scrub off the nastiness.

A car pulled up, and Jane went to talk to the driver. She told him to park and she'd meet him in the lot. As she stepped away, the arresting officers went on alert, waiting for her signal.

I caught sight of Terri returning from the motel. Since she just made an arrest and Jane was about to, I should step up my game. *You got this, Lexie.* But my inner voice had doubts.

Terri stopped to bum a cigarette and struck up a conversation with her next mark. So far, we'd gotten the name of a local drug dealer who traded sexual favors for smack. Once we had proof, patrol would make the arrest. It wasn't much, not quite the big fish the brass wanted us to stop, but it was better than the guppies we'd been propositioning.

"Hey," I said to an actual sex worker, "are you having a slow night?"

She gave me a look. "Fucking cop."

"Who?" I looked around. "Where?"

"Quit the Barbarino act, honey." Her lip curled in disgust. "You're not a regular around here. That can mean only one thing."

"I'm new to the area."

She snorted. "Yeah, and you smell like bacon."

"Breakfast for dinner. I have to stop doing that."

She laughed, despite herself. "Y'know, I'd like you if you weren't out to get me."

"I'm not."

"Then what are you doing here?"

"Working, the same as you."

"Uh-huh."

I stared across the street. "Is there anyone I should watch out for? Predators? Pimps? Anyone dangerous I should avoid?"

"You'll figure it out soon enough." She gave me another look, a little less certain about my identity. "All I can say is you better not be costing me work."

"A girl's gotta eat, right?"

She gave me an uncertain look, unsure how I meant it. "Yeah."

After she left, I ventured a little farther from the corner. Since we were in the red light district, I passed a few other sex workers. When I spoke to them, they didn't seem as hostile, but they weren't helpful either. No one had anything to say about the Shark.

"Who's in charge around here? I'd like to pay my respects. Ask permission. Whatever."

"Keep to your own business and you'll be fine," one guy said before walking away.

No one else had anything useful to share either. Based on the suspicious looks and angry glares I received, I wasn't sure if they thought I was their competition or if they realized I was a cop. Either way, asking questions wouldn't get me anywhere.

"We're calling it," a voice said through the earpiece. "Meet at the rendezvous. We'll give you a lift back to the station."

Terri concluded her conversation and performed a one-eighty, heading back to the agreed upon pick-up. Jane was coming from a nearby parking garage and would take a side street. Being the farthest away, I took a deep breath, readjusted my skirt, and headed for the rendezvous at a fast clip, keeping my head down.

A passerby grabbed my arm. I jerked out of his grip.

"Look. Don't touch. Otherwise, that'll cost you," I said.

"Don't be like that, baby." He flashed me a roll of bills before tucking it back into his pocket. "I got the cash."

"How much?"

A lecherous grin lit up his face. "Why don't you reach in and pull it out for me?"

"I need the money up front."

He reached into his pocket and peeled off a handful of twenties. "Blow me."

"Whatever you say." I pulled him into the nearest dead end alley and reached for his belt. Once it was unfastened, he pressed his palm against the top of my head, attempting to force me to my knees. "Hang on. I don't want to get a run in my tights." That was the codeword we were using. The affirmative sounded in my earpiece. Officers were en route. I just needed to buy a couple of minutes. "Help a girl out and let me kneel on your jacket."

"Yeah, all right."

While his arms were stuck in his sleeves, I pulled his belt

free.

"I didn't realize you were that excited," he said. "You like to play it cool, huh?"

"Oh yeah, so cool." I grabbed his elbow and shoved him around, forcing him against the wall as his jacket fell to the ground. Quickly, I grabbed his other arm, leveraging it behind him while I bound his wrists together with the belt.

"I'm not paying extra for this."

I snorted. He'd pay, all right. "Sir, prostitution is illegal. You're under arrest. You have the right to remain silent." I Mirandized him while I waited for the uniforms to arrive.

Once they took over, I returned to the street and made my way to the rendezvous. My cover wasn't blown, which meant vice could keep me in play. I'd also made an arrest, which would keep the brass happy and keep Jane off my back about being gun shy when it came to vice operations.

"You always have to show us up," Jane teased as I climbed into the back of the waiting van. "You couldn't just meet at the pick-up. Instead, you had to make a final arrest."

"It was his fault. I told him I was closed for business, but he didn't take the hint."

While the team chatted on the way back to the station, I stared out the window. It was dark. Thick clouds had moved into the area and blocked the light from the stars. The impending storm would go perfectly with my mood.

After filling out paperwork on the arrests we made, the potential CIs to be cultivated, and updating the boards with the few tidbits I'd learned, I leaned back in the chair and rubbed my eyes. It had been a long day, the first of many to come. A small part of me wished I hadn't used all my sick days being sick. But I said I could do this. I needed to prove it to myself.

"Y'know, you didn't have to finish the paperwork tonight," Jane said.

"I like to know it's done, so it's one less thing to worry about in the morning."

"C'mon, let's grab a drink."

"Not tonight. The last thing I want is to go to a bar with the potential for some jackass to hit on me. I'd probably arrest him."

"That would be better than shooting him."

"That depends."

"True." She laughed. "How about we go across the street? It's a cop bar. You're way less likely to get hit on there."

"You'd think so, but past experience tells me otherwise."

"Really?" She steepled her fingers and tapped her fingertips together in a diabolical fashion. "Do tell."

"Maybe some other time. Right now, I'm going home and taking a very long, hot shower. Then I'm ordering pizza and watching cartoons or some family-friendly programming where married people sleep in separate beds until I fall asleep on the couch. I don't want to think about today or the things we heard and saw or the way we've been objectified as nothing more than real life sex toys. I don't know how actual sex workers do it. I hate that so many of them feel like they have no other choice or that they really don't have a choice."

"What I'm hearing is you've missed working vice."

"Yeah, even more than I miss having a root canal."

"Is that some new sex thing?"

"I hate you sometimes." I laughed at the stupidity of our conversation. "Until tomorrow?"

"Looks like it."

SEVEN

"Lexie," Kemper called when he spotted me on the stairs, "congratulations."

"Thanks."

"Yeah, well, you deserve it."

I stopped. "What are we talking about?"

"The detective's exam. You ranked fourth. That's freaking incredible. Do you have any idea how many people took the test?" He glanced around. "You practically have top pick. What are you going to choose?"

"Uh..."

He did his best to avoid the eye roll, but the sentiment came across loud and clear. "Gangs, right?"

"I dunno. I can't think beyond this thing I'm doing for vice."

"You mean they won't let you out of that now that you're more than a lowly patrol officer."

I plucked my badge from my belt. "Not according to this."

"But you could pull strings, right?"

"Bobby, what do you want?"

Kemper snickered. "I still love it when you call me that."

"It's your name."

"Yeah, but you never use it." Deciding this was a waste of time, I continued up the steps, hoping I wouldn't be late. However, Kemper didn't take the hint and fell into step beside me. "So," he waggled his eyebrows, "where did we land on you putting in a good word for me?"

I stopped on the landing. "You want to work vice?"

"Hell yeah. You get to go undercover. No uniform. No paperwork."

"There's still paperwork."

"Yeah, but not the mountain we get from working intake or fielding calls. Come on, please." He stuck out his bottom lip.

"Why do you want this so badly?"

"It'd look good. It'd add to my experiences. Maybe that could lead to something permanent."

I didn't have time to argue. "I'll see what I can do."

"Thanks, Lex. You're the best." He looked like he wanted to hug me, but I pushed my way through the door before he could try. I'd worked with Kemper long enough to know he wanted to be a hotshot, a hero. When things took a turn and we were both almost killed, I hoped he'd wisen up. After all, I had to stop Michael from knocking some sense into him, but now that his ribs had healed, he'd forgotten how to be smart.

"What's wrong?" Jane asked when I dropped into a chair beside her desk.

"Kemper wants to volunteer to assist. He was hoping I would put a good word in for him."

"Why don't you? Sgt. Hunter's desperate for decoys and support teams. I'm sure he'd appreciate having someone else to order around."

"I don't know."

Jane eyed me. "Kemper. He was your partner when that went down?" She nodded to the mark on my arm. "You don't trust him to have our backs?"

"I do." Well, at least that's what I'd told Michael, written in my reports, and said to every single IAD investigator who asked.

"Are you sure about that?"

"Vice scares me, and Kemper's a glory hog."

Jane gave me a knowing look. "There's your answer."

I considered that while I changed for another day of decoy work. Kemper considered it being undercover, but that's what Michael was doing, as far as I knew. What we were doing was more akin to painting a target on our backs.

We were bait. Plain and simple. And whenever someone moved in for a bite, we'd bite back.

On our way out, I spotted Detective Lightman. He was in the middle of a conversation with Lt. Peterson, but when Jane, Terri, and I moved past in short skirts and fishnets, Lightman stopped mid-sentence to watch us leave. Unlike some of our other colleagues who whistled or catcalled, earning themselves dirty looks and raised middle fingers, Lightman wasn't ogling.

He caught my eye, giving me a disconcerting look. It wasn't confusion or attraction. I'd almost consider it a question, but he should have known where I'd been assigned, unless Peterson had just given him the news.

As we drove to a different neighborhood from the one we'd visited yesterday, I finally realized what bothered me about the look on his face. The wheels were turning in his brain, as if he had been struck by an idea. Lightman had a plan for me. Given what I was wearing and my current assignment, I already knew I wouldn't like it.

"You good, Sarconi?" Officer Reynolds asked. He tapped his right ear. "Do you want to do another sound check since the last one was staticky?"

"Yeah." We went through sound check again. He heard me, but the static hadn't gone away. "Do you think the weather's interfering?" Dark clouds filled the sky. Low rumbles of thunder could be heard, along with the occasional flash of lightning, but the storm wasn't that close to us.

"It's possible. It could also be a loose connection or something." He checked the equipment in the van. "We can read you, so we should be set."

"I hope so."

He winked at me. "Knock 'em dead."

"I don't think the brass would appreciate that."

He laughed. "Probably not."

By the time I left the van, Jane and Terri had already selected the corners they wanted to work. So I adjusted the bustier I was wearing and called to everyone who went by, like a person working one of the kiosks in the mall. Idly, I wondered if any of these passersby could accuse us of harassment. It seemed likely. We were being a nuisance. While contemplating the elements necessary for entrapment to stick, a voice caught me by surprise.

"Hey."

I turned, unsure how someone had snuck up on me. I hadn't been that in my head. It's almost as if he'd come out of the building behind me or emerged from an alley. I glanced in that direction before hitting him with my most alluring smile. "Hi yourself." I did a little head nod and checked him out. "Looking to have a good time?"

The speaker was in his early thirties and nicely dressed. Either he was great at hiding the insane factor, or he was married. Then again, it took all kinds. He could be traveling, lonely, or any of a million other things. But something about his sudden appearance made the hairs at the back of my neck prickle.

He smiled but didn't respond.

"How about a little bang for your buck?" I asked.

"Anything I want?"

That type of question often indicated some sort of kink. I wondered what kind of fetish he had. His eyes hadn't settled on any specific part of my body, so I didn't know what to expect. He didn't appear to be armed, but that didn't mean he wasn't dangerous. "I wouldn't say anything, but most things are on the table for the right price." I winked at him. "Even me."

"Can I buy you a cup of coffee so we can talk?"

"A lot of guys like to talk, but they prefer to do it while my legs are behind my head or when I'm on my knees. Do you have a preference?"

"That's not talking."

"What do you want? The girlfriend experience? I can do that no problem, but it'll cost you."

He indicated the illuminated coffee shop sign two blocks away. "Let's sit down and discuss." He moved his hand, as if to place it against my lower back and guide me down the street, but he stopped before he made contact, as if he already knew the rules.

"While that sounds great and all, time's money."

"I'll buy you the coffee."

"I'm gonna need a little more than that."

"Well, when you put it that way," he stepped closer and put his hand on the wall next to my face, "maybe I should just cut to the chase."

A plainclothes officer lingered nearby, pretending to read a magazine. At times like this, I was relieved backup was so close. Hopefully, I'd shake that fear one of these days.

"I'd like to get to know you, to find out what you enjoy," he said.

"Whatever you want, baby. It's your money." I indicated the motel two doors down from the plainclothes officer. "If you're interested, I have a room."

He smiled. "I see how it is. You want to go somewhere more private before you tell me what you like and how you like it."

"Are you into dirty talk?"

He held the grin. "You'll see."

The warning claxons buzzed in the back of my brain. Something was off about this guy.

"Works for me. Let's go."

EIGHT

He didn't touch me. Instead, he followed half a step behind on my right, keeping me on the inside, away from traffic. Some could construe that as a chivalrous gesture. It was something Michael did subconsciously whenever we were out together. It had taken me a while to realize why he did it, and then another few weeks to stop thinking of it as ingrained misogyny, like he thought I was incapable of not wandering into traffic. But this guy wasn't doing it to keep me safe. He was doing it to make sure I couldn't get away.

When I passed the plainclothes officer, I coughed a few times. It wasn't the signal, but I wanted him to be aware of what was happening. Something told me I'd need backup.

"Right this way." I led the potential offender down the dimly lit hallway with its stained walls and patchy carpeting. Surveillance equipment was set up to monitor the two rooms we had rented. The other officer providing backup was in the room across the hall, monitoring the camera feeds. Pulling the key from between my breasts, I stuck it into the lock. "Shall we?"

The suspect followed me into the room and swatted my ass as I closed the door. I turned to him, painting a phony smile on my face. "Spanking costs extra, sweetie."

"Fine by me." He peered around the room, almost as if he suspected it might be a trap. "Do you mind if I..." He indicated the bathroom.

"I'm adding it to your time." I wasn't sure what he planned. Since I hadn't been able to frisk him, I had only been able to perform a visual assessment to determine if he was armed. For all I knew, he had a weapon concealed somewhere I wouldn't have noticed. A blade could have been strapped to his thigh or a twenty-two could be holstered at his ankle. The last thing I needed was for this guy to disappear from view. "And I get paid by the minute."

"Minute? Really?"

"Yeah, I'm that good."

He snorted in disbelief and went into the bathroom.

I looked around the room. We hadn't made many modifications when we set up because we didn't want to alert our potential suspects what was going to happen to them. We needed the element of surprise to catch them with their pants down, literally and figuratively, in order to push them for information in exchange for a deal.

No wonder I hated working vice. This entire operation felt sleazy, including our part in it.

The toilet flushed. A moment later, he emerged, wiping his hands on a towel. He tossed it onto the bathroom counter behind him and looked around the room again. "You're too pretty for a place like this."

"Thanks."

He took a seat at the table, the top covered in a grimy, sticky film. He sneered at it before turning his full attention back to me. "Is this really where you like to conduct business?"

"Do you want to do this or not?" I nodded to the nightstand beside the bed. "I need to see the money. Once I know you're not going to stiff me, we can get down to business." I crossed my arms over my chest. "If you're not interested, stop wasting my time. There are plenty of people who'd be more than happy to pay."

His tone changed, as did his demeanor. "Come here."

"Cash first."

"That's the last thing you need to worry about."

"Is that so?"

"Yeah." He stood, reaching into his pocket and pulling out his wallet. "I'm good for it." He tossed his wallet onto the bed and moved forward, pinning me between him and the wall. "Now tell me what you like."

"Whatever you want."

"That is what I want." His eyes were so dark they were nearly black. "Say it, slut."

Again, the elements of entrapment went through my mind—inducement and lack of predisposition. Saying anything without being asked or paid, which hadn't happened yet, could be construed as inducement. In fact, the guy said he wanted to get coffee and talk. Defense counsel could argue we met the burden of the second element since I lured him into the motel.

"Are you a lawyer?" I asked.

"Why? Do you get a lot of them around here?"

"You'd be surprised."

"Were you hoping for free legal advice." He moved closer. "I don't think that's the kind of help you need right now." He was so close we were breathing the same air. His chest brushed against mine with every inhale.

"Money first," I insisted, turning my head to the side.

He inhaled deeply and eased half a step backward. "Fine, we'll do it your way." He grabbed his wallet off the bed and tossed a hefty stack of bills onto the spread. "I want the rest of the night. Does that cover it?"

"It should. It looks like we're all set." That was the phrase we were using for today's op. Any minute, backup would be knocking on the door to educate this guy on the error of his ways.

He grinned and held out his hand. "In that case, it's time you answer my question."

I tried for flirty. "Whatever, baby."

"Do you like it rough?"

That question made the warning bells blare louder in my brain. "Sure."

He grabbed my shoulders, spun me around, and threw me face first onto the bed. He grabbed my ponytail and yanked me backward against him. Before I could do anything, he was on top of me, his fingers on the zipper of my skirt and his lips at my ear.

"Good, I'm glad we're in agreement." He bit my earlobe before flipping me onto my back.

I couldn't help the shudder that traveled through me.

Every instinct told me to fight back, but backup was on the way. Taking action would be premature. It'd blow my cover.

Taking both of my hands in his, he yanked my arms over my head and pressed them into the mattress before kissing me.

I jerked my head to the side. "Stop."

He tugged on my zipper. "You said whatever I wanted."

"And now I'm saying stop."

"Is this how you treat a paying customer?"

This asshole was nothing more than a predator. "Fine. I'll show you what I like."

He grinned. "That's more like it."

Kneeing him before he could unzip my skirt, I slid to the side and scrambled to get up. He reached for me, but I was faster than he was. I was halfway to the door when he tackled me.

Backup should have been here. Why weren't they coming in? Should I announce?

He was acting like this was a game, but his eyes said otherwise. He was a cat toying with a mouse before moving in for the kill. I rolled away from him, but he grabbed my ankle before I could make it to the door and dragged me toward him.

Memories from that night in the liquor store came to mind. Panic set in, my breathing becoming erratic and my vision blurring. Sucking in a breath, I forced myself to concentrate on the present. The past couldn't hurt me, but this guy could. And I'd be damned if I let that happen.

Since this deranged asshole wanted to fight, we'd fight. He pinned my wrists again. Something dangerous twinkled in his eyes. "You said spanking's extra. What about slapping?"

"Do you really wanna know what gets me off?"

The question caught him by surprise, causing his grip to loosen. "Tell me."

In one swift move, I shifted my hips and escaped his hold, courtesy of all that self-defense training they taught us at the academy. Locking out his arm, I twisted it around his back which would result in a dislocated shoulder or elbow if he didn't cooperate.

"Ooh, you're feisty," he said. "I knew you'd be fun."

Before I could announce and arrest him, the door burst open. "Police." The cop I passed earlier had his weapon out. "Miss, let the man go."

I wasn't sure what was happening. This was the gotcha. The part where we asked questions to gain compliance. Sure, it was important we keep our covers intact on the streets, but in a private room with a man who would be arrested, that should no longer be a concern. Someone had changed the play.

"He attacked me." I released the suspect while the other officer cuffed him. "He paid for services, but that does not give him the right to attack me. I didn't consent to that."

"You said you liked it rough, whatever I wanted," the man said.

"Prostitution is illegal." The officer who'd spoken to me went to the bed and picked up the man's wallet. "Jeff Stark," he turned back to the guy in cuffs, "we're going to arrest you for soliciting sex. You have the right to remain silent." He finished reading Stark his rights.

"What about her? She's the professional. She enticed me. She came on to me," Stark insisted.

Again, I wondered if he was a lawyer.

"Don't worry. We've been after this one for a while." The cop helped me up and forced me against the wall. After a quick pat down, he cuffed me.

What the hell's going on? I thought. Instead, I waited for him to read my rights. Once that was done, he told his partner to take Stark to the car and he'd call for another unit to pick me up. At least that would be the end of it.

"Sorry about that," he said once they were gone.

"It took you long enough." I rubbed my wrists the moment he took off the handcuffs. "What's going on?"

"I'm not entirely sure. Lt. Peterson said we needed to make sure you stayed in play."

"Just me or all the decoys?"

"You specifically." He examined the rumpled bedding. "Are you okay?"

I straightened my clothes and secured my zipper. "Yeah, but make sure you run Stark through the sex offender database. That one's a real winner. There's something off about him. Sexual assault is definitely a possibility, so let's see how many counts we can stick him with."

"Yes, ma'am." He paused, listening to something in his earpiece. "Terri needs an assist. Stay here until I get back."

"Go." Hopefully, she was having a better time than I was.

Disgusted and a little dizzy, I leaned against the doorframe and stared down the hallway, needing to see something besides the inside of that room. My hands were shaking, and my heart pounded in my ears. It was over, which meant I finally had the luxury of reacting instead of pretending what happened was a typical Thursday.

The only solace was Stark had picked an undercover cop instead of a pro. That made this worth it. Still, my backup took their sweet time. That couldn't happen again. Not to me. Not to any of us.

A moment later, I heard the all-clear in my ear. Terri was fine. Another offender had been apprehended.

Tilting my head to the side, I wondered why I hadn't heard the updates earlier. As soon as we got back, I'd report the equipment malfunction. That was another thing we couldn't afford to have happen while conducting an op like this.

"When it rains, it pours." I stared at my hands, hoping to force the shakes away. Flashes from my memories inside the liquor store mixed with memories from helping stop that serial killer. I hated to admit it, but I needed another session or two with the department shrink. This wasn't healthy. I had to get my head on straight.

Movement at the end of the hallway distracted me from my thoughts. A blonde woman who looked exactly like Detective Samantha Preston knocked on the door to room 214. When a man answered, she pulled him into a hug. Piercing blue eyes stared past her shoulder and zeroed in on me.

Michael? My brain formed the question, but he dragged her inside and slammed the door a millisecond later.

My heart leapt into my throat. Was I hallucinating? Had I already crossed over into looney tunes territory?

No. I didn't imagine it. That was Michael. It had to be.

But why was he meeting Preston in some shitty pay-by-the-hour motel? As far as I knew, he wasn't part of this op. Someone in vice would have mentioned it, and the look on his face told me he hadn't expected to see me, that I was the last person he wanted to see. What was going on?

NINE

"Sarconi, hold up," Jane called, halting my beeline to the door. "Hey," she jogged to catch up, "what the hell happened out there?"

"One of the johns got a little rough." I saw the worry in her eyes. "I'm okay. I put a stop to it before it even started. It just brought back some bad memories. I might have overreacted."

"I doubt you overreacted. Something about that perve must have triggered something. Are you good?"

"I'm cool as a cucumber." I forced a smile onto my face. "See?"

"You're full of shit is what you are." She assessed my expression. "What aren't you telling me?"

"Nothing. That's it. End of story."

"I know you better than that, partner. Are you sure you're okay?"

"I'm fine." I pushed the door to the locker room open. "I'll meet you upstairs."

On my way, I stopped by the gangs unit. Detective Preston wasn't at her desk. There was no sign of her in the conference room either. She wasn't here, not that I expected her to be since she was across town with Michael.

Forcing the pointless thought away, I returned to the stairwell and continued the trek to vice. I had more important things to worry about, or at least that's what I hoped to convince myself.

As soon as I took a seat at Jane's desk, I felt better. I was at work. I had a job to do, and I knew how to do it. Rolling my eyes at my own insecurities, I started on my reports. I was halfway through when Jane appeared.

"Lexie, the sarge wants to talk to us," she said.

"Now what?"

"It has something to do with your final arrest of the night."

"Does this have anything to do with why they wanted to keep me in play?"

"Maybe."

"It's either that or Stark filed a complaint, saying it was entrapment or his rights were violated." Perhaps that would be enough for the sergeant to pull the plug on my temporary reassignment to vice. Could that derail my chances at making detective? Sure, I passed the exam, but I hadn't gotten my badge yet. How badly did I screw up?

"I don't know. No one's told me anything," she said.

I sighed. "What's your backup plan?"

"For what?"

"In case the cop thing doesn't work out. We used to talk about this all the time. Weren't you going to be a rodeo clown or something like that?"

She laughed. "I'm sure I must have said that at one point. Lately, I've been leaning toward race car driver. It's male-dominated. It could use an infusion of estrogen. Why do you ask?"

"I was hoping to steal your idea, but driving doesn't interest me." That meant rideshare, limos, buses, and taxis were out of the picture too. "What do you think of waitress?"

"Come on, Lex. I'm sure it's not that bad." She led the way to the sergeant's office.

"Shut the door," Sergeant Hunter said as soon as Jane and I stepped foot inside. "Take a seat." Once we did, he cleared his throat and leaned forward. "Prior to three months ago, the man you arrested didn't exist. Jeff Stark was supposedly born in Colorado, moved here in 2010, and is an investment banker. However, he has no tax records. His driver's license is bogus. His address leads to an empty lot, and his phone number is disconnected. He's a ghost.

We're running his prints through the federal and international databases, but it'll take time."

"Clearly, he exists. We have him in holding. So who has the power to pull off something like that?" I asked.

"Witness protection, a clandestine government agency, or someone well-connected to a powerful crime syndicate," Hunter replied.

"Is there an option D? Because none of those are particularly comforting."

"No, they aren't," Jane agreed.

"Until we know more, we're keeping him on ice. Right now, units are checking the area for any evidence or clues as to who this man really is." Hunter stared at the intel on his screen. "His papers look good, but my gut says they are expensive forgeries. We should know more in a few hours."

"Okay, so what do you need me to do?" I asked.

"The detectives want a full play-by-play of what happened. Maybe Stark said or did something that will provide us with some clue as to who he is or where he came from, so go talk to them. If they want you to hang around, I'll authorize you to work a double."

"Great," I muttered. "Is there anything else?"

"I was just looking through your record. You had a close call recently. Well, a few, if we count the last time you worked vice. I'm going to assign a detail to shadow you to be on the safe side." He held up his hand before I could protest. "It's out of an abundance of caution. I don't expect there's any reason you'll need backup close by, but in case a government agent or mafia kingpin decides to have a word with you, I want to make sure we know about it."

"All right. Thanks."

When I didn't get up to leave, Hunter cocked his head to the side. "Is there something else on your mind, Sarconi?"

"I was told to keep my cover intact and not to announce. There must have been a reason."

Hunter turned his attention to the paperwork in front of him. "That came from Lt. Peterson. Since you'll be transferring to the gangs unit soon, they thought you may be of some use to their current op."

"Do you have any details?"

"No."

I glanced at Jane, wondering if that's why Hunter wasn't more forthcoming. "Come on, Sarge. You can't expect me to believe that."

"I'd say ask them, but finish up here first."

I sighed and left the room. Nothing was ever simple, and somehow, I managed to get myself into another mess.

Knocking on the open conference room door, I offered an uncertain smile to the detective inside. Despite my two years in vice, he didn't look familiar. Maybe he was a recent transfer.

He returned the smile and gestured to the empty chair. "Please," he reached across and slid the files and papers out of the way, "have a seat, Officer Sarconi."

"Lexie."

"Dean Petrocelli." He held out his hand. "It's nice to meet you. Care to tell me what happened today?"

After giving him the rundown, I massaged my temples. He had made a few pages of notes, but instead of reviewing what he had written, his chocolate brown eyes observed my every twitch and mannerism. Normally, scrutiny like that would make me uncomfortable, but something about his demeanor was calming.

"Close your eyes," he instructed as he pushed away from the table.

"Why?"

"Humor me."

Reluctantly, I shut my eyes. "Now what?"

"I want you to tell me what Jeff Stark was wearing."

"Why? Did something happen to his clothes while he was being booked?"

Petrocelli laughed. "I hope not. No one wants a naked guy in lockup. We'd have to disinfect the benches, and no one wants to do that." He hid another chuckle by clearing his throat. "What was Stark wearing?"

"A suit, dark grey, brown shoes and matching belt. He didn't have a tie." I opened my eyes.

"Keep your eyes closed."

I complied, unsure what the point of this exercise was. I rested my elbows on the table and propped my head in my hands. Petrocelli walked around the table. The soles of his shoes made soft, measured thuds against the floor as he came to stand behind me.

"The officers reported you subdued him. Why didn't you wait for backup?" Before I could answer, he placed his hands on my shoulders. I tensed, my breath hitching in my throat. I felt his warm exhale on the back of my neck, teasing the shell of my ear. "What did he want to do to you?" he whispered.

My eyes shot open, and my pulse raced. Practically leaping out of the chair, I pulled away from him, edging around so the table was between us. Without even realizing it, I was hyperventilating.

"Easy, Lexie." He held up his hands in surrender. "You're inside the station. You're safe. No one's going to hurt you." He sat in the chair I vacated. "Why don't you sit down and take some deep breaths?"

"What the fuck's wrong with you?"

He cocked his head to the side. "It was a simple question. I'm sure you included everything he said in your report. So what's the problem?"

I sat, unclear what just happened, and then I realized it was a test. Surveillance equipment was inside the motel room. Detective Petrocelli knew exactly what had gone down and he did his best to recreate that experience inside this conference room. He must have known I freaked out and wanted to see how unstable I was.

"No problem, sir." I glared at him. "Did I fail your test?"

"I'm not sure, but at least you didn't deck me." He reached across the table, grabbing a file while I pushed my chair farther away from him. "Let's talk about your history."

"Let's not."

"You were attacked recently while responding to a crime in progress. From what I read in the incident report, two men got the jump on you inside a liquor store."

"What does that have to do with anything?"

"Like they say, once bit, twice shy." He closed the folder, picking up another one. "From these records, it looks like you've had three or four close calls throughout your career. Granted, I'm not the best at math, but I'm guessing that's three times too close for your comfort."

"Stark deserved to be arrested. I didn't do anything wrong. He became too aggressive. I told him to stop. When he didn't, I responded with an appropriate amount of force to subdue him until officers could arrest him."

"I don't doubt that, but you knew backup was seconds away. Why didn't you wait? Did you believe you were in danger?"

"I didn't blow my cover. I never announced. I was told not to announce. Do you know why?"

Petrocelli reached for a pen and grabbed a sheet of paper. "What did Stark say to you before you fought him off?"

"Why don't you listen to the tapes?"

"His words weren't picked up on the recording."

I didn't buy it. "Do you work for IA?"

"You think I'm with Internal Affairs?"

"That's not a denial."

He rocked back in his chair and put his feet up on the edge of the table. "You're not in trouble, Sarconi. I'm just trying to understand what happened. You could have busted him, but you didn't."

"I had orders."

"You didn't know you weren't supposed to announce until after backup arrived. Right? So why did you hesitate?"

"That's not how these stings are being conducted. Decoys wait for backup."

"Terri announced."

Petrocelli was giving me a headache. "I didn't think it was necessary."

"But you thought it was necessary to physically subdue him. See, that's where the problem comes in."

"I was doing the best I could, given the circumstances. Everything's in my report. If this is going to turn punitive, I'd like my union rep present."

"I already said you weren't in trouble."

"So why the hell did you stage this little reenactment? Sergeant Hunter said Stark's using a fake identity. The guy is clearly guilty of something, so why are you questioning my actions?"

"There's no reason to be defensive. I'm just trying to

understand why you reacted like that. Do you suffer from post-traumatic stress?"

"If I did, I'd be chained to a desk."

"So what happened today?"

"I was alone with an aggressive predator. He wanted it rough, so I showed him how I do it rough."

"And that's the only reason you reacted like that?" Petrocelli asked, his pen poised over the paper.

"Yep."

"Okay. Thanks for clearing that up, Officer Sarconi. You can go now."

Rolling my eyes, I went out the conference room door. Reeve was waiting nearby. After taking one look at me, she grabbed my elbow and dragged me into the ladies' room.

"How'd it go with Petrocelli?" she asked.

"How should I know? The guy's on a witch hunt. He lures me into the conference room and acts like he's my best friend. Then he sneaks up behind me, scares the shit out of me, and wants to know why I reacted the way I did."

"That sounds like Dean. He likes to pretend he's a profiler. The blowhard watches too much TV. We've been hoping he'll go back to robbery-homicide, but apparently, they can't stand him either and don't want him back, no matter how much we beg."

"He's a homicide detective?"

"Yeah, RHD. With this crackdown on crime agenda, he asked to assist. Now he's a pain in vice's ass." She glanced underneath the stalls. "I think he gets off on it. Terri thinks he requested the transfer so he wouldn't accidentally get picked up for going into the wrong kind of club or paying for an escort that was actually an undercover officer."

"When did he transfer in?"

"A few weeks ago. Maybe a month or so. Why does it matter?"

"Do you think there's another serial killer operating in the area?"

"Lexie," Jane gave me that annoying look that meant she thought I was seeing ghosts everywhere, "this isn't a slasher flick sequel. This is real life. Stranglers and killers aren't waiting around every corner for unsuspecting hookers."

"Who said anything about a strangler?"

"Oh my gosh, you're incorrigible. Let's finish up the paperwork and get a drink. One of us needs it, and at this point, I'm thinking it might be me."

"I have something else I need to take care of first."

TEN

After completing the paperwork, I searched the police database for recent violent crimes with a sexual component. There were dozens of entries, so I scanned the list, looking for a pattern.

Jane was probably right. I was jumping to conclusions or letting my imagination get the best of me. Normally, I wasn't a conspiracy nut, but Detective Petrocelli was an oddball. The fact he was a homicide detective who volunteered to assist vice didn't help matters. If he needed a break from violent crimes, he would have asked to assist larceny, auto crimes, or cyber division. He wouldn't pick vice.

Maybe it was a coincidence, but everything about today felt like part of something bigger. My assignment. Jeff Stark. Spotting Michael and Preston in that motel room. Today really was one of those days.

Since the computer wouldn't provide answers, I excused myself and went in search of Lt. Peterson. According to what I'd been told, he'd instructed me not to break cover, but how did he know I wouldn't? If backup hadn't arrived when they did or Stark had been harder to handle, I would have announced.

I knocked on Peterson's open office door. "Sir?"

He looked up. "What is it, Sarconi?"

"I was hoping you could tell me." My internal voice warned to be better behaved, but I was tired of listening to her. "I was told to keep my cover intact. That the order came from you. What gives?"

"Lightman may have something for you sooner than he anticipated."

"What does that have to do with vice?"

Peterson's cheek twitched. "I heard you were at the Park Motel today."

"Is gangs using that location for something?"

Peterson looked up at me and pointed to the badge hooked to my belt. The only perk of working for vice was not changing back into uniform when we were inside the station. "That doesn't say detective yet. Are you hoping to practice your questioning skills? Because I don't appreciate an officer interrogating me."

"I just want to know what's going on, sir."

"You'll be told what you need to know, when you need to know it."

"With all due respect, I almost identified myself to a suspect today when backup was late to arrive. It was only after that incident that I was told not to do that."

"I'll make sure we don't cut it as close next time." Peterson glanced at my exposed forearm. "We'll have your back, Sarconi. You have my word on that."

It didn't feel like it. Before trudging back up the steps, I ducked into the department psychologist's office. Since it was near the end of shift, I expected him to be working on paperwork instead of seeing a patient. He looked up when he noticed me lingering near the outer door.

"Is there something I can help you with, Lexie?"

"Do you have a minute?"

He gestured at the chair. The only good thing about this was I didn't have to worry about compromising operations or cases. The bad part was anything I said could be reported to the brass if the doctor deemed it appropriate to have me removed from active duty. "Are you still having trouble sleeping?"

"Occasionally."

"That's not uncommon." He eased back in the chair. "That's not what brings you here."

I told him about the call and the resurgence of my memories, leaving out everything about my orders and Michael and my odd encounter with Det. Petrocelli. "Any call, any encounter can turn rough. I know that."

"You've been there several times."

"Yeah."

"And you don't want that to happen again."

"Damn right, I don't. But that's the job. There are no guarantees with this or anything. That's life, right?"

"Right."

"So what am I supposed to do?"

"Do you want an honest answer or a professional one?"

"Both."

"Honestly, I have no idea." He winked. "From a professional standpoint, I think it's good you're asking these questions. You're paying attention. You want to make sure you take care of yourself, but you are aware of other factors and you want to overcome this and stick it out. If you didn't, you would have taken Jane's offer. You also would have pulled your badge the moment Stark approached you."

"What about the flashes and the panic?"

"Did it prevent you from acting or reacting?"

"No."

He made a note. "Right now, I'd say you're handling this appropriately. Everyone gets scared. You may be more sensitive to that or more aware, but it isn't preventing you from doing your job. However, you know the warning signs. We've been over the symptoms of post-traumatic stress. You know what your stressors are and you know when it gets to be too much. If that happens, come see me, and we'll reassess. How does that sound?"

"I expected you to tell me I'm crazy."

"That's what everyone who walks through that door says."

I laughed. "Yeah, well, some of us are."

"Off the record, all of us are."

My brief stop didn't solve any of my problems. I still had the same questions and self-doubt, but maybe the doc was right. Maybe that's how we all felt. And who was I to argue with a professional?

In my absence, the bullpen had grown quiet. Several of my colleagues had called it quits. I didn't spot Terri, but Jane remained at her desk. I took a seat beside her and watched as she finished the last of her reports.

"I still don't see how you always get the paperwork done so quickly," she said.

"That's the fun part."

"You're joking, right?"

I shrugged. "It means I can stop thinking about things, and after a day like today, I kind of need that."

"I have an even better solution to that problem."

Once Jane handed the last of her files to Petrocelli and a few other detectives working the case, we went across the street to the bar. A patrol car with two uniformed officers watched me. I gave them a wave, which they returned. At least I wasn't paranoid enough to believe my protection detail was comprised of stalkers. They were just bored cops doing their job.

Jane dragged me to a booth in the corner and ordered a pitcher of beer. Unlike my best friend Amber who always tried to force me to talk about my problems, Jane was a fellow cop. She knew what happened. Besides tossing around a few theories concerning the mysterious Jeff Stark, we didn't do much talking.

"He could be a spy," she said when we were halfway through our second pitcher.

"The CIA's rigorous background checks should have ruled out sexual predators."

"Maybe. Maybe not." She knocked back more beer and refilled her cup. "What do you think he is?"

"My money's on lawyer. A rich lawyer."

"If he has that much money, he wouldn't bother with the fake ID. He'd buy his way out of trouble or have things buried. He could have a fixer on speed dial."

"That would mean he's working for someone with a lot of money or he's a criminal."

She laughed, a little tipsy. "Both of those scenarios mean he's a criminal."

"That is the one thing we know after the way he behaved in that room." I drained my glass, putting my hand over the top before she could refill it.

"Did you freak out?" she asked. "I won't say anything, but is that what happened in there? Is that why you were told not to break cover?"

"I don't know. All I know for sure is backup was slow to respond. Stark could have had a weapon. Even without one, he still posed a threat. I had every right to defend myself."

"That's not what I'm saying. Of course, you did. I just meant—"

"I know." I sighed. "I spoke to the LT. He said another unit may need my decoy status intact for something. It didn't make much sense to me, but nothing about any of this makes any sense. Stark, Petrocelli, whatever the hell gangs is doing in the mix, it's all a big giant tangled ball of yarn."

"Well, it's a good thing you acted. Whoever Jeff Stark is, he's dangerous. He wouldn't bother hiding his identity if he wasn't."

Before this conversation circled back around again, I said, "I'm calling it."

"Come on. We can get another pitcher and forget all about this shift."

"The only thing I want to do is go home."

"Okay, Lex. I'll see you tomorrow. It's the last day of phase one. Then the real fun begins. Aren't you stoked?"

"Sure. Only two more weeks until I'm back in uniform."

"You mean toting around a shiny detective's shield."

"After today, I wouldn't be so sure. Petrocelli said a lot of things which make me think my promotion could get rescinded."

"They wouldn't do that. You're worrying for nothing."

"I hope so." I laid some cash on the table. "Take it easy. We have work tomorrow. The last thing you need is a hangover."

"Yeah, yeah. I know."

I went out the door, spotting the patrol car immediately. On the bright side, it was comforting to know I had my own personal bodyguards. However, I doubted they felt that way.

After making sure I was sober enough to drive, I started the engine and headed home, wishing I could call Michael and hear his voice. I wondered what his take on this situation was. He would tell me if I screwed up or if I had reason to worry. Unfortunately, that wasn't a possibility. Instead, I found myself wondering why he and Preston were meeting at that sketchy motel.

ELEVEN

I twisted and turned all night. By morning, I was ready to get back to work. I wanted answers. Correction, I needed answers. I didn't know what was going on or what was in store for me. Jeff Stark couldn't remain a mystery for long. We'd figure out who he was and what he was doing. He had to be someone important for a homicide detective to be running the investigation. And what was going on with gangs that Lightman asked Lt. Peterson to make sure my decoy status remained under wraps? Being a decoy wasn't exactly the same as working undercover, but it was close. Why would gangs want me to masquerade as a sex worker?

After filling the coffeemaker, I brewed a full twelve cups, poured the contents into three separate thermoses, and went outside to the patrol car.

"Slow night?" I asked, passing them two of the thermoses and a handful of non-dairy creamer and sugar packets I had grabbed during one of my many trips to the neighborhood coffee shop.

"I'd go so far as to say humdrum." The officer unscrewed the top of the thermos and inhaled. "Thanks, Sarconi."

"No problem. Thanks for keeping an eye out. Any idea who or what might be coming for me?"

"We were told to watch for anyone suspicious or dangerous. That was it."

"That's vague."

"You know how it is when we're looking for threats. They

could come in any shape or size."

"True." I tapped the side of his door. "I'm heading to the station. Hopefully, that means you get to clock out."

"We'll see. Be safe, Sarconi."

"You too."

I walked across the parking lot and climbed into my car. Today was a new day. A fresh start. It was the last day Jane, Terri, and I had to prowl the sketchier neighborhoods.

Phase two sounded more promising and less chaotic. There would be more police officers on-site and plenty of them in uniform. Everything was starting to look up.

I greeted the desk sergeant before going up the stairs to vice. I nodded to a few officers I passed on the way. When I made it to the bullpen, I caught sight of Detective Petrocelli and followed him into the conference room.

"Hey," I said, leaning against the doorjamb, "any progress on determining who Jeff Stark really is?"

"Not yet." He cast a cautious look in my direction. "Are we okay? Yesterday, you seemed ready to kill me."

"Wasn't that the point of your exercise? Weren't you hoping for that kind of response?"

He observed how I lingered in the doorway. "Is there anything else I can do for you, Sarconi?"

"What's your interest in Stark?"

"Same as yours."

"Somehow, I doubt that."

Petrocelli went back to the paperwork, but when I remained, he looked up. "Is there something I can do for you?"

"Not at the moment, but if I think of anything, I'll let you know." Turning, I went to Jane's desk and took a seat. She wasn't in yet, and I didn't feel like reviewing the progress we'd made. If anything major had popped, Petrocelli should have mentioned it. And I didn't want to get bogged down in the details since I was determined to hold on to my good mood for as long as possible.

"Yo, Sarconi," someone called. I swiveled around at the sound of my name. Coming up the steps was Detective Preston. She waved me over. "Do you have a sec?"

I joined her near the stairwell. "What's up?"

"Your name was mentioned in the Jeff Stark file. When was he brought in?"

"Last night."

"Why?"

I resisted the urge to say something snarky. This was vice. There were very few reasons why we brought anyone in. "He was looking for a good time, but this isn't Nevada. Prostitution's illegal."

"That's it?"

That question surprised me. She was in the motel when Stark was. But that didn't seem like his kind of neighborhood. "Detective Preston," I paused, "Sam, what is going on?"

"I don't know what you mean."

But she did. I opened my mouth to mention seeing her, but she shut me down before I could utter a word.

"When is Stark getting cut loose?" she asked.

"He isn't. It turns out his identity is bogus. We can't let him go until we know who he is. To top it off, he strikes me as a violent offender. The last place he needs to be is back on the streets."

"Did you make the bust?"

"I assisted. Decoyed. I almost announced, but backup arrived half a second before I did." I searched her face, but she was playing it cool. "Do you want to tell me why Lightman said I shouldn't announce and keep my cover intact?"

"Who knows why Jack does any of the things he does?"

"That's bullshit. You said there aren't secrets within your unit. You know what's going on. You know who Stark is, don't you?" Another thought came to mind. "Riley was there. Stark was there. Was that a coincidence?" My mind said no, but I couldn't figure out how the two connected. Preston could fill in the blanks.

Instead, she looked as if she had no idea what I was talking about. "Why do you think Stark's violent?"

"When I said no, he got aggressive."

"I'm glad you're okay."

"I'd be better if I knew what was going on. Why am I being kept in the dark? My promotion should be a surefire thing. Can't you read me in?"

"Are you still working for vice?"

"Yes, but—"

She cut me off. "Who's in charge of the investigation into Stark?"

"Detective Petrocelli."

"Petrocelli? As in Dean Petrocelli?"

"Yeah."

"That makes no sense. He's with robbery homicide division. What is he doing here?"

"He volunteered."

"Of course, he did." She shook her head, resisting the urge to roll her eyes. "Where can I find him?"

I jerked my thumb at the conference room. Before I could say anything else, she strode past me without so much as a thank you, entered the conference room, and slammed the door. Compared to Preston, I was positively bubbly.

Once Jane arrived, we received our assignments and went to change into less appropriate attire. On the way to the locker room, I heard angry voices coming from the closed conference room. I couldn't make out the words, but it sounded like Preston was tearing Petrocelli a new one. Tabling that thought for later consideration, I put my game face on and changed into a faux leather dress.

"You still with us, Lexie?" Terri asked.

"Uh-huh."

"So what do you think?"

"About what?"

"How we're supposed to work when you have a protection detail following you around. If they really think that asshole you collared last night poses a threat, they should have you in protective custody, not out working. Plus, since he's locked up, who do they think is going to come after you? The boogeyman?"

Jane finished dressing and poked her head around the side of the locker. "Lexie's dealt with a lot of shit lately. Give her a break. She didn't ask for the detail. They assigned a unit to shadow her. It's precautionary. All that means is we have an additional unit to provide backup. They aren't going to charge in every time a john approaches her."

"They wouldn't have me working the streets if I had a babysitter. I'm sure they've been reassigned. When I spoke to them this morning, there was no mention of a relief team."

"What even happened yesterday?" Terri asked. "I heard the official version and some whispers that a john attacked you. How does that translate into a protection detail?"

"We don't know who the guy is. They figured he could be connected to some scary people." Again, I hated that Preston didn't answer my questions. Why did everyone want to keep me out of the loop?

"But you didn't announce you were a cop. Why would he come after you? As far as he knows, you were arrested too," Terri pointed out.

"I don't know why the brass is freaking out. I wish I did."

"They want to avoid lawsuits," Jane said. "You've been in enough scrapes. At this point, you may have grounds for a complaint about an unsafe work environment or failure of the administration to take appropriate steps to keep you as safe as possible."

"We're cops," I said. "Unsafe work environment is part of the gig. It's why we get hazard pay."

"Still, if it happens repeatedly and not through any fault of your own, it could look like a pattern, like the brass is specifically assigning you to rough neighborhoods or giving you dangerous assignments."

That sounded crazy, but people sued for everything. Most of the time, civilians were suing us, but I knew enough cops who had taken settlements when they'd been injured. Maybe that was the only reason I'd been assigned babysitters, but I doubted it.

"It seems like overkill to me," Terri muttered.

"How many close calls have you had, Terri?" Jane asked. "Since we've been working together, I can't think of a single one. Yeah, sure, you get groped occasionally, but not once have uniforms had to rush in because your life was in danger. So don't run your mouth. Lexie's been there. I've been there. And if you talk to most of the decoys in this department, they've been there. You should consider yourself lucky."

"That wasn't what I meant." Terri shook her head. "Whatever. I'll meet you guys downstairs." She slammed the locker room door, annoyed Jane backed me instead of her.

"You're supposed to side with your partner," I reminded her.

"You used to be my partner. And in this instance, you're right. She isn't." She reached for a brush. "Seriously, you were freaking out last night. Are you sure you can hold it together today?"

"Yep."

Jane assessed me carefully. "You suck at making friends, Lex." She turned so I could zip her dress. "The truth is Terri's one of the lucky ones. And I'm glad. I really am. But one of these days, someone's going to get too aggressive. I hope she's prepared for it and remembers this conversation."

"I'm sure she will. After all, aren't you teaching her everything you know?"

"I taught you everything you know, and we see how that turned out. You ran from this department as soon as an opportunity presented itself."

"That's because you taught me well."

"Maybe too well." Jane checked her reflection in the mirror a final time.

TWELVE

We met Terri and the uniformed members of our team. We split up into two mobile units of six each. The ride was pleasant enough, minus the cracks being made at my expense. But they weren't malicious. It was the usual teasing and ribbing.

"Next time, make the john take his socks off first, so you can shove one in his mouth before he starts yelling about you being a cop," Officer Jones said. "Then you don't have to worry about anyone else finding out if you choose to announce."

"Thanks for the tip."

"Was the sarge afraid some lowlife was gonna follow you home?" Officer Bullock asked. "Is that why you had a detail following you around?"

"You're just jealous because I brought them coffee this morning."

"Did you make them breakfast in bed too?"

"A girl never tells."

Jane tossed a look in my direction. "Don't be jealous, Bullock. Sarconi can't help it that's she out of your league. You can't expect a smoke show like her to slum it with a guy like you."

Bullock chuckled. "I make up for my looks in other ways."

"That's not what your wife says," Jones teased.

And just like that, the conversation was no longer focused on me. "Thank you," I mouthed to Jane.

I didn't request a patrol car on my tail. One of the white

shirts had made that call for no real reason I could discern. My gut said Jane was right. The brass didn't want me involved in another incident. The last time some crook had come to my apartment, he nearly killed me. It wouldn't look good for the department if that happened a second time.

Unlike our last shift, today went much more smoothly. By the end of shift, another dozen arrests were made, including six working girls who had been particularly obnoxious and threatening. The mayor would be thrilled, and the district attorney would prosecute as many as possible.

"At least it's over," Jane said, once we made it back to the station. "Now for phase two."

"Doesn't this sound like some crazy scheme in a superhero movie?"

"I was thinking more of a heist flick."

"You mean the ones where things go sideways halfway through and hijinks ensue?"

"Yeah, just like that." She finished filing her last report. "Come on, the team's going out for drinks to celebrate. You're coming with. I'm not taking no for an answer."

"Didn't we drink enough yesterday?"

"You're a cop. How can you even ask me that?"

"Fine. I'll go, but no more beer."

"Only if we get the guys to buy us something better."

As usual, the place was crowded with cops. Since the tables and booths were occupied, we sat in a row at the bar. I couldn't hear much over the noise. From the sounds of it, every department had some major operation in the works due to the mayor's mandate. And since the week was up, everyone had gone out to celebrate. You'd think it was a retirement party or a wake.

"I hate politics." I picked up my cranberry vodka and took a large sip. "Who thinks this week was pointless?" Jane, Terri, Jones, and Bullock raised their hands. "Me too."

Last call was quickly approaching. I sat at the end of the bar, next to Jane. Terri was desperately trying to get the bartender's attention so we could get another round.

Normally, I didn't drink this much unless I was out with Amber, and even then, I tried not to drink when I knew I had to work the next day. Being hungover on the job was asking for trouble. But it had been a week since Michael left, and with all the confusion over my role at vice and the secrets gangs was keeping from me, the only thing I wanted to do was find comfort in the bottom of a bottle.

Drowning my woes and worries seemed like a great idea, even though I knew it wasn't. We were starting phase two tomorrow. And no matter how drunk I got tonight, it wouldn't make anything better. It'd only make it worse.

Jane tapped my arm. "What are you thinking about?"

"Have you ever dated someone on the job?" I asked.

She shook her head.

"Don't. Particularly if they might be stuck working an undercover assignment and their last girlfriend is Police Edition Barbie."

"Oh-kay. Is that really what you're thinking about? I figured you were focused on Stark."

"I can multitask."

She slid another glass in front of me. "What do you think his deal is? The brass must be worried since they assigned you a car to follow you home again tonight. Do you think he's in witness protection? He could be a mob hitter. That would explain it."

"I doubt it. The mob would know better than to put a hit out on a cop."

"Okay, so maybe he's a secret agent for some foreign power."

"He's no secret agent." I sipped my newly refilled drink. "He's probably some sicko who turned state's evidence and changed his name to stay off the registry."

"If that's true, how did he come by a quality fake ID?"

I shrugged.

"The brass thinks he's working for someone powerful—an arms dealer, the cartel, the mafia," Terri said from two stools over. She hadn't heard my rationale that Stark wasn't working for the mob. "That's why Sergeant Hunter assigned you a couple more babysitters." She swallowed her shot of tequila. "Are you going to make them breakfast in bed too?"

"You betcha." Saying such things would only add fuel to the rumors which always circulated, but I was at the point where it was easier to go with the flow than to think about the more serious implications. Joking was safer, easier. It meant the danger wasn't real, and since no one wanted to tell me anything, I had no way of knowing if it was. "How did you find that out?"

"That's the scuttlebutt around the watercooler," Terri said.

"You're mixing your sayings," Jane pointed out, "which means it's time someone cuts you off."

Terri stood, slightly wobbly, and moved down the bar to close the tab. Since she was done drinking, she wasn't paying for us to drink anymore either.

I stretched, glancing around the room. Two of our drinking buddies had disappeared while I was talking to Jane, and now that Terri closed our tab, there wasn't much left to do except call a cab and go home. Perhaps I could convince the patrol car outside to give me a lift. They were supposed to protect me. Right now, I needed them to protect me from myself.

Before I could ask Jane if she thought that was beyond reasonable, she headed to the ladies' room, effectively causing our conversation to come to a crashing halt. Swallowing the remainder of my cranberry vodka, I surveyed the rest of the bar and spotted Kemper and Hawking.

I waved. They waved back, but since they didn't wave me over or get up to talk to me, I had to assume they didn't know anything about Stark or why I had babysitters watching me for a second night in a row. If they knew, they'd tell me.

My eyes settled on Samantha Preston sitting alone at a booth. Getting up, I approached her table and took a seat.

"Does that contain the answers to life's questions?" I asked.

She snickered at the beer bottle she'd been staring at. "I was hoping they were printed on the label. Instead, all I'm getting is the surgeon general's warning."

"That sucks."

"Yeah." She leaned back in the booth. "What are you doing here, Lexie?"

"Just thought I should say hello." She wouldn't make eye

contact, which made my insides wither. My gut said she felt guilty about something. And only one thought came to mind. *Michael.* "Did you get whatever it was straightened out with Petrocelli?" I asked.

"Not really. He thinks his case is more important than ours. He doesn't want to play ball. He's such an asshole sometimes."

"What is his case?"

"He didn't say?"

I was on to something. "So he's not working for vice because he thought he should help out? RHD has something else in the works?"

"Is that what he told you?"

"That's what I heard."

"He thinks Stark connects to one of his other cases."

"That's why I never noticed Petrocelli working for vice before." I shook my head. "For a guy without a real identity, a lot of people are interested in Jeff Stark."

"Yep."

Preston wasn't giving me much to work with. I hoped the booze would have loosened her lips, but that was probably her only beer of the night. I was much closer to being overserved and saying whatever popped into my head, so I had to be careful. I had too much to lose.

"Is gangs working on something big?"

"You know we are." She took a swig of beer. "Is there any chance you could convince Petrocelli to expedite the paperwork or fudge a little to get Stark released from lockup?"

"I don't think he holds my opinion in high regard." I thought about our encounter, but I couldn't read the RHD detective or his motives. And the last thing I wanted to do was help the woman sneaking into a motel room to meet my boyfriend. "Why would you want Stark released? It sounds like he's a murder suspect."

"We don't know enough about that, but if he did kill someone, he may have done it on someone else's behalf," she said. "We need him freed, so we can figure out what's what."

"We?"

"You're not going to let this go, are you?"

"I don't understand why Lightman won't read me in. He tapped me to join his unit. The results are in. Maybe I haven't gotten my new badge yet, but isn't that a technicality? Am I not part of the team? You treated me more like a member of gangs when I was nothing more than a gofer. Even when I was attacked working patrol, everyone in that unit banded around me. You, Frank, Jack, Michael." I knew I was drunk since I was using everyone's first name. "You wanted my help then. Why don't you want it now?"

"It's not that we don't. It's complicated."

"Like whatever was going on inside that motel room?" I glared at her. "How's Michael?" Clearly, I was inebriated. If I wasn't, I wouldn't have asked. "Did the two of you sneak in some cheap thrills?"

"You're drunk."

"Let's call it tipsy. Stop changing the subject."

"He said you saw us." She grabbed my wrist. "Listen, no one's supposed to know what's going on. But he needed to get a message back to the station, so he called me."

"Right." I sighed in disbelief.

"He was in trouble, Lexie. His meet went sideways. There were some miscommunications. He wanted to make sure we knew what was what in case of anything."

Those words removed my jealous and betrayed feelings and sobered me. "Is he safe? Where is he? Are they going to pull him?"

"As far as I know, it's been worked out. But at the time, he thought he'd been made." She lowered her voice to something barely audible. "He wanted to turn over the evidence he had in case of anything. I told him it was ludicrous, and he needed to scrap the operation. But you know exactly how stubborn he is. The last I heard, he spun something and got back in their good graces. He just needs me to do him a favor, and I can't seem to get it done because Dean is being the world's biggest pain in the ass right now."

"Whose good graces?" I asked, desperate to find a way to verify Michael was alive and breathing.

"That doesn't matter. It's need to know. You don't, unless Jack says otherwise. However, what you need to know is me showing up at that motel was meant to look like a lover's rendezvous, but it wasn't. He would never betray you, least of all with me."

I pulled my wrist free from her grasp. "Yeah, okay." I didn't know what to believe.

"He loves you. Don't ever doubt that."

My throat had gone dry. "I should go. If you talk to him again, tell him to be careful."

She picked up the beer bottle and toasted in my direction. "Will do."

Jane caught up with me before I made it out the door, and we split a cab. I didn't speak about Preston's revelation or mention Michael. Jane may have been my old vice partner, but this was too personal to share, even with her.

"Hey," she nudged me, "are you okay? You got quiet."

"I'm just tired," I said as the car slowed to a stop. My brain kept twisting over the one thing Preston said that made no sense.

"Get some sleep, Lexie. You look like you could use it." She hugged me. "And we need to be bright-eyed and bushy-tailed to take down some pimps tomorrow."

"Good night, ho," I called as she went up the walk to her apartment building. The cab driver looked at me through the rearview mirror. "It's okay. We're cops. Now drive the damn car."

My temporary amusement at the cabbie's disconcerted look was squelched once the car was in gear and my alcohol-addled brain tried to wrap itself around the issue with Stark, Preston's feud with Petrocelli, and the possibility that Michael was in danger.

Jeff Stark connected to all of this. He must have something to do with Michael's assignment. There'd be no other reason Preston would want him released from custody. Given where I picked up Stark and where I found Michael holed up with Preston, I had to assume that was the meet that had gone south.

Did Stark know Michael was a cop? Was that why a patrol car was following the cab back to my apartment? But there was no way Stark could connect me to Michael, not the real me and definitely not the decoy version of me. After all,

Michael wasn't himself. I didn't know who he was, but his cover identity and mine weren't linked.

None of this made a bit of sense, and I didn't think that had anything to do with the four cranberry vodkas I had. The cab came to an abrupt halt, as had my thoughts. After tossing some cash at the driver, I marched to my apartment, aware of the patrol car parked near my front door. Tonight, I'd sober up and get a good night's sleep. Tomorrow, I'd figure out what was going on, one way or another.

THIRTEEN

The next morning, I woke up with my brain on fire. I forgot how horrible a hangover could be. Getting up, I drank some water, popped a few aspirins, and threw up multiple times.

After showering and rehydrating, I felt slightly better. I played Michael's message a dozen times. I didn't doubt he loved me. But I still didn't understand what was going on or why the gangs unit insisted on keeping me out of the loop. Was that his doing?

My stomach clenched, and no matter how hard I tried to convince myself it was the hangover, I knew the sick feeling was fear. Was Michael alive? Was he safe? I looked at the wilted roses which I refused to throw away and picked up the teddy bear and hugged it.

"Please be okay."

When I could no longer stand the loneliness of my apartment or the oppressive feeling of impending doom, I put the bear on the couch and left for work. The patrol car remained out front. I wasn't sure why the brass thought it was safe for me to work but too dangerous for me to stay alone in my apartment at night. What did they think was going to happen here that wouldn't happen on the streets?

I had to find out who Jeff Stark was. RHD wanted him. Gangs wanted him. And thanks to me, he was vice's problem.

I arrived at work an hour before parade. That would give me enough time to get some answers. Detective Petrocelli was still holed up inside the conference room, wearing the same thing he had on yesterday. With any luck, that would make this easier.

I knocked, not waiting for permission before pulling the door open. "Did you sleep here?"

Petrocelli rubbed his chin, scratching at the stubble. "Is that the nice way of saying I need to shave?"

"I have no qualms about a man with a five o'clock shadow, but I'm getting tired of seeing that same suit. Is it the only one you own?"

"I spilled coffee on myself this morning and happened to have this in the car. Does it really look that bad?"

"You look fine, I guess."

"Thanks. For the record, so do you."

I rolled my eyes. "What's your deal, Detective?"

"Nothing. I'm just feeling you out." He leaned back in his chair. "Tell me what makes Alessandra Sarconi tick."

"Well, if you want to know what ticks me off, keep calling me Alessandra."

"Noted." He steepled his fingers and tapped them absently against his lips. "You have issues being back in vice. You're on edge. You hate working as a decoy. It makes you jumpy."

"That's called cautious, and I don't think anyone enjoys being objectified or sexually exploited."

"Did you react inappropriately toward Stark?"

"No, I did not. Are you still stuck on that?"

"No. I was waiting for you to realize you didn't screw up. The plug got pulled because of Stark, not because of you."

"Is that the same reason I have a protection detail on my ass? Is that also Stark's fault?"

Petrocelli didn't say anything.

"Cut the crap." Wincing, I reminded myself this jerk outranked me. "Sir."

"You don't have to sir me. I'm not here to make friends. You don't have to like me. Hell, you don't even have to be nice to me. I'm here to do a job. That's it."

"What job?" Again, my question was met with silence. "I heard Stark connects to a homicide."

"Stark connects to a lot of things."

"That's why you want him and why gangs wants him. But the last I heard, we don't even know who this guy is. So why is bagging him at the top of everyone's wish list? How do you even know you have the right guy?"

"Close the door," Petrocelli said. Once I did, he pulled out a file from the bottom of the stack. It was a different color from the rest. He opened it but didn't put it down for me to see. "Jeff Stark is one of many aliases this man uses. He's known in black market circles as the Procurer because he can get anything for anyone."

"He sounds like a clichéd villain in a B movie."

"Don't let the moniker fool you. Stark's very good at what he does. He's never been caught. We know him by reputation only."

"Again, I'm wondering how you know this guy is that guy."

"We have our ways."

Michael? I wondered if he IDed Stark. "Did someone witness Stark committing one of the Procurer's crimes?"

"You could say that."

I sighed dramatically. "I'm going to need more."

Petrocelli put his badge on the table. "Huh? See, that says detective. It doesn't say suspect or informant. And that," he pointed to my badge, "says officer. Which makes me wonder why you think you can interrogate me."

"I deserve answers. I brought this bastard in."

"Deserve isn't the right word. You're a cop. You did your job. However, I may need your help, so I can play ball for now." He gave me a playful look, almost as if he were flirting. "Let's see. Where should I begin?"

"The beginning would be good."

He pointed his finger at me. "Is that the kind of deductive reasoning that allowed you to make detective?"

I held my tongue, not wanting to get him off track again. I didn't have time. I couldn't miss roll call.

When I didn't offer up a quip, Petrocelli focused on the folder in front of him. "Stark is suspected of dozens of crimes, including human trafficking. Unfortunately, the FBI and Interpol don't have anything solid on him. We're the only department to ever bust him for an actual crime. If you hadn't tried to pick him up, he'd still be roaming free."

"He doesn't know I'm a cop."

"We're not sure about that. That's what we've been trying to figure out."

"He doesn't. I didn't announce. The support team cuffed me. He saw it happen."

"We can't be sure of anything. It's best not to assume. And it'd be smart for you to remember that."

"Why does RHD have an interest in him?"

"The Procurer obtained a valuable ruby necklace through less than legal means. The owner and two security guards were killed in the process. That's why I want this guy. But that's just the tip of the iceberg. I'm supposed to be patient." The look on Petrocelli's face said that was the last thing he wanted to do.

"So he's dangerous?"

"Weren't you paying attention? That's why there's a detail. If he thinks a cop made him and can testify against him, he'd want to remove the problem. Getting caught isn't an option for a guy like this, and he's caught."

"Has he been arraigned? Surely, the judge wouldn't grant bail when we don't even know the guy's real name. If he's in custody, why worry? He can't hurt me."

"He could have friends."

"Do we know who they are?"

Again, my question was met with silence.

"Do we know anything else about this guy?" I asked.

"All I know is it's hard to file charges against someone you can't identity. Plus, the longer we keep him here, the better."

"Preston doesn't think so."

"She's wrong."

"Are you sure about that?"

He snorted. "Of course you'd be loyal to gangs. You're going to work for them. Did she send you in here to ruffle my feathers?"

"No one sent me. I want to know why I have babysitters watching me every night."

"That must screw with your sex life."

"Is that a vice joke?"

He held up his palms. "It was an observation. I know it'd mess with mine. Anyway, Samantha need not worry. Stark's lawyers will get him out. As it is, they're ripping apart our actions as unconscionable for law enforcement officers. Like he declared when he was brought in, it's entrapment and police brutality, and he announced it loudly enough that there are alleged witnesses who will corroborate that fact. Once he's arraigned, if we even get to that point, he'll be in the wind again. I don't have any hard evidence to pin him to the murders, and gangs refuses to share whatever they have on him." Petrocelli rubbed the bridge of his nose. "That's why I've been trying to find something we can use to prove he's the Procurer, but there's nothing concrete. We have a lot of suspicions, but no evidence. Not yet, and I doubt we'll find it in time."

"Are you sure gangs has something on him?"

"They must."

"Do you know anything about the op they have in play?"

He scrutinized me as if he suspected that was a trap. "Do you?"

"No."

"I have a hard time believing that."

"Believe whatever you want." I indicated my badge. "Remember, it doesn't say detective. According to you, that means I don't deserve to know anything."

"I didn't say that."

"Didn't you?"

"I'm not your enemy, Lexie. We're on the same side. We're in this together. We both want this guy. I'm sure your pals in gangs want this guy too, just not yet."

"Which means they have something bigger in the works."

Petrocelli pointed at me. "Gold star. However, they won't tell me who they have in their sights, just that they need Stark to lead them to him. But I will be damned if I let a killer loose on the streets. Who knows what he'll do or where he'll disappear? I don't care what Samantha says. She can't guarantee he won't slip their surveillance and get away."

"I don't see how we can cut him loose. We have a case against him. Even if soliciting sex falls through—"

"Which it will because the brass wants your cover to

remain intact, which means you can't testify against him. If you were to go on the stand under the guise of sex worker, you'd perjure yourself with the misrepresentation."

Petrocelli had given this more thought than I realized.

"We still have the fake ID. That has to be fraud or identity theft. Isn't that enough?" I asked.

"It's not enough for a judge to deny bail."

"He's a violent offender and a flight risk."

"We don't know that."

Except that was what Petrocelli had been harping on this entire time, but I understood his point. The judge would never see it that way without hard evidence. "Except we do," I said.

"That's the kicker. We can't prove it. His attorneys are saying the fake ID is a clerical error, that Stark was born in another country but has all the proper documentation to be here now. I'm sure they're fabricating those things as we speak."

"This is bullshit."

"I know. That's why I've been inside this room for so long, but I can't find anything and time is running out."

"Preston wants him released. They must have a plan."

"I don't like it."

"You told me you didn't know what it was."

Petrocelli gave me a look. "I don't have details."

I wasn't sure what to believe. All I knew was he wouldn't tell me. I'd have to get that information from someone else. Someone in gangs.

"This would be easier if you could testify that he's dangerous. But that's off the table for now. Your history isn't particularly helpful either." He sighed and flipped through the files again. "We need solid proof."

"My history?" I balked.

"Yeah, your skittishness, which is why I questioned you and tested your reactions when we first met. Defense council will find some cockamamie headshrinker to testify with enough psychobabble to make you out to be suffering from post-traumatic stress." He looked apologetic. "For the record, I don't think you have post-traumatic stress. But I'm sure that's what they'll say."

"There has to be something else we can do."

"Not with the legal team he has assembled. We're talking the top defense attorneys in the country. One thing's for sure. Stark has deep pockets."

"Or his boss does."

"You're starting to think Samantha has a point." Petrocelli gave me a look. "But you always thought that. You want to be one of them so badly, you don't realize how dangerous this could be."

"Don't talk to me about danger."

"I've heard stories. I thought they were embellishments."

"They are not," I said.

"In that case, I'm sorry you had to go through the things you did. For what it's worth, the city's better for it. Everyone's lucky you're on the job." Glancing at the time, he added, "Don't you have somewhere to be?"

"Yeah, on a street corner, searching for a pimp."

"Have fun with that."

"I'll try."

FOURTEEN

That conversation did not get me any closer to figuring out what was going on. I had no idea if Michael was safe. All I knew was Jeff Stark, a.k.a. the Procurer, was trouble in capital letters. Michael must have been keeping tabs on Stark. He must have been targeting Stark's boss, client, whatever the proper term was, when Stark showed up on the scene. Maybe Stark was Michael's way in. That would explain why Preston was adamant about having Stark released from custody.

A chilling thought ran through me. Preston said Michael wanted to meet because he feared he was compromised. Did vice's op compromise whatever play gangs had in the works? Did Stark's arrest solidify that? Is that why she wanted Stark released? Was that the only way to save Michael? Did someone think he informed or suspected he was an undercover cop?

"Stop jumping to conclusions," I mumbled to myself. But the thought made me even queasier. Deep down, I knew that must have been it. It would explain why I had a protection detail. I'd worked with Michael before. I was the cop who lured Stark to the motel room. If Michael was compromised, I could be too. And to think, we weren't even working on the same case. He would hate this, thinking his assignment put me in jeopardy. After all, that was the entire reason he kept me in the dark.

Once roll call was finished and I was allowed to return to

my duties, I detoured to the gangs unit. When I stepped through the double doors, the sight of Michael's empty desk tore at my heart. *Don't go there, Lexie. Michael will be back.* He promised, and he knew better than to break a promise.

Preston wasn't at her desk. Neither was Detective Frank Devereaux. I checked the conference room, surprised to find Detective Lightman standing in front of a corkboard. At the sound of my intrusion, he spun around.

"What do you want, Sarconi?"

Lightman was the last person I wanted to ask. He ran the unit. Unlike everyone else, his shield said sergeant, even if he preferred the title of detective. Once my promotion became official and my transfer went through, he'd be my boss. Starting off on the wrong foot again wasn't advisable. But I didn't think I had a choice.

"I...uh...was hoping we could discuss Jeff Stark," I said.

"What about him?"

"You didn't want him to know I was a cop. If backup hadn't shown up when they did, I would have announced. For future reference, I need advanced notice."

"That's what you want to talk about?"

"No, sir." I stood a little straighter. "I wanted to know why it was important he didn't find out."

"Did he find out?"

"Not that I'm aware."

Lightman nodded. "Relax, Sarconi. You're not in trouble, for once."

"Is Riley?"

Lightman licked his lips. "What did he tell you?"

"Nothing. I haven't spoken to him since he left. All he told me was he was working undercover and had to cut ties. But I saw him at the motel after we arrested Stark. I assume that's not a coincidence. According to Det. Petrocelli, gangs wants Stark released. I'm guessing there's a reason for that and it relates to Riley's undercover assignment."

"Vice doesn't want to cut Stark loose. They busted him. They want him prosecuted. I spoke to Lt. Peterson and the captain, but they're deferring to vice on this. Do you think you can do something about that?"

"It's not vice that wants to keep Stark. Sgt. Hunter

wouldn't dig his heels in like this. It's Petrocelli."

Lightman nodded. "He doesn't want a killer walking around free."

"Can you blame him?"

"No, but it's imperative Stark walks. Riley's cover depends on it." Lightman assessed me carefully. "Do you think you can make that happen?"

"I'll try."

"Get it done. Once it is, I'll bring you on board." He turned back to the photos and notes, not waiting for my response. He already knew I'd do everything I could to make it happen.

On my way to speak with the sergeant, Jane called me to her desk. One of our reports had been misfiled. By the time we found it and straightened everything out, everyone had been called into the conference room for our briefing on phase two, which meant I had to wait until after it was over to speak to Sgt. Hunter.

Two dozen officers filed into the room. The mood was only slightly better than it had been when we were originally corralled for our phase one briefing. Jane and I stood near the back. I tried not to eye the door like it was an escape hatch. All that mattered was the sergeant didn't slip away before I had a chance to speak to him.

"Since many of the smaller prostitution rings are controlled by the local gangs, the gangs unit has offered us their intel on prime locations." Hunter drew circles on the map tacked to the board behind him. "These territories are controlled by area gangs who consider the drug dealers and sex workers their property. Our goal is to shut them down."

"Won't that lead to a gang war or open season on the police department?" someone asked.

"We just had open season on the police department," someone else said.

Several sets of eyes peered in my direction. I'd been targeted and attacked due to the last time we pissed off an area gang. It'd be best to avoid poking the bear a second time.

"That's why we're doing this quietly," Hunter said. "To start, we're putting a few decoys on the otherwise occupied corners to lure out upper management. If we can pick them off individually without anyone being the wiser, it won't look like we've declared war on them, so they won't retaliate by coming after us." The sergeant shook his head, displeased with this plan but unable to change it. "Worst case, we'll make sweeping arrests and shut them down for the short-term. A few tactical units have been briefed. We are prepared to go in hot if necessary. Are there any questions?"

"We're supposed to paint ourselves as sex workers who want to move in on gang territory," Jane said. "That sounds like suicide."

"Believe me when I say I have the same worries and concerns, but these orders are coming directly from the commissioner's office. The mayor wants this done, so we're going to do it the best way we know how. Above all, be careful. Work this however you like. If you want to make an approach by trying to join the gang for added protection, go for it. Do whatever you have to in order to keep yourselves safe." Hunter looked increasingly uneasy. "Make sure your radios are working, people. This isn't busting a few johns and streetwalkers. This is serious business. A tactical unit will be stationed five minutes out from each of these locations." He pointed to the circles again. "The goal is to arrest the pimps that way our detectives and the prosecutor's office can bleed them for information on their gang affiliations. Is everyone clear?"

Once we were dismissed, I made my way to Hunter before he could escape to his office.

"Sarge," I said, "may I have a word in private?"

"Given what you went through, if you want to—"

"It's not about that."

"Oh-kay." He gestured to the door. "I can spare a minute to chat."

Before we even made it into his office, I launched into the Stark dilemma. "Gangs has their own operation in play. A detective could be compromised if Stark isn't released. I understand Detective Petrocelli's point. Releasing a suspected killer isn't something anyone wants, which is why I know Detective Lightman wouldn't be pushing for this if he had any other choice. Whoever Stark's working for must be that much worse, that much more dangerous."

"I understand all of that, Sarconi. Detectives Preston and Lightman already pled their case."

"But you know me, Sarge. You know I wouldn't ask for this if it wasn't life or death." Again, my stomach was in knots.

"It's not entirely up to me since homicide stuck their nose into this matter. Murder trumps just about everything. But I'll see what I can do. The homicide lieutenant owes me a favor."

"Thank you," I said.

"Don't thank me until I see if we can get this done." He rolled his eyes. "I swear, everything is falling apart. Damn election year. Damn politics. Damn it all."

Leaving Hunter to fight that battle, I figured it'd be best not to cause any more waves, so I went in search of Jane. Instead of changing and heading to our assigned destination, the twenty of us had been divided into three groups for a second briefing.

The person in charge of our group was a new vice detective I didn't know. She went over the intel they had gathered on our target—the Sixth Street Slayers. We were shown maps of the neighborhood, schematics of what was believed to be their base of operations, and photographs of their leadership, including the four men who controlled the sex trade in that neighborhood.

"The goal is to collar these four. Anyone else you bring in is your prerogative. Do what you can to maintain your cover for as long as possible. Once your cover is compromised, the whole op is blown. Is that clear?" she asked, her gaze resting on me.

There was a round of ayes and plenty of head nods.

"Sarconi, you're staying here today," the detective said, reading a note someone had handed her. She held up her palm as if I were about to protest. "If you have a problem with it, take it up with Sgt. Hunter. I'm just the messenger."

"Lucky you." Jane bumped against my shoulder on her way to the door. "It looks like you have standing orders not to reveal your true blue self."

"Ma'am," I said, halting the vice detective's retreat, "any

idea who made that request?" If it had been Hunter, he would have told me when we spoke earlier.

She showed me the sticky note. It didn't have the source listed, but I recognized the handwriting. *Lightman.*

I went back to Jane's desk and took a seat while the room emptied. Terri tossed a confused look in my direction and waved goodbye before disappearing with the five other members of our team. Perhaps this is what detention felt like, except no kid who served detention was ever this happy to do it. At least, I wanted to be happy about this, but I couldn't, knowing Michael's life was on the line.

Once everyone cleared out, leaving me with nothing to do, I went down the hall and knocked on Sergeant Hunter's office door. A few seconds later, Detective Preston opened the door. She attempted a smile that didn't make it to her eyes and gestured that I join them. Petrocelli and Sgt. Hunter were waiting inside.

"Maybe I should come back later. I just needed clarification on what I should be doing."

"Stay put, Lexie," Hunter ordered. "This little meeting of the minds is about our current predicament, which has plenty to do with you."

"Jeff Stark," Petrocelli eyed me, "is getting released. It seems you have more sway than I do."

"I—"

"Save it," Petrocelli stopped me before I could explain myself. "I don't want anyone to be in danger, especially one of our own. So we're going to do everything we possibly can to make sure Stark can't hurt anyone." He looked at Preston. "And I mean anyone."

"That's where you come in, Sarconi," Hunter said. "Right now, we have no basis for thinking Stark realized you were a decoy. The patrol units keeping watch haven't noticed any suspicious activity. As far as we know, Stark hasn't made contact with anyone except his legal team. They are unaware of the role you played. We withheld that from them, which is why they were so adamant our case wouldn't hold up, but it'd be best to take precautions. On the off chance Stark overheard police personnel talking about our current operation, we don't want to risk him locating you and blowing your cover while in the field."

"Instead, Jack's thinking we can use you," Preston said.

Hunter looked uneasy. "One thing at a time, Detective."

"Use me how?" I asked, but Preston shook her head. She didn't want to overstep for fear the brass would change their mind about setting Stark free.

"If Stark's smart, he'll go to ground," Petrocelli said. "It'd be the best thing for him, and we know he's clever enough to avoid charges sticking to him. So we shouldn't discount the possibility."

"Except he has a job to do," Preston said. "He won't be going anywhere until that's finished."

I stared at her, wanting answers or an explanation, but she didn't provide one. Instead, she picked at the chipped clear polish on her fingernail.

"Sarconi, until Stark's back in custody, you will assist Detective Petrocelli and the gangs unit in whatever capacity they assign you." Hunter nodded at me. "It was nice working with you again."

"Thank you, sir."

"I'll meet you in the conference room," Petrocelli said, jerking his chin at the door.

"*We'll* meet you in the conference room," Preston insisted.

Clearly, I wasn't allowed to stay in the room while the grown-ups were talking. Hopefully, that'd change after my promotion.

FIFTEEN

"All right, what's going on?" I asked the moment Preston and Petrocelli walked through the door.

"By all means, Samantha." Petrocelli gestured that she go ahead. "This is your show. As always, you want to be on top. So please, take charge."

She glared at him before turning her attention to me. That look made me wonder what their story was, but I already had enough drama in my life. I didn't need any more.

"Rumors have been circulating about a local syndicate hoping to make it big. They've conducted a few power plays, but organized crime has been keeping them in their place. At least, that had been the case until the mayor's crackdown led to a lot of arrests and a giant mess. The syndicate saw this as their chance to take control."

"Control of what?" I asked.

"All things related to human trafficking—sex workers, laborers, those scam farms. Usually, OCU would handle this or assist, but the police department is in a mess." She muttered several derogatory things about the mayor before shaking it off and getting back on topic. "Anyway, we're still piecing things together and hoping to gather intel. We don't know what connections the syndicate has, how they are moving people in and out, or even who is in charge of this."

"You don't even know who's running this alleged syndicate," Petrocelli scoffed. "That's rich."

"Shut it, Dean. We've been investigating, gathering intel, hoping to figure things out. We think it might be the Shark."

"There may not be anything to it. This could all be for nothing," he insisted. "If this syndicate had that kind of power, OCU would do something about them. Hell, the FBI would be all over their asses."

"What do we know about them?" I asked. "Are we looking at the Italians? Russians? Irish? Mexicans?"

"If Jack thought this had anything to do with the Italians, he would have read you in sooner," Preston said.

"Ha ha." Though her joke may not have been that far off. My immediate family wasn't connected, but that didn't mean I wasn't distant relatives to people who were.

"Organized crime doesn't have anything on them, so we're not looking at mafia-types. However, the syndicate has connections to get people in and out of the country undetected," she said.

"So cartel?"

"Not necessarily, but they most likely connect to that network and use coyotes."

"They could be shipping them over on cargo ships."

"Also a possibility," Preston said, "which is why Detective Riley went undercover to find out. His intel led to Stark's network, hence our dilemma."

Petrocelli let out a grunt. "You realize the syndicate could be providing Stark the connection, not the other way around. By having him released, you're allowing them to get back to business as usual. What kind of intel has Michael even offered up? Has he identified any of these syndicate members? Do you have surveillance set up?"

"Don't worry about what we're doing," Preston said. "That is need to know."

"I can't believe you'd send one man in alone. He needs backup," Petrocelli said, "especially when your entire unit is operating blind."

"We're not blind." Preston turned back to me. "Lightman thinks we may be able to use you, the sex worker version of you. It all depends on what Stark believes. But he and Riley were in that neighborhood for a reason. They're recruiting."

"You mean looking for people to traffic," Petrocelli said.

"We don't know for sure. Riley was unclear about the reason they met in that location, but once we know more, we may need you, Sarconi."

"Sure, anything I can do to help," I said.

Preston sighed. She didn't say it out loud, but I could read the look in her eyes. Michael would not approve of this. Unfortunately for him, he didn't get to dictate my actions. "As soon as we have more details, we'll let you know what we want to do. Until then," she pointed at Petrocelli, "you're stuck with this guy."

"Hey," he said, "be nice, Samantha."

"You never liked it when I was nice."

He grinned at her. "I always liked it when you were nice. You just never were."

Rolling her eyes, she pushed open the door.

Petrocelli returned to his chair and reached for the stack of folders. "You heard the lady. You're all mine until gangs decides you should play with them instead. I don't know about you, but I wouldn't appreciate being treated like a pawn."

"I'm an officer. It's part of the job description," I said.

"They won't treat you any differently when you have a detective's shield. A piece of advice. Tell gangs to shove it. You could do better."

"Oh yeah?" I took a seat across from him and opened the file he pushed toward me.

"Yeah." He glanced up. "I'm sure we could find a spot for you at RHD."

~*~

Petrocelli's phone chimed. After picking it up and studying the message on the screen, he put it down. "I'm calling it." He flipped the folder closed. "Time of death 9:24."

I glanced up briefly before going back to what I was doing. Today had been the epitome of boring. I'd been tasked with pulling records on every known gang suspected of sex trafficking. The syndicate, as Preston referred to them, appeared to be an off-shoot of the Sixth Street Slayers. They had ties to southeastern Asia as well as alleged connections to criminal organizations south of the border.

However, since we hadn't been given much to go on, I was looking into everything, hoping to figure out how the syndicate or the Sixth Street Slayers connected to Jeff Stark. My best guess was they were all S names. The syndicate, the Slayers, the Shark, and Stark. They must have had club meetings or something, and that's how they met.

"Sarconi, didn't you hear me?" he asked.

Shit, I was an S name too. Maybe I was involved. "Oh, sorry. I didn't realize I was required to laugh at your joke." The one my internal voice made was much funnier.

"Well, you are supposed to fulfill whatever role I require, but it wasn't a joke. Okay, no one actually died, but this place is dead. It's time to call it quits."

"Y'know, this is vice, not homicide. You need to lose that morbid sense of humor and don't think that sexual innuendo is acceptable because it's not."

"There was nothing sexual about what I said. Why would you take it that way? Are you thinking impure thoughts?"

"Detective, I've spent the last six weeks studying protocol and procedure. You don't want to split hairs with me on this. I'll win every time."

"Was that from studying for the detective's exam, or do you just have an unquenchable thirst for reading regulations?"

"What do you think?"

"I don't know. That's why I asked."

"Has anyone ever told you you're annoying?"

"Are you sure saying that doesn't violate a rule? That sounds like insubordination."

"We aren't military."

He rocked back in his chair, grabbed the apple that had been sitting beside him for the last two hours, and rubbed it against his shirt before taking a bite and putting his feet up on the edge of the table. "No, but we have a command structure. The system relies on orders and respect."

Closing the folder and making one final notation, I rubbed my eyes. "Right, the same way you respected Preston."

"That was different. We have a history."

"I might have picked up on that."

He put the apple down, took the stack of files off the table, and dumped them into the nearest filing cabinet. "To clarify, there was no innuendo. You've spent too long decoying for vice if you think there was."

"Tell me about it."

He stuck the apple in his mouth while he slipped on his jacket. "I've got something else planned for us that's far more exciting than paperwork. We're gonna get a drink."

"No, thanks." This guy needed to learn boundaries. I wasn't above reporting him. I'd dealt with enough during this temporary reassignment.

"Trust me. This is definitely not what you're thinking." He ushered me out of the chair and toward the door. "Get changed. Put on something elegant but slutty. Think high-end hooker."

My eyes widened. Was he serious, or was this another joke? "What?"

"Elegant but slutty. Y'know, some black, low-cut, slinky number and heels. Strappy stilettos would be a nice touch. I'm partial to a lace bustier and garter belt, but the undergarments can be a surprise. We're on a timetable, so beggars can't be choosers."

"Maybe we should continue this conversation in Sergeant Hunter's office or with my union rep and a few IA investigators. You wouldn't have a problem repeating what you just said in front of them, would you?"

"No, but can we do that afterward?" He tapped his watch. "I need someone to work with undercover, and since you've been stuck inside all day, I thought you'd like to go out and play." He held up his palms. "But if you want to call it a night, I'll get Reeve or one of the other decoys to fill in. After all, that paperwork is mighty draining."

"What's the play? Why are you going undercover? And how come this is the first I'm hearing about it?"

"It isn't the first you're hearing about it." He checked his watch. "Look, I need an answer. You've already made detective. The rest is a formality, which means you're the most qualified, especially since you've done decoy work before. Say yes, and I'll explain everything while you get dressed." He could see the hesitation on my face. "Fine. You can say no. I'd hate for you to accuse me of sexual harassment, but I have a job to do and not a lot of time to waste debating this with you. Nothing indicates Stark will be there, so this may not connect. You can bow out, but we need more background info. Your buddies in gangs could definitely use it. From the sounds of it, they've been operating blind. What do you say? Take some initiative? Help a guy out?"

"Fine, I'll help, but if this is a ploy, you're gonna need a good lawyer and you might want to start checking the classifieds." I headed toward the wardrobe room. The city had spent quite a few dollars to appropriately attire us with evening wear. The assortment had vastly improved since the last time I checked. I held up a backless dress with a deep v, earning a nod. "Start talking," I said, stepping into the ladies' room and finding an empty stall to change.

Petrocelli hesitated for a second and then entered the bathroom. "That message I got was from Lightman. After Stark was released, he paid a visit to one of the high-end escort services and inquired as to hiring several escorts for a party. Given the amount of cash he flashed, we're assuming none of that is aboveboard. Since most of those ladies and gentlemen work out of the nicer hotels, we're trying to figure out which hotels and where Stark is planning this party."

"What kind of party?"

"It's a giant bash because he got out of jail."

"Seriously?"

"That was sarcasm. Are you sure you made detective?"

"Bite me."

"That sounds like something I should report or at least discuss with my union rep."

I sighed. Petrocelli was enjoying this way too much. "Are you sure I should go with you? I thought Lightman wanted me to stay out of sight."

"Surveillance has Stark in their sights. He won't be there. However, Lightman has another idea in mind, if you can pull it off." He held out his phone, so I could read the message.

The gangs unit wanted to see if I could get hired on as a

high-end escort in time for whatever event Stark was hosting. It'd put me in the perfect position to get scooped up by the syndicate for trafficking or worse, which would get us one step closer to getting the details needed to make sweeping arrests and get Michael out of there.

"According to Sgt. Hunter, phase three will be taking down the madams. Lightman's hoping to convince vice to move up its timetable. If it does, you'd already have a presence and be an easy shoo-in when the shit hits the fan. With a shortage of escorts, they'd have to take you, and Stark would have to accept that."

"That's a lot of ifs," I said.

"That's how assignments like this work. Operations aren't made in a day. Insertion of an asset takes a lot of time and a lot of luck, most of which we make ourselves by being in the right place at the right time and having exactly what is needed. I was told you did undercover before."

"Not long term. I was a plant, a decoy, that was it."

"Did you go through any training?"

"Academy basics."

Petrocelli rubbed his eyes. "Jeez. Maybe you should sit this one out."

That made me want to dig my heels in. "I can handle it."

"Are you sure? It's not just your life on the line."

Michael. But I wouldn't botch this. "I have lots of practice pretending to be a sex worker. This should be in my wheelhouse."

"We'll see. Tonight we're gathering intel on the hotels, how things work, who may be working there, and getting you seen. Vice has eyes on some concierges who have madams on speed dial. But Sgt. Hunter wants us to scout the locations and make sure no one is pulling our chain."

"Fix my knot." I spun, and Petrocelli brushed my hair to the side and retied the halter's straps around the back of my neck. "Don't ask where my badge and gun are because that's privileged information."

"And I don't need to know."

"Precisely." I glanced in the mirror, realizing I needed to do my hair and makeup, but Petrocelli tugged gently on my elbow.

"You can finish getting ready in the car." I must have looked nervous because he added, "This is only recon. There's absolutely nothing to worry about. I'm your date for this evening, not some lonely high roller. You won't be in any danger. Backup won't be necessary since you have me."

That was debatable, but I said, "Okay."

SIXTEEN

Despite his words, the nervous energy settled around me. This wasn't an attempt to whore myself out to some random john or piss off a pimp. This was to gather intel on the escorts and call girls and see if hotel management was a willing or active participant in the sex trade. Vice would need that to shut things down.

There had been rumors that managers and concierges were taking money under the table to turn a blind eye or to request escorts for a few of their guests. While there were legitimate escort services, it was a slippery slope between paying for a dinner companion and paying for sex.

Phase three would be the hardest to execute, but if Lightman needed to have enough women arrested so I could get invited to the party and provide Michael backup, I was game. My gut said Sgt. Hunter would be too.

"What's really going on?" I asked.

"What do you mean?" Petrocelli tried to play innocent, but I wasn't buying it.

"You volunteered to assist vice before Stark was arrested. You wanted him all along, but you didn't say anything about it. You said you were volunteering. Why the secrecy?"

"You ask a lot of questions."

"Yet, you don't like to provide any answers."

"There are things you don't need to know."

"How can I change your mind on that?"

"Careful, Sarconi. It sounds like you're attempting to

bribe me. That could be a violation, possibly even a crime."

Resisting the urge to call him an unkind name, I dug through my bag. Putting eyeliner on in a moving vehicle was tricky business, but amazingly, Petrocelli avoided most of the bumps and potholes. By the time he pulled into the parking garage across the street, I was painted up like a porcelain doll. After running a brush through my long brown hair, which was wavy from being in a braid all day, I settled on putting it half up and hoped for the best.

"Take a seat at the bar and wait for me," he instructed. "I hear you're quite the overachiever. Refrain from picking up any other men in the meantime."

"Should I beat them off with a stick? Or is that too dominatrix-y for a four-star hotel?"

"I'll join you in ten minutes. Work the room a little but just enough that management notices. Then you'll have to do your best to pick me up. I want a real spectacle that leaves no doubt in anyone's mind. Make it blatantly obvious."

"Sure, but you better keep your hands to yourself because that costs extra, sweetie."

If this was an elaborate hoax or a hazing ritual, I'd have Petrocelli's badge. But I knew this wasn't a joke. I'd seen the text. For Lightman to ask for help, things were dire. Was Michael safe now that Stark was roaming free? Originally, that's how Preston made it sound, but given the givens, I didn't believe that. If anything, I feared he was in worse danger now than before.

Strutting through the door, I winked at the man working the front desk and continued to the bar. My heels clacked suggestively against the hard tiles, echoing in the exquisitely decorated hotel. A few businessmen were seated on the couches and armchairs, working on laptops and tablets. A few looked up when I passed.

Once through the entryway to the hotel's bar, I scanned the area, sizing up potential targets and the competition. The problem with identifying escorts in classy joints was they dressed like the other women in the bar, sometimes even more conservatively than the average woman. At least on street corners, it was obvious who was for sale and exactly what they were selling. Here, it was a charade filled with finesse and quiet exchanges.

I found an empty stool and took a seat. Crossing my legs so the slit of the gown exposed my thigh, I put my forearm on the bar and leaned toward the bartender. "What's good tonight, sugar?"

"We have a special on mojitos."

"I'll take the Macallan 18, neat." I wasn't a scotch drinker, but it was a favorite of quite a few lonely businessmen that I had encountered back in the day.

"Macallan for the lady, coming up," the bartender said, drawing the attention of a few nearby patrons.

I smiled at a forty-something gentleman, doing my best to make bedroom eyes at him. The bartender poured the glass, zeroing in on my gaze for a second. He studied my appearance while he toweled off the bar.

"Business or pleasure?" he asked nonchalantly.

"Why do I have to pick?" I batted my eyelashes. "If you derive enjoyment from what you do, then is it really nothing more than business?" Internally, I cringed, but my face remained neutral.

"I've never seen you here before. Are you traveling?"

"No, I'm new." I took a sip from the glass.

"Do you have a room?" He produced a receipt to explain the question, but he was suspicious. Hopefully, he assumed I was rentable by the hour.

"Not yet, but I've only been here five minutes. Give a girl some time to work her magic."

A few minutes later, Petrocelli entered. His appearance had drastically changed, despite the fact he was wearing the same suit from earlier. He had lost the tie, unbuttoned the top two buttons on his shirt, tousled his hair into something much sexier than it had looked at the station, and exuded an air of self-assured cockiness that reminded me of Michael.

He stood at the end of the bar, smiling at the closest woman and beckoning to the barkeep. The nearest bartender poured a gin martini for him. Instead of taking a seat, Petrocelli circled the room. He was on the prowl. He hovered at a table and shamelessly flirted for five minutes before striking out with all three women. To anyone paying attention, it was obvious he was determined to get laid.

"Hey, handsome," I called once he was within earshot, "what are you drinking?"

He stepped closer and rested his elbow on the bar beside me. "I was thinking a bottle of champagne would be nice, but I want to share it with someone special."

"Oh yeah? How special are we talking?"

The bartender glanced in our direction. I wasn't sure how long this ruse would have to go on before he called hotel security or told us to take it upstairs.

"Are you waiting for someone?" I asked.

"I might be." Petrocelli slid onto the seat beside me. "It depends. Are you waiting for someone?"

"He just arrived."

Petrocelli made a pretense of looking around, and I giggled. I ran a hand up his arm to his shoulder. Without hesitating, he gripped the stool beneath me and yanked, pulling my chair flush against his so that my crossed leg was resting over his knee. The sound of the stool sliding against the tile drew the attention of the bartender, who returned to ask if we needed refills.

"What do you say to sharing that champagne?" Petrocelli asked me.

"It sounds lovely, but it might take a bit more than champagne."

"How about we work out the specifics in my room?" He produced a hotel key from his jacket pocket. "Or will that be a problem?"

"No problem, sugar." I fingered the card he laid on top of the bar. "Why don't you have that champagne sent upstairs?"

He turned to the bartender. "The lady drives a hard bargain, if you know what I mean." Petrocelli sounded sleazy saying it. I was impressed by his undercover ability. Until now, I pegged him as a suit who investigated crime scenes and screwed with suspects' heads once he had them in the box.

He ordered a bottle of mid-priced champagne to be delivered, signed a room number on his receipt, and pulled me onto his lap, suckling against my neck for a second before placing me on the ground and snaking his arm around my waist.

"C'mon, I can't wait, and I know exactly what I want," he said.

He kept his arm around me as we made our way to the elevators. The door opened, and we stepped inside. He continued the charade inside the elevator car and as we made our way down the hall. He led us to the room at the end of the corridor and slid the keycard into the lock.

After pushing the door open, he pressed against my back and whispered in my ear, "There's a camera at nine o'clock, so please don't slap me." Then he spun me around, covered my mouth with his and walked us into the room, kicking the door closed behind him.

SEVENTEEN

"What the hell is wrong with you?" I wiped my mouth with the back of my hand, resisting the urge to spit. "I didn't agree to tonsil hockey." I gestured around the room. "Did you seriously rent this room to run recon, or did you hope to actually get laid? I thought we were supposed to be feeling out the bartender and the hotel staff. What are we doing up here?"

"You'll see." He took his jacket off and began unbuttoning his shirt. "The champagne will be here in a few minutes. Get on the bed."

"No." What was he thinking? There wasn't a chance in hell I was going to screw his brains out.

"Look, either you can answer the door half-naked, or I can. I assumed you'd prefer to remain dressed, but that's up to you. One of us will be waiting on the bed."

He removed his wallet and laid a crisp stack of hundreds on the dresser in clear view of the door. Then he placed a ribbon of wrapped condoms on the dresser next to the cash. It'd be obvious to anyone what was going on. Newlyweds and one night stands didn't leave the money out in the open.

"I want to see if they kick us out or threaten to report us."

"Fine," I growled, moving toward the king-sized bed. Haphazardly, I tossed a few of the pillows onto the floor and hopped onto the mattress. "Let me guess, you want me to roll around a bit to make it look like we were in the middle of something."

"It couldn't hurt." He snorted. "It's nice to have a seasoned decoy helping out."

"Shut up."

After giving the bed a slightly used appearance and adequately mussing my hair, I settled near the pillows and waited. Petrocelli took a seat at the table. His belt was on the floor near the foot of the bed. His pants were unbuttoned but still zipped, and his shirt was completely open, hanging loosely from his shoulders. He was in decent shape.

He felt my eyes on him and cocked an eyebrow skyward. "See anything you like?"

"I expected to find an eight pack and at least eight inches underneath that nice suit," I teased. "Sadly, I'm disappointed. That's gonna cost ya extra, sugar."

"Do you really want to see what's underneath this suit? Because you were the one spouting off about sexual harassment earlier this evening." He fought the smile off his face. "Despite what most feminists want me to think, that train runs both ways, sister."

"Says the man who assaulted me with his lips." I shook my head, turning serious. "If you do it again, I'll hurt you. I'm okay selling my act, but I'm not okay making out with you in order to do it."

"I'm sorry," he said sincerely, "but you know what this job is and what it entails. You shouldn't be surprised."

"You could have warned me."

"I play it by ear. Pro tip, that's the only way to survive undercover."

Footsteps sounded outside our door. He pressed a finger to his lips to shush me. There was a knock, and then someone called out, "Room service."

Petrocelli stood, facing away from me and unzipping his pants so they'd hang lower on his hips as he went to the door. He opened it wide, making sure the money and other evidence of his pay-by-the-hour tryst were in plain sight.

"You showed up just in time. A minute later and I would have had to cancel that order, if you know what I mean." He rummaged in his pocket and pulled out money for a tip.

"Is your guest staying all night, sir?" the bellhop asked.

"She's staying as long as I can afford her," Petrocelli

replied. "Is that a problem?"

"No, sir. Just phone ahead to the front desk if she needs to catch a cab home. We wouldn't want anyone to get the wrong idea or for the young lady to have to wait outside for a ride."

"Sure thing." Petrocelli took the champagne bucket, and the bellhop disappeared down the hallway. We didn't speak again until the door was locked. "I guess that answers our question." He zipped his pants and retrieved his belt. "I hope you didn't have plans tonight. I wasn't sure how things would turn out, but it looks like we'll be stuck here a while longer."

"No plans." I climbed off the bed, straightening my dress and then my hair. "Now what do we do?"

He picked up the remote. "We can watch TV. In about an hour, we'll head out."

"That's a lot of money for an hour." I jerked my chin at the table.

"Don't worry, you earned every penny."

I slapped his arm.

"Pain doesn't do it for me," he said.

"Good," I laughed, "then again, if it did, we could probably get out of here in twenty minutes or less."

"Ha ha."

"Fifteen?"

"You're enjoying this, aren't you? Granted, I guess I deserve it for failing to prepare you for tonight."

"I've learned to adapt. It's part of the job."

"You didn't seem like that earlier. You seemed pissed you didn't know about any of this until the last minute."

"In this situation, I could have used more time to prepare. The more intel I have going in, the better the outcome."

"Are you talking about Stark?"

"It would be nice to know what's going on with that situation, but the more intel I have on any situation always proves useful. Prior experiences have taught me that."

"You seem the type who likes to prepare for everything."

"Again, I'll direct you to my previous comment." I shook my head and stared at the TV. "It's been a rough week. A rough few months, actually."

"It really has." He flipped through the channels, finding nothing to watch, and turned off the television. "I'd ask if you want a glass of champagne, but we're on the clock. And despite what you may think, I don't break the rules. The sip of scotch and martini we had downstairs was more than enough."

"Why are you going after Jeff Stark?"

"It was my case, so I volunteered. I like to see things through."

"You weren't being punished?"

His right eyebrow raised. "Is that why you were asked to assist vice?"

"I wasn't asked. I was forced." I stared at the dark screen. "I don't know if it's punishment, but it feels like it."

The psychologist in him found that interesting. "How about we get to know one another a little better?"

"Sure," I snickered, "most men just want to talk."

"Is there an off switch?"

"Most men can't find that either."

He glared.

"Okay, I'm finished." I giggled. "Damn. Sorry. Really, that's it." I sat on the edge of the bed and scrubbed a hand down my face.

"Is humor a defense mechanism or what you do when you're nervous?"

"Maybe I'm just a smartass."

"That I don't doubt." He stared at me. "Come on, I'm serious. Tell me something."

This felt like a trap, but sitting in silence or refusing to play along could be construed as hostile. He seemed the type to bring up the whole disrespect, insubordination thing again.

"The first thing you should know is that I tend to make inappropriate remarks or have irrational emotional responses when I'm nervous or stressed out."

"So it is a coping mechanism." He tucked his shirt in and went to work on the buttons. "Do I make you nervous?"

"No, it's the job. I hate vice. Frankly, that's why I asked to transfer out."

"It's not because of the situation with gangs? That is your new unit, after all."

"I'll help them if I can."

His brows knit together. "Correct me if I'm wrong, but every time you try to help them, you end up in peril. Why would you want to go anywhere near that unit?"

"I have my reasons."

Petrocelli quirked an eyebrow. "You avoid vice because of that situation. I'd think they'd be the same."

"It's different. The work is different. More rewarding, more respectful."

He considered what I said. "I remember that hostage situation that occurred at the station. That was you, wasn't it?"

"Yeah, fun times."

"And that was before you were attacked at the liquor store."

"It wasn't just me. A local gang declared war on the police. My partner was shot. He had a vest on, so he was okay, but—"

"They made a few attempts to kill you."

"I'm lucky like that."

"Gangs caught those guys. Is that why you want to work for them? It's paying back the debt you owe."

"I don't owe them anything."

"Maybe they owe you." Petrocelli considered what I said. "Is that why you decided to go out for detective? You realized patrol was too dangerous?"

"You make it sound like I tried out for cheerleading."

"Were you a cheerleader?"

"Fuck no. Why would you ask that?"

"I'm just trying to figure you out."

"Do you think I'm bubbly enough to be a cheerleader?"

"No. I think you may have been into emo, dressed in black, and smoked pot under the bleachers."

"Not exactly."

"So the job made you like this?"

"Do other people like it when you poke around in their heads?"

"No."

"So stop it."

"Do you want to ask me a question?"

"Not unless you have some intel you haven't divulged on Stark or this op."

"I thought you'd ask me something personal."

I waved my hand at him. "We're on the clock. Keep your personal matters to yourself."

He chuckled. "I don't know anything else. Samantha hasn't been particularly forthcoming. I can tell you about the homicide investigation and my suspicions, but the evidence is flimsy. I need more time and a warrant before I can prove anything. I would have gotten it too, if we hadn't cut Stark loose." His gaze shifted around the room. "Right now, I'm just hoping Samantha's on the level. Gangs may have their sights set on whoever hired Stark, but I have every intention of making sure he goes down too." He looked at me. "You don't need to worry. I have every intention of making sure that man won't be free to hurt anyone else."

"I'm not worried."

"Could have fooled me."

"Since you think you're so good at reading me, why don't you tell me what makes you tick? Why are you like this?" I asked.

"What can I say? Things didn't turn out the way I thought, so I signed up for the police academy and never looked back."

"For someone who didn't look back, it sounds like you might regret it."

"It depends on when you ask the question." He crossed the room to tuck the money back into his pocket. "The big busts make it worth it. Any day I pull a deranged piece of shit off the street makes it worthwhile."

"I can relate to that," I said. "You have a psych degree, right?"

"Yeah," he folded up the ribbon of condoms and put them into his jacket pocket, "but you turned down my offer for free psychotherapy."

"How come no one calls you Doc?"

"I don't have a Ph.D. I stopped after my M.A." He continued to place the important items back inside his pockets while making the room look like the scene of a wild sex party. Turning back around, he sighed. "You can't decide if you want to grill me about my past or our current op."

"It's not that. You're the one being selective about the kinds of questions you'll answer."

"There's a reason for that."

"Rules and regs?"

"You have no idea what to make of me, Sarconi. Or do you prefer Lexie? See, I don't always have to be that serious. Although, I do recall you hate it when people use your given name, even though Alessandra is a beautiful name." He narrowed his eyes. "You don't want your heritage to define you."

"Seriously, stop it." I despised how well he could read my inner thoughts and feelings when we barely knew one another. "That's creepy. It's why people don't like you."

"That's not why they don't like me."

"Then why don't they like you?"

"You'd have to ask them."

"I'm not buying it." I tapped my nails against the table. "Being in the field with questionable backup is something I despise, so should I despise being here with you?"

"I follow the rules when it comes to dealing with perps, but my personal life is messy. I've made a few enemies."

"Did you cheat at poker?"

"Worse."

"What would be worse?"

He shook his head. "My record's clean. I'm strict about following the rules for a reason."

"Did you snitch on your partner?"

My question touched a nerve. "New topic."

I grabbed the remote and turned the television back on, abruptly halting the conversation. Annoying Petrocelli wouldn't lead to him sharing information on how our current mission connected to Michael's undercover work, so it was best to let him cool off. I flipped through the channels, finding a sitcom and hoping the laugh track would ease the tension in the room. Eventually, Petrocelli ran out of things to rearrange and sat on the end of the bed, focusing on the television.

"Are you friends with Samantha?" he asked out of the blue.

"Detective Preston?" I practically choked. "She's been in my corner quite a few times. I'm not sure friends is what I'd call it though. The gangs detectives took me under their wing when I was first tasked to assist."

"That's why Lightman requested you?"

"I guess. Why do you ask? Are you friends with Preston?"

"You could say that." He turned to look at me. "I take it you've heard the rumors about her?"

"What rumors?"

"For someone with experience as a decoy, you could sound more convincing." He stared at me. "Are you going to ask me what you want to ask?"

I already knew how Preston had gotten that reputation. The rumor was she tried to sleep her way to the top. She was Michael's ex. But he never outranked her, so that story never made much sense. Kemper insisted she'd slept with lots of top brass, but I didn't know. And I didn't want to.

"I don't want to ask you anything. Rumors are rumors. People say terrible things about me that aren't true. I don't want to be part of the gossip mill," I said.

"That's refreshing."

"Am I supposed to believe you live under a rock and haven't heard the things the other officers say about me?"

"Oh, I've heard a few, but I don't believe them. Well, most of them. The one about you threatening to rip off a guy's balls is probably true."

"That actually didn't happen, but I'm glad that's the rumor you chose to believe."

We fell silent as I thought about the nasty rumors that circulated. Nothing was ever substantiated. Jane had spread plenty of gossip and started some rumors of her own as a joke. It was the nature of vice, but once they were out there, there was no escaping them or the looks and whispers that followed.

Petrocelli reached across the bed and touched my forearm. "Hey, don't worry about it. Anyone who's worked with you will know what's true and what isn't. Don't dwell."

I focused on where his hand rested against my forearm,

the scar nearly invisible beneath the caked-on makeup I used to conceal it. "So you didn't think you'd get lucky on our stakeout? That's always a favorite urban legend in the police department."

"We did get lucky. We know this hotel has no problem with guests inviting sex workers to their suites, and they do what they can to keep it on the down low. From here, we'll grab up the concierge and maybe the bartender, get some names, and quietly shut down the madams and escorts working from here. That's about as lucky as I want to get." He followed my line of sight and withdrew his hand. "But to satisfy my own curiosity, was that kiss really so terrible?"

"I don't know." I put my palm up as if to push him and the question away. "That wasn't a line to encourage a repeat or to spare your feelings. When it was happening, I just wanted it to stop."

"You're seeing someone."

"Yeah."

"That explains a lot." Petrocelli sat up straighter, increasing the distance between us. "Does he know what you do for a living?"

"That's not something I could keep secret."

"And he's okay with it?"

"I guess. He doesn't have a choice." A smile crept onto my face as I thought about Michael's constant encouragement to take the detective's exam.

"Wow, you're practically glowing. He's a lucky man. Do you want to share whatever memory or thought is floating through your mind? We could use some cheering up."

"It's nothing. He hates the idea that I could be in danger, but he's always incredibly supportive. He's a great guy."

"I'd love to meet him sometime. What does he do?"

I glanced at the clock. "We should get out of here. I don't want to spend the entire night in a hotel room when there's paperwork to be filed."

EIGHTEEN

Once I was settled inside my apartment, I checked the time. It was a little after midnight. Preston might still be awake. Surely, midnight wasn't too late to call someone, right?

Chewing on my bottom lip, I put the phone down, circled the kitchen, and returned to the spot where I placed the device. It was now or never, and I had to know what was happening.

"Hello," she answered. My mind went blank. I remained silent, attempting to determine if she sounded awake or asleep. "Sarconi, I know it's you. What do you want?"

"Is he okay?" I blurted out before my brain could reengage and develop a realistic excuse for calling.

"As far as I know. There's been no communication since you caught us at the motel. He's not supposed to be in contact. You know this, so why are you calling me?"

"This afternoon you said you could use me. That's why Petrocelli and I went to the high-end hotels to gather intel. I thought when we returned you or Lightman would have had something waiting for me, but you didn't. I want to know what's going on, what you expect me to do. I don't want to walk into this unprepared. Lives are on the line. Michael's life is on the line."

"You don't have to tell me that. I know." She let out a huff. "I hate it when he does this. I always have. But you know Michael. He'll do whatever he's asked and more. It's that damn sense of right and wrong, protecting the innocent, and all that. I don't know why he can't get it through his thick skull that this is a job. He doesn't need to volunteer for these insane things or put himself at risk like this. I thought things would be different now that he's with you. But they're not."

I bristled. "You think this is my fault?"

"No," she said, her voice softer, "that's not what I meant. I...I don't know what I'm saying."

"You're worried."

"Yeah." She snickered. "So are you."

"That is why I called."

"I know Michael trusts you. But he specifically wanted you left out of the loop." She sighed. "Look, you were briefed on the syndicate. That's pretty much all you need to know for now."

"Do you think Stark's providing the network for them, or do you think the syndicate has its own network Stark is piggybacking off of?"

"We're not sure. Michael's working the inside angles to find out. Either way, we'll take them all down."

"Why isn't organized crime dealing with this? From everything you've said, the syndicate sounds pretty damn organized."

"OCU has enough on their plates. With this major crackdown in the works, the crime families are positioning themselves to grab up more territory and control. OCU has to stay on top of that. It's whack-a-mole for them. So they're leaving the syndicate to us. If left to their own devices, they will build a criminal empire. Jack wants to nip it in the bud before it gets to that point. We're on the cusp. We need to figure out what kind of overseas connections the syndicate has. If they can't traffic, their operation won't be able to expand. Maybe they'll crumble, or maybe they'll remain small potatoes. Either way, we take down whoever is in charge, and we'll grab Stark while we're at it."

"So that's the plan? You want to clip their wings?"

"In a manner of speaking."

"Do you think Stark is part of the syndicate or an outside contractor?"

"Michael wasn't sure. Stark knows a lot when it comes to syndicate business, but he's answering to someone.

Michael's been there when calls and texts have come in."

"I thought Michael infiltrated the syndicate. Shouldn't he know who's running it?"

"They operate the same way the cartels do. The person in charge doesn't waste time on nobodies. But Stark's not a nobody."

"Which is why Michael's been trying to get close to him."

"Exactly," Preston said.

"That's why gangs wanted Stark released."

"Didn't we have this conversation earlier?"

"Not in so many words," I said. "I need more, Sam."

"Wow, Lexie, you must be serious to use my first name."

"You said Michael feared he was compromised. With Stark out, does that suspicion go away or get worse?"

"I don't know. The syndicate is looking for a rat. Michael's cover will only hold up for so long. He won't let us pull him out until he gets the evidence he needs to bust everyone. The only way he gets that is if Stark leads him to it. That's why we needed Stark released. If he blames Michael for setting him up, we'll know soon enough."

"Is that why Lightman wants to add me to the mix?"

"Jack wants someone on the inside he trusts in case things go south. He knows you and Michael work well together. In fact, you may be better together. Michael could work Stark from the syndicate angle, and you could work it from the inside out."

"You want me to get trafficked?"

"No, but if you find out where they're taking these people or how they're moving them, it'll lead back to the source. It's two sides of the same coin. You and Michael would be working the operation from opposite ends. You can meet in the middle."

"Does Michael know this is the new plan?"

"No. He'd never agree to it. That's why Jack won't ask permission, not that he has to. It's his unit. He can do whatever he wants."

Maybe Petrocelli was right. Gangs would always treat me as a pawn since that's how Lightman was treating Michael.

"Jack will brief you with the official version once he's ready to put you in play. Until then, keep an ear to the ground on local prostitution rings and let me know if anyone goes missing or gets recruited or hired by Stark," she said.

"Will do."

~*~

"Sarconi," Lightman was waiting at the door to the roll call room when I arrived to start my shift, "walk with me."

I gave the door a questioning look.

"Peterson knows we're having this discussion. You aren't going out on patrol. There's no reason you need to go through parade. You're a detective now."

"Yeah, okay," I said skeptically.

Lightman cocked an eyebrow before reaching into his pocket and pulling out a case. "Here. Peterson was going to do a whole thing in his office, but we don't have time for that now. The fanfare can wait until things settle. Don't worry. We'll have cake and a celebration so you don't feel like you missed out on anything."

"Seriously?"

"No." Rolling his eyes, Lightman pushed open the door to gangs, expecting me to obediently follow behind. As usual, I hurried to keep up. We strode through the bullpen. Detective Devereaux was on the phone. Preston was nowhere to be seen. "Sam said you were briefed yesterday."

"Bare bones," I said.

Lightman led us to the conference room and waited for the door to shut behind me. The boards he'd been staring at the other day remained where they were. As far as I could tell, nothing had been added or updated. "How bare?"

I told him what I knew.

"All right, that's a good starting place. Your position with vice makes this easier. You've already established your cover as a sex worker. Uniformed officers busted you when they busted Stark. Should the two of you cross paths again, the reason should be self-evident. Hopefully, that will be enough to throw off any suspicion he might have."

"If we cross paths again? Don't you think that'll happen? Detective Preston made it sound like the entire point was to figure out how Stark connects to the syndicate's operation.

I'd think that would put us on a collision course."

"Let's hope not. What I want you to do is stay the course with whatever vice has planned. Last night, you scouted a ritzy hotel. Vice will make another massive sweep, taking a lot of escorts out of play before going after the madams. That should prevent everyone else from moving in on that territory. Once everything's been taken care of, you saunter onto the scene. The madams will be desperate and less picky, making you an obvious shoo-in as an escort. What I need from you today is making sure a lot of people recognize you as a hooker. Your reputation has to precede you. Do you think you can do that?"

"I guess." My head was spinning. Petrocelli explained the nuances of undercover to me last night. "But couldn't this backfire?"

"What do you mean?"

"Common denominator. If everyone arrested remembers me being there, won't they realize I'm a cop?"

"Not if you get booked and processed too." Lightman stared into my eyes. "You have nothing to worry about. This is basic. Go with the flow. You've decoyed plenty. It's the same premise. Think of this as the extended edition."

"That's what she said."

He looked confused, then annoyed. "My opinion on wisecracks hasn't changed."

"That's too bad."

"What was that, Sarconi?"

Dammit. "Nothing, sir. Nervous tic."

"Sgt. Hunter's been briefed. He'll be in charge of assigning you whatever placement has the most visibility. Under no circumstances do you announce. Do I make myself clear?"

A million worst-case scenarios played through my mind that would require me to flash my badge, but I resisted the urge to ask about any of them. Lightman wanted the affirmative. "I'll make it work."

"Good. That's what I like to hear."

NINETEEN

I didn't have time to bask in the golden shine of my new badge. *Detective Sarconi, gangs unit.* Whenever things calmed down, I'd have to practice that in the mirror. Amber would mock me. Michael would too.

Fear and sadness crashed into me like a wave. I didn't have time for that either. I had a job to do, even if I felt like an imposter playing dress-up. Maybe that had something to do with the neon pink tube top, black sequined miniskirt, and clear plastic spike heels I wore. Maybe being a sex worker made more sense than being a detective.

"Hey," Jane came up beside me, "stop that."

"I thought we lost the psychic connection when I transferred out. Stop reading my mind."

"Shut up, Detective. You deserve that shield and the respect that comes with it. The paperwork, well, you did always have a strange fascination with keeping things organized and getting everything done ASAP, so I guess that aspect fits your personality too."

"What if I screw up?" I stared at my reflection in the mirror.

"Don't."

I turned to look at her.

"You heard me."

With that kind of logic, how could I argue? "Okay, so since you and Terri did this yesterday, tell me what I should expect."

"Undercovers will be spread out over the area. We want to be enough of a nuisance to attract the attention of the neighborhood pimps. Yesterday, we took down a few gang lieutenants and cleaned up two different neighborhoods. Twenty-eight arrests were made. The plan is to do the same today. A tactical team will remain in proximity. No one wants to become a victim of a drive-by or a casualty of gang violence."

That would be even harder to avoid if a pimp decided to eliminate me as the competition and I couldn't announce.

"What's wrong?" Jane asked.

"Nothing."

"Stop catastrophizing. You know how to do this job. The fundamentals are the same." She gave my badge another look. "I'm surprised that wasn't your one-way ticket out of this."

"It was my one-way ticket into this."

"Want to share with the class?"

"Another time."

"Okay."

The decoys and vice cops were dropped off at several different locations nowhere near our target area. We made a staggered approach. I was one of the first to arrive, and I'd be the last to leave, most likely in cuffs.

For the first hour, no one paid me any heed. The local talent kept their distance, but after catcalling a few men and disappearing into an alleyway with an undercover officer posing as a john for twenty minutes and returning in a state of disarray, I'd made my intentions known. I was here for a payday and I didn't care whose territory I encroached on.

"Yo," a tattooed man called after I returned from performing another trick with a second undercover officer. He wore a stained wifebeater and baggy cargo pants beneath a long coat. From the way it hung, I was certain he had heavy artillery tucked in the back of his pants, probably to make up for whatever he lacked in the front. "Get your ass over here." I surveyed the area, waiting for one of the neighborhood girls to scurry over, but no one made a move. "Bitch, I'm talking to you."

Oh, you did not just call me bitch. I turned my head in

his general direction. Two of the closest neighborhood girls scowled and proceeded to talk smack about me. It looked like our plan was working.

Taking an uneasy breath, I ignored the man. Undercover officers and a few patrol cars were in the vicinity. It'd be fine. Someone had my back. Despite the internal pep talk, an uneasy tingling coursed through me.

He stomped across the street, stopping once he was towering over me. "Who the hell do you think you are?" His spittle covered my face. Before I could say or do anything, he slapped me, grabbing my elbow before I could hit the ground, and dragged me in the direction from which he had come. "This is my neighborhood." He looked around. "My neighborhood," he bellowed loud enough that everyone in a two block radius could hear him.

"Sarconi, stay cool," the voice in my earpiece said. "We have you in our sights."

I didn't make a peep as the man put his other hand on the back of my neck and led me down the street. If I said the word, units would roll in, but I could handle this. If they arrived too quickly, he'd think this was a setup, and I couldn't afford that. Michael couldn't afford that.

My heart raced, but it was just nerves. I was a trained police officer. Anyone worth her salt ought to be able to handle herself in this situation. There was no reason why I couldn't. The uneasiness was a result of prior bad experiences, but I could hack it. It was time to get back on the horse.

Once we were almost to our destination, I jerked free. "Let go," I snapped. "Get your grubby paws off me. If you want a date, you gotta ask nicely."

"I don't gotta ask for anything." He grabbed my ponytail and jerked my head back. "If you want to work this street, then you're working for me." He studied my appearance for a second. "Hand over whatever you've made today."

"No."

He hit me, this time busting my lip open. My face stung, but I didn't see stars. Only red. "You're mouthy for a whore. Someone didn't train you right. I'm gonna teach you how to behave." He leaned in close. "There are better uses for that mouth than speaking."

"Oh, that's what you like. Okay, I can play along, sugar, but normally, that costs extra." I cowered slightly, casting my eyes downward submissively. "I'm sure there are better uses for my mouth, sir. Maybe you could tell me exactly what those are." I gave him a wicked smile, upping my act. "I've been a very bad girl. I need to be punished. Do you want to punish me?"

His entire demeanor changed. "Shit, you're crazy." He returned the smile. "Crazy's always fun. How 'bout you show me what you got, and I'll take good care of you from now on. I could use some fresh meat. You give me my cut, and I'll make sure you get whatever you need." He manipulated my arm around, looking for track marks. The makeup didn't completely conceal the scar, but it did a good enough job that he didn't notice I'd already been branded. "What's your poison?"

"Anything that doesn't require a needle."

"All right, that I can do." Tentatively, he released his grip, but I didn't run. I held my ground. "You see that car wash over there? Go around back. I'll be there in a minute." He grabbed my hair again and pulled. "And you better be waiting." He squeezed my ass hard enough to leave a mark and shoved me in the direction he pointed before turning on his heel to bark orders to a few of his girls.

Wobbling slightly, I went around the dilapidated side of the car wash, finding a padlock and chain to keep the doors closed. A few thugs lingered nearby, taking hits from a crack pipe and eyeing me.

"Do you have visual confirmation?" I whispered into the tiny comm hidden in my watch.

"Affirmative. Once he takes you inside, we'll wait for your word," the voice said in my ear. "Be careful, Sarconi."

A minute later, the man returned. He nodded to the others and unlocked the doors. Then he pushed me into the dark, cavernous space that looked like a storage area. Inside were stacks of tires and cleaning supplies. The floor was filthy, littered with towels, fast food wrappers, empty liquor bottles, and various odds and ends. A workbench and disgusting mattress appeared to be the only pieces of furniture inside.

"I'm Ray." He pressed against my back. One of his hands went between my legs, and the other wrapped around my neck. My entire body tensed. He inhaled deeply and dropped his hands. "Take your clothes off so I can see what I have to work with. I don't want to put a subpar product on the street. I got a reputation to protect."

I stepped away, moving deeper into the room. In two seconds, I'd say the word and the place would be raided. "You never said how you planned to reimburse me. How much of a cut will I make working for you?"

"I'll let you keep what you earned today." He was unbuttoning his pants when the group from outside walked in. "What? Can't you see I'm busy?"

"Ray, we got a problem," one of them said. "Word came in that we have to move the product early. Someone said the cops are on to us. Antonio's getting antsy. He's sending his guys to make arrangements for the exchange."

"Who told you that?" Ray, the not-so-friendly neighborhood pimp, asked. "And when are Antonio's boys getting here? That paranoid prick needs to learn how to use a damn cell phone." His focus drifted back to me. "C'mon, move it along." He snapped his fingers. I wasn't sure if I was supposed to strip faster or leave. "Out. If you're still hanging around my 'hood, I'll hit you up later so we can work out our arrangement. Now go."

There were too many men to handle on my own, and backup would take at least two minutes to bust through the door. So I had to walk away.

Once I stepped back into the fresh air, I spotted three undercovers lingering at the side of the car wash. After shaking my head, they disbanded. It was nice to know they were worried.

"Bring me in," I whispered into my wrist, heading away from my previous position. "There's been a snag."

A dark sedan pulled up. I made the pretense of leaning into the car and asking if the driver wanted a date. Once we finished putting on our show, I got inside. Petrocelli kept his eyes on the road while I tugged on the hem of the skirt to maintain some level of modesty. He reached behind my seat and grabbed his suit jacket, passing it to me.

Once I was covered, he cleared his throat. "Are you okay?"

"I'm fine. I didn't ask to get pulled because of this." I gestured at my scantily clad body beneath his jacket. "That guy, Ray, is in charge. A second ago, a few of his guys warned him someone named Antonio wanted to move up the timetable for their trade. He's sending his people to meet with them. I figured that would be a better time to move in on the bust. We'll get Ray's gang and Antonio's, and in the confusion, they won't have any way of knowing why they're getting busted."

"And we pick up enough hookers along the way to make it look like we're street cleaners."

"Pretty much."

Petrocelli grinned. "I'm glad to see that badge suits you."

I smiled. "Thanks."

"When is this going down?"

"Soon. Antonio's guys are on their way."

"Which means you'd get scooped up too because you're still in the vicinity." He picked up the radio and barked orders to the standby units to meet at the agreed upon location. "Did they say what they're trading? Or who would be there?"

"They didn't say much. Ray wanted me gone more than he wanted to score, so it had to be urgent."

"Aren't you conceited?" Petrocelli offered a smile before turning serious. He slowed the car and parked in an alleyway not far from where he picked me up. "You know you're going to have to head back there."

"Yeah." I fixated on the side mirror, but nothing was happening yet. "Do we have any intel on Ray or Antonio?"

"Last names would help."

"I'll work on that next time."

Petrocelli chuckled. "You could always check IDs when they have their pants down."

"Thanks for the tip."

"I don't suggest you say that to them."

"I didn't realize you had prior experience decoying for vice."

"Guess I'll leave the quips to the pros."

I gave him a sideways look, realizing the joking was for my benefit. He remembered what I said in the hotel room the night before. "Thanks."

"Don't mention it." He tapped his ear. "I'll be right here. Be careful."

"You too." I reached for the car handle.

"I hate to say it, Sarconi. But I'm gonna need my jacket back."

TWENTY

Since units were set to move in and take down whoever showed up to the trade with Ray, I took my time making my way back to my starting position. I had little to worry about, so I turned up my game and propositioned anyone I could find. The few regulars I passed scowled at me.

"Didn't Ray set you straight?" a woman asked.

I smiled. "Afraid of a little friendly competition?"

She cursed at me, but I kept walking. Fighting wasn't worth it, definitely not for this job. That told me one thing. Ray didn't inflict a quota on them. My brief encounter with the man left a bad taste in my month, figuratively only, thank goodness, but he could be worse. I'd seen worse.

Shaking it off, I reminded myself I had a job to do. Originally, when I started in vice, I had wanted to take down all the Rays, but that wouldn't solve the problem. Ray was a symptom. He didn't help matters, but removing him didn't fix things. Sometimes, it made them worse.

Instead of having another one of my internal debates about the socioeconomic factors and societal stigmas associated with sex workers, I turned my thoughts to more pressing matters. Two alleged gangs were making a trade. I assumed drugs. That's how it sounded, but I couldn't be sure.

However, I wanted to stay close in case of anything. So I went back to my original street corner where I could keep an eye on the car wash. By now, the thugs outside had gotten into three waiting SUVs. The chrome spinners may have been stereotypical, but Hollywood took those liberties for a reason. Maybe the writers and directors drove through these neighborhoods to get a sense of things. I wouldn't doubt it.

"We have movement," the voice in my ear said. "Two dark colored, armor-plated SUVs." I listened to the plate numbers, but they meant nothing to me. "They're heading for the car wash."

"Wait until they settle, then we'll surround them. Maintain a tight perimeter. Arrest everyone suspected of any illegal activity," Petrocelli said.

The rush of adrenaline hit hard. I shook it off as best I could, bouncing a little like I was hyped up on something, as I made another attempt to pull over a slow-moving vehicle. The driver looked like he may have been interested in a date but didn't like the looks of things.

Thirty seconds later, another car stopped. The driver got out. Jimenez winked while he said something sexy and inappropriate in Spanish. He pinned me between him and the brick, keeping a respectable distance, while he placed one hand on the wall behind me, the swagger evident in his every move.

"I didn't think it'd be a good idea to leave you all alone," he whispered, turning up the flirtation.

"Afraid I was going to run into danger?"

He shrugged. "You have a reputation for finding trouble."

"It finds me."

"So I hear."

Another voice in my ear said they had eyes on the exchange. It was taking place not far from the car wash. I could see the two armored-SUVs, which I believed belonged to Antonio, idling on the opposite side of the parking lot from the SUVs with the chrome spinners that Ray's guys had gotten into. From here, it looked like a duel or the world's lamest auto show.

"What do you think they're waiting for?" I asked, running my hands up Jimenez's chest while keeping an eye on the SUVs in the periphery.

"I'm not sure." The tension radiated off him. I could feel

it in his shoulders, which were solid steel. But to the casual observer, he appeared loose and uninterested in anything except whatever I had to offer. "I'm hoping they aren't about to get into a shootout."

Taking the lead, I switched our positions and shoved Jimenez against the brick before brushing my body against his. The sound of car doors opening made me turn. Four men stepped out of the lead SUV. From the looks of them, they were providing protection. A few of the thugs I'd seen outside the car wash stepped out of their SUV. The scrawny, twitchy one gave Antonio's guys a head nod, which was returned.

"They seem friendly," Jimenez said. "That's usually a good thing."

"Yeah." But my internal voice reminded me *not always*.

More guys stepped out of the second vehicle. That's when Ray appeared. He offered a wave before approaching someone and giving him a fist bump. I couldn't see much from here.

"Hold position," the voice in my ear said. "We need contraband in plain sight. Remember, this has to hold up."

"They're armed," I said into my wrist. "They're all carrying."

"I can't see that. The weapons are concealed," the voice replied.

Jimenez looked at me. "Don't worry. We'll get them."

The doors opened on the second armored SUV. Two men got out. Even from here, with his hair longer than normal, I recognized him. "Shit." I pressed against Jimenez, my lips on his neck so I could speak into his comm. "Riley's here. Brown jacket and jeans."

Petrocelli cursed. "No one make a move. We have an asset in play."

Michael and the man who'd been inside the SUV with him moved to the rear and pulled out an aluminum case. Once Ray caught sight of it, he signaled for his men to bring out two large crates.

"As soon as we have visual confirmation, let's light them up," Petrocelli said.

A moment later, the top of the crate opened. From this

angle, I couldn't see what was inside. Neither could Jimenez. But whoever had eyes on the exchange had a clear shot. I could barely hear the voice in my ear over the sudden sound of sirens.

Michael turned, shouted something to the others, and raced toward the SUV. Before pulling open the door and climbing in, he looked in my direction. This time, I was the one caught in a compromising position. Then he got into the car and slammed the door.

Unlike most action movies, the thugs didn't seek cover and open fire. They scurried, like rats who'd been discovered hiding in a dark basement. The second SUV, the one Michael had gotten into, was the first to peel away.

"Let them go," Petrocelli ordered. "Let's focus on stopping everyone else from leaving."

"You should make a run for it," Jimenez reminded me.

Several sex workers had taken off the moment the sirens blared. I ran, like they did. My feet protesting such action as the clear plastic cut into my skin. If this wasn't for show, I would have ditched the shoes. Instead, I followed the others while I listened to the sounds of Ray and his pals being apprehended.

When I rounded a corner, I came face to face with half a dozen police officers. Guns out. Four sex workers had already surrendered, hands behind their heads.

"Stop right there," the nearest cop said. "Put your hands up."

"You have no right to arrest me," I said.

"The hell I don't." He approached, spun me around, and pressed me against the brick while he patted me down and cuffed me. "Sit down, ma'am." He waited until I took a seat beside the woman I'd passed earlier.

She glanced at me and scoffed.

"What?" I asked, mustering as much street as I could.

That's when she laughed. "It's not your day, is it?"

"I had a better day than you."

She turned, possibly to spit on me or to headbutt me. Either way, one of the cops dragged us apart. She winked, and that's when I realized she was another decoy.

"Let's get them out of here. Don't let these two ride

together unless you want to clean blood out of the back seat," the officer said.

We were the last to get picked up. By now, Ray and his pals had been taken in. Every patrol car drove by us at a slow enough pace that the men could see us lined up on the street, waiting to be brought in. It was for show, but given the number of arrests, so far I'd counted fourteen, not counting us, it made sense why this was taking so long. No one would question the parade of cars going past us. No one would have any doubt I was another streetwalker. Not Ray and not the other women beside me.

Once we made it to the station, I was taken through booking and processed like everyone else before being tossed into one of the holding cells. No one said a word. I assumed the other women had been arrested enough times to know it wasn't a good idea to cause trouble or run their mouths.

After almost two hours, most of them had been taken to speak to the arresting officers. From there, they were transferred to central booking to await their arraignment or released.

When Officer Kemper appeared outside the holding cell, I feared he'd blow my cover. But to my surprise and relief, he played it cool.

He pointed at me. "It's your turn."

"Great," I said sarcastically.

He waited for the cell to be opened before cuffing me and leading me down the hallway. After we made it to vice, he stuck me in the conference room. "That promotion didn't turn out the way you planned, huh, Lex?"

"You have no idea."

"Yeah, well, after seeing what they put you through, I'm glad they didn't pick me to assist." He nodded at Jane who had entered the room with my bag from the locker room. "I'll leave you ladies to it."

Jane took one look at me and shook her head. "I'll get the blister band-aids."

"Thanks." I slid out of the painful shoes, seeing the marks they left on the tops of my feet. No wonder I was so cranky.

I hadn't heard anything since I'd been brought in. The

officers had confiscated the earpiece before putting me into the holding cell. I had to assume Michael had escaped, but I didn't know who he'd been with or what he was doing.

By the time Jane returned with the band-aids, I'd changed back into my normal clothes. After taking care of my blisters, I put on the extra thick socks she grabbed for me and put on my shoes. The boards inside the conference room hadn't been updated.

"Where's Petrocelli?" I asked.

"He hasn't come upstairs yet. The last I heard, he was hanging out with gangs."

"Shouldn't I be down there?"

Jane shook her head. "You can't leave this room until everyone we arrested is squared away. You can't afford to run into someone being brought back to holding or being taken into interrogation. It'd ruin everything."

"Did Petrocelli say that?"

"No. Sergeant Hunter did."

"Any word from Lightman or Preston?"

"No one said anything to me, but why would they start now?" She pointed to the detective's shield on my belt. "Does that mean you're gonna stop speaking to me too?"

"It depends."

"On what?"

"On what I'm allowed to say."

TWENTY-ONE

"It's a good thing you were there," Petrocelli said. "If not, we would have arrested one of our own."

"You arrested me," I reminded him, "and several decoys."

"That wasn't my point."

Preston rolled her eyes. "You did good, Sarconi. Michael's already on thin ice. A patrol officer could have ruined everything if he recognized him while making the arrest."

"Are you sure the raid didn't ruin everything? The syndicate was already suspicious of Riley. A second bust happening so close could have spooked them even more."

"I doubt it," Preston said. "Michael got away, and he took Antonio Vargas with him. If it wasn't for him, Vargas would have been arrested. That save should have solidified Michael's position within the syndicate, and hopefully, it'll make the syndicate look elsewhere for a snitch."

"All right." I wasn't nearly that optimistic, but I hoped she was right. "Here's what I don't understand. Riley didn't know who was in charge. Now we find out it's Antonio Vargas."

"It's not Vargas," Lightman said. "Vargas isn't that big of a player. He arranged the deal with your buddy Ray, but Vargas is not running the syndicate."

Petrocelli pushed a folder toward me. "I pulled Vargas's rap sheet. There's not much to him. He's a local with local aspirations. I doubt he has the contacts or networks necessary for someone of Jeff Stark's caliber."

"Vargas used to run a gang a few years back. I'm using the term loosely. They didn't have more than eight guys at any one time. They worked a one block radius, providing protection to businesses. In their spare time, they performed some armed robberies and otherwise made a lot of noise. There was never much to them. So when someone bigger and stronger came along, they got absorbed into that mess. Vargas and his guys are nothing but foot soldiers. They're on the front lines. Should things go south, they're the first to be arrested." Lightman pointed to the board where he'd drawn a rudimentary sketch of what looked like circles and ladders. Was that supposed to be something out of a football playbook? "This is why Riley can't determine who's in charge. He's been stuck with them while Stark was detained."

"But Stark's out and Riley is still with Vargas," I said.

"He has to rebuild trust," Preston said. "Michael got them to safety. He made sure Vargas avoided arrest. The only people we picked up were Ray and his thugs."

Petrocelli chuckled. "That sounds like a garage band from the nineties."

Preston snorted, giving him a genuine smile for once.

"All right, so what do we do now?" I asked.

"We stay the course," Lightman said. "Sam and I will see what we can get out of Ray and his friends. In the meantime, vice is making real progress. A lot of people saw you get arrested. You were in holding for hours. Since we have no evidence to use against you or any of the other sex workers we brought in, they won't be surprised to learn you were released. But we're going to hold everyone as long as possible. In the meantime, vice has to shut down as many escorts as possible, so you can continue with your mission."

"Should I choose to accept it," I said.

Petrocelli stifled his laugh with a snort. Again, Lightman's glare reminded me I needed to cool it with the quips. Damn nerves.

"Get back to work, Sarconi. Keep your head down until we need you. Sgt. Hunter is aware of the situation. We want to keep you out of the public eye for a while. Do you think you can manage that?" Lightman asked.

"Yes, sir."
"All right, Detective. Get to it."

~*~

Word had spread that the police department was gunning for pimps and gang-run prostitution rings. A lot of the sex workers were pulled off the streets until the heat died down. No one wanted the hassle of getting arrested, which was sure to happen with so many patrol cars circling.

"The neighborhoods are quiet," Jane said. "Only a few people were working out in the open, and they got scooped up, which means it's about time we start phase three."

Petrocelli pushed away from the table. "Good job."

"Uh...thanks." Jane gave me a bewildered look. "I'll be at my desk if you need me."

Petrocelli slid a tablet to me. "Here's everything we have on Ray. I thought you might want to take a look."

One of the three SUVs with the chrome spinners managed to get away, but inside the other two vehicles we found assault rifles, frag grenades, a significant amount of cash, and half a dozen handguns.

"I'm surprised they didn't open fire."

"Me too." Petrocelli scratched at a spot behind his ear. "Given the cash, I'd say that's only a fraction of whatever else they planned to trade."

"So it wasn't drugs." I recalled the conversation I had overheard, but Ray had been careful not to divulge anything. "How many weapons do you think were in the third SUV?"

"More than I want to think about." He nodded at a photo of the bags of cash. "The cash came from Antonio Vargas."

"Why do you think he wants that kind of firepower?"

"Gang war?" Petrocelli suggested.

"Does that fit with what we know about Stark?"

"No, but we don't know how Stark figures into this. All we know is Vargas and Stark are working for the same person."

"Whoever that is must have some pretty intense interests."

"Intense, huh?" Petrocelli cocked his head to the side.

"That's one way of putting it. Guns, girls, and whatever Stark is procuring for him."

"Unless it is Stark's network that he needs and not whatever Stark can obtain."

"Unless Stark is using this guy for his network. After all, whoever is pulling these strings has a lot of liquid assets at his disposal. He may not need Stark's network. He may already have his own connections. Stark could be paying him instead. It might explain some of the cash."

"Possibly." I flipped through the photos taken at the raid. "Why would someone this well-connected bother making deals with common crooks like Ray?"

"Ray isn't a common crook." Petrocelli took the tablet and tapped a few times before handing it back to me. "Raymond Pascal has ties to a major cartel. He keeps his business to himself and only operates locally, but his family is another story. When I spoke to him, he said he didn't know anything about what was inside the SUVs. Those vehicles belong to his cousins, that whatever was inside must be theirs."

"Don't tell me you're buying that."

"Of course not."

"Good." I scanned the info on the tablet. "Who are Ray's cousins?"

"As far as I know, he doesn't have any."

"You think his relatives are cartel members?"

"I'm looking into the possibility." Petrocelli studied me carefully. "Explain something to me."

I felt like I'd been caught sleeping in class. "What?"

"On one of your first days out, you pick up a guy that no one has ever been able to touch."

"That's because he wanted me to touch him."

Petrocelli didn't appear amused. "Then today, you walk into this mess."

"That's my luck."

"I'm not buying it. Did Riley leak these details to you?"

"How dare you?" Petrocelli was an outsider. Until I was reassigned, we'd never met. He had never seen me and Michael together. Why would he assume that?

"You are the newest member of the gangs unit. You have

a history. You saved his life. He saved yours. Circumstances like that can lead to strong bonds."

"I haven't spoken to Riley since he was told to cut ties."

Petrocelli looked like he believed me, but it was making his brain glitch. "Michael Riley has a reputation as a ladies' man."

"Again, I'd like to ask if you want to have this conversation with someone from human resources or IAD."

"I'm not—" Petrocelli sighed. "Why are you always so defensive?"

"What choice do I have? It sounds like you're accusing me of something."

"I just want to understand."

"What's to understand? I've had the weirdest career in the history of the LAPD. You've read my file."

Petrocelli held up his hands in surrender. "I'm surprised you still want to be a cop."

"Me too."

He jerked his chin toward the door. "Good luck with phase three. I'll have SWAT prepped and ready. Given the givens, I'll make sure we're prepared for a terrorist takeover or a nuclear holocaust. Those seem likely since you're on the case."

Resisting the urge to say the million snarky things that went through my head, I went out the door and met Jane at her desk. We had a briefing to attend.

TWENTY-TWO

Officer Jane Reeve grinned. "Hey, Lex, are you ready to become one of the city's premier escorts?"

"Gag me."

"Don't tell that to your dates. I hear a lot of the rich and powerful have BDSM fetishes."

"Are you sure that's not what Hollywood and smut writers want us to think?"

"I guess we'll find out."

Sgt. Hunter opened the conference room door. "Ladies, if you'd be so kind as to join us."

Once we were inside, he picked up a laser pointer and chronicled phase three of the assignment. Since we had already performed recon inside the upscale hotels and clubs, our intel was sound. While vice had been busy with phase two, patrol had stepped in and shut down several escorts for everything from business license violations to solicitation.

Most charges were unlikely to stick since the madams made sure any appearance of impropriety would not befall their establishments, but we only needed them out of the way for a few days. However, I couldn't help but think the PD would be facing dozens of harassment claims in the weeks to come. And I wasn't sure we didn't deserve them.

"A hotel concierge let it slip that certain events were being held this coming week. Rooms have already been booked and the staff has been told to keep things quiet. Madam Sinclair's agency was supposed to provide the entertainment, but since we arrested several of her employees, she'll be in the market for fresh meat to fill-in. We're sending you out in teams of two and three to the most utilized and requested venues where Sinclair's people usually hang out," Hunter said. "Work the room like you did the corners, but the goal isn't to pick up a john, it's to get invited to work for Sinclair. Lexie, you already had a run-in with one of her girls the other day. They have no reason to doubt you're in the business. So put that to good use."

"Yes, sir."

"If you spot any of these women," he flicked his laser pointer to photos of Sinclair's escorts that hadn't been arrested, "make a good impression. You need this job. Got it?"

A round of affirmatives echoed through the confined space, and then we were sent to prep for the evening and hope the fish were biting.

"You ready for this?" Jane watched as I carefully applied a thick layer of liner before selecting a brush and eyeshadow to make a smoky eye.

"No."

She laughed. "We're cops. We're supposed to be prepared for everything."

"You have us confused with the boy scouts."

She settled in front of the sink beside me and pulled out some lipstick. "I'd say send them instead, but child molesters are the worst." When I didn't respond, she nudged me. "What's wrong? You haven't been yourself since you were arrested. Did something happen in holding?"

"I'm fine." I finished with my eyes and reached for her tube of lipstick. "Do you mind?"

"Not at all."

I checked the color before applying it to my lips. After blotting the excess with a tissue, I turned to face her. "For some reason, I thought making detective would mean I had a clue as to what was going on and why it was happening. Instead, I'm even more confused. I don't know what's going on or how any of it makes any sense. Everything is moving at warp speed, and I feel like I'm standing still. How do these raids make sense? How did we know Stark was looking for escorts or that he connects to any of this? I can't wrap my head around where these facts are coming from or how we're one step ahead or at least in the right place at the right time when I can't even determine which way is up."

"That's because this isn't your case, Lex. You're assisting. All these moving parts and pieces, the facts, the intel, all of that was being compiled while you were out on sick leave or while you were working patrol or answering phones."

"But I found Stark. Did someone know he'd be there? Is that why they put us there?"

"I wouldn't doubt it."

"But you don't know for sure?"

"I try not to ask questions," Jane said.

"I always ask questions."

"Which is why you're always in trouble." She took the tube of lipstick back and put it in her bag. "And it's why you have a detective's shield and I don't."

"You're a P3. You could pursue detective if you want."

"I wasn't saying that for pity. I know my options. I'm good with where I am. I don't mind working vice. I kind of like it. All I'm saying is there are a lot of factors in play that we are not aware of. Did you know the mayor carved out a special task force from the intelligence unit to put together this plan?"

Suddenly, a lot of things made more sense. "They knew. That's how the phases were planned. It's how the locations were chosen."

"That'd be my guess, but I can't say for certain."

"And since I wasn't with a specialized unit, I wouldn't know."

"I'm surprised gangs didn't tell you."

"I was on sick leave when all this started, and ever since I came back, I've basically been pulling desk duty and occasionally walking a beat."

"No wonder you're out of the loop. Hopefully, that'll change soon."

"Yeah, I hope so." This would explain why Michael had been given an undercover assignment. But that started weeks ago. He should have told me. Maybe not the specifics of his op but what was going on in the department. We were both cops. He knew I'd been left out of the loop, that I was stuck playing catch-up. The next time I saw him, I'd give him a piece of my mind.

~*~

It didn't take long to get to the hotel Petrocelli and I had visited. By now, it was late, a little after midnight. That didn't give us a lot of time to make much of an impression. Luckily, the bar was at half capacity, which meant we'd be noticed. Hopefully, that'd be enough.

The same bartender from last time was working. He eyed the two of us suspiciously. "You brought a friend?" he asked.

I winked at him. "Two's better than one."

"All right." He pointed to the sign behind him. "Does that mean you want two for one cocktails?"

"Yes, please." Jane leaned forward, giving him an eyeful in her asymmetric dress.

"Coming right up." He filled a shaker, poured, and placed the martini glasses down in front of us. "Drink up, ladies."

"Thanks," I said.

Twenty minutes later, I spotted the escort I'd seen last time. Jane texted an undercover john to make an appearance and got up to work the other side of the room. I sipped my drink and waited. Within ninety seconds, the undercover cop appeared.

I propositioned him, but we had a different play in mind tonight. When he turned me down, I sipped my drink and made eyes at another gentleman who also had no interest in me.

Jane giggled from across the room as the undercover cop offered her his arm. Now there should be no doubt why we were here. Jane went past me, running her fingertips along my back. "Sorry, sweetie. He's only interested in solo play tonight."

"Good for you." I spun on the stool, searching for other prospects while Jane headed out of the bar. I continued to scope out the room as if I were waiting for a rich sugar daddy or high roller.

Fifteen minutes later, my mark took a seat beside me. She

ordered a martini and gave me a lengthy sideways look. "Fish aren't biting tonight for you either?" she asked, sliding a business card across the bar with a perfectly manicured, fire engine red nail.

"One almost did, but he wanted something cheaper." I glanced at the card. "I'd ask if you were looking for a date, but it seems we're in the same business."

"I saw you the other night," she said. "How did things end?"

"Like they always do. With a bang."

"Do you have representation?"

"Not anymore. Cops have been closing down a lot of places."

"Aren't you afraid of getting caught?"

"What's the worst that will happen? I spend a night in jail while I wait to get arraigned. This is a victimless crime. My attorney can do wonders to get me off." I smiled at her. "We have what you'd call a quid pro quo. He gets me off. I get him off." I flipped her card over, finding a direct line. "Are you sure you aren't looking for a date? Because I'm an equal opportunist."

"I'll keep that in mind, but I wasn't shopping for myself. I was looking for someone else." She nodded at the card. "Madam Sinclair is always looking for young, attractive talent. It's upscale. The job includes protection and healthcare."

"I carry my own protection," I replied.

"No, protection from the clients who get too rough or legal protection if you encounter trouble, but I guess you already have that handled."

"It'd be easier if I didn't have to handle his business." I tapped the card on the bar. "Are you serious?"

"Madam Sinclair needs a few extras to fill in. Consider it a job interview. If you perform well, she'd be willing to hire you on permanently."

"When's the party?"

"Party?"

"Whatever job she wants me to do. And trust me, sugar, I'm great at all jobs. Ask any of my satisfied customers. Or my lawyer."

"Give me your number."

I did as she asked. "Now what?"

"Now you wait for a text with details." She finished her drink in one sip and left me alone at the bar.

A minute later, a man in a suit sat down beside me. "Buy you a drink?" he asked.

I gave him my best bedroom eyes, noticing the woman from earlier watching from the closest table. She must have sent him over. Perhaps he was one of Sinclair's regular customers.

"That depends. Does the drink come with a hotel robe?" It was a silly line, but he smiled.

"All night?"

"If you can afford it." I gazed pointedly at his expensive watch. "I'm guessing you can."

"Is anything off the table?"

I looked him up and down. He was around forty, slightly balding, and a bit overweight. His finger had the telltale sign of a removed wedding band. "Are you here on business or looking for a regular liaison?"

"Aren't you forward?"

I might have pushed too hard and wondered if he'd walk away.

Instead, he offered his arm and produced a room key. "Let's see how tonight plays out first. Shall we go upstairs and discuss terms?"

"Absolutely." I slid off the stool, took his arm, and allowed him to lead me to the elevator. Backup was in the lobby, but I had to let this play. However, I wasn't about to service this guy, so keeping my cover intact and satisfying whatever test Madam Sinclair's lackey was throwing at me would be harder than I thought.

As the doors closed, he slid his key into the slot and pressed his floor number. "I'm not into any hardcore bondage, but I like to be spanked and called a dirty boy."

"Not a problem, dirty boy."

His hand ran gently up and down my back. The elevator doors opened, and he guided me to his room. When the door closed, he took a deep breath and avoided eye contact as if he were shy.

"Just so we're clear, are you paying for the entire evening or for a few hours? I'm sorry, but I need to see the money up front."

"Right, sure." He fidgeted, searching for his wallet. He held up a stack of hundreds. "Is this enough?"

"Sure, put it on the dresser."

He put the cash down, and I heard a voice in my ear. The department was hoping to leverage him to ensure my position as one of Sinclair's newest hires. They needed his name to see what kind of dirt they could find on him.

"Why don't you make us a drink?" I nodded at the mini-bar. He turned around, and I picked up his wallet, reading the name off his license so our team could run his background. An affirmative came through my earpiece, and I was instructed to stall. I leaned against the wall, striking a sexy pose. "Have you ever done this before?"

"A few times, mostly when I travel. Business trips can be lonely."

"I'm sorry."

He looked confused. "Thanks." He handed me a glass and offered his to toast. We clinked them together, and then I put mine on the table. He drank his and put the empty glass beside mine. He ran his hands down my shoulders and leaned in for a kiss. I turned my face away.

"You don't kiss?" he asked.

"Do most escorts?"

"I guess not. It just seemed nicer and more normal than getting straight to it."

"Well, we haven't exactly discussed what you want yet. Why don't you paint me a picture, and we'll work out the business before we get to the pleasure? You said you wanted me to spend the night." I pointed to the cash. "That shouldn't be a problem, unless you want something specific. So let's talk specifics."

He sat on the edge of the bed. "If money's an issue, I can get more. The woman downstairs said you'd agree to anything."

"Do you work with her or her boss normally?"

"I've done this a few times, but I'm not a regular customer." He looked uneasy, like he was caught with his pants down. "What's going on?"

"Nothing. I just got hired to work for them, I think. It's all very confusing. I want to make sure I make you happy, that I make a good impression. In order to do that, I'd like to get to know you a little better."

He brightened. "I'd like that too."

"How do you feel about room service?"

"Sure. Let's get some champagne."

"Don't forget the strawberries and whipped cream," I said, "unless you aren't interested in that."

"Oh, I'm interested."

Before he could pick up the phone, I grabbed it. "Since you're paying for this, at least let me do the heavy lifting." I pretended to call room service and spoke to the dial tone. Meanwhile, the radio in my ear said they found leverage on this guy.

At the sound of knocking, I opened the door and let in the room service cart manned by two undercover officers.

TWENTY-THREE

The door closed, and the two disguised officers produced badges, identifying themselves. My date turned crimson. He wasn't expecting to get busted. We questioned him about his ties to Madam Sinclair and Olivia Getting, the headhunter who hoped to add my name to the ranks of Madam Sinclair's escorts. Within an hour, we convinced my date to cooperate, and the two of us returned to the bar in an affectionate embrace.

Olivia had taken up a permanent spot at a back table, watching the happenings around the bar with rapt fascination. She was on the hunt, not for a date but for working girls to serve as temporary replacements. A few nicely dressed women were working the room. I wasn't sure if they were more of her tryouts or if they already worked for Sinclair. But Olivia was keeping an eye on them.

Jane was gone, dealing with a similar situation to the one I had found myself in. Apparently, she also got tapped to audition for Madam Sinclair.

My date bought a round of drinks for us, gave me a lingering peck on the cheek, whispered something in my ear, and returned to the elevator, leaving his room key behind. Not a single detail was lost on Olivia.

Once he disappeared, she sidled up to me. "Finished already?"

"No," I palmed the room key, "he has to video chat with his wife, and then we'll move on to round two." I gave her a look. "Is he one of your usual clients? He was nice and gentle. Very respectful, which is hard to find."

She smirked. "I take it you approve of this arrangement."

"What's your cut?" I asked.

"Seventy-thirty. Dates don't always require sex. In fact, as far as Ms. Sinclair is concerned, sex doesn't happen. That's your choice." She raised an eyebrow, making sure I understood the official line. "Are you clean? Disease free?"

"Yes."

"Good." She withdrew a pen from her purse and scribbled a room number and time on the napkin. "Tomorrow, we're providing entertainment for an event. It's short notice, but due to issues beyond Ms. Sinclair's control, we're in need of some fill-ins. Show up tomorrow and make a good impression. If Ms. Sinclair or the client finds you to their liking, we'll find a permanent place for you at the escort service. Oh, and you should be aware this is a black-tie affair. I don't imagine that will be a problem."

"No problem at all."

Before I could ask anything else, Olivia pulled another vanishing act. The woman would have made a great ghost.

Stuffing the napkin inside my purse, I returned to the elevator, slid the key through the slot, and exited on the proper floor. My date and the two officers were waiting.

Once everything was handled, they escorted him to the service elevator. At least they were kind enough to avoid the front door. Although, I doubted we could continue to run the sting if we were caught hauling guests through the lobby in handcuffs.

Despite his illegal activity, my date wasn't a violent offender. I wouldn't even consider his actions criminal, even if the penal code disagreed. He was lonely. The possibility he was a cheater made me bristle, but that was a personal hangup and not one I thought should be criminal, at least not in his case. But this was the job. Lucky for him, no charges would be filed if he provided a statement and answered a few more questions at the station.

Vice was tough. Sometimes, decent humans got caught up in things they should avoid. Other times, the treatment of the sex workers was so depraved and horrible that I wanted to murder the pimps and johns. It was a tossup where the crime would fall on the spectrum.

Some people argued prostitution was a victimless crime, and maybe in some instances it was, but there was so much to consider, human trafficking, sex slaves sold on the black market, and violence. Then there would be an instance like this that would make me wonder what the harm would be if a willing, non-coerced individual wanted to be reimbursed for providing a lonely traveler with sexual favors. There was just no winning. Luckily, I didn't have to make the laws or policy. I just had to enforce them. Well, most of the time.

I straightened my dress and gave the hotel room a final once-over before taking the elevator back to the lobby. As the door whooshed opened, the elevator across the hallway was closing. The brief glimpse inside made my blood run cold. Jeff Stark was on his way upstairs.

~*~

"You're crazy, Sarconi," Petrocelli said, "and I am somewhat a professional on the matter."

"Is that because you're certifiable?"

He pressed his lips together and offered his best rendition of a reassuring look. "It's understandable why you thought you saw Stark. You were undercover, which was how you spotted him the first time. Until two days ago, you had a car assigned to tail you because he might pose a threat. But no one else spotted him. We had officers all over that hotel. He wasn't there. We even checked the hotel registry."

"That doesn't mean anything. You don't even know what his real name is. Jeff Stark is one of his million aliases."

"Fine, but you said you barely caught a glimpse of the guy. A nice suit and shitty attitude doesn't mean he's our untouchable target. That describes most of the men in this city."

"If your suit was nicer, I'd think you were talking about yourself."

He tilted his head to the side, not amused.

"Fine." I lifted my purse off the table. "If there isn't anything else, I have paperwork to do. Reeve and I have to go over everything before tomorrow evening, and I'd like to catch her before she leaves."

"The two of you are infiltrating Sinclair's escort service at nine p.m. tomorrow, right?"

"Yeah."

Petrocelli made a note. "Teams will be in the vicinity. I've been digging into her business. On the surface, she's clean. Dare I say squeaky? But I spoke to the guys in intelligence and a few contacts I have on the street. There are rumors circulating that Sinclair's involved in human trafficking. If so, she may be supplying the girls to whoever the Shark is."

"Shark, Stark," I shook my head, "I'm so over this."

"You and me both." He jerked his chin at the door. "Get going. I'll see you tomorrow."

I left the conference room and tried to shake off the turmoil concerning the Stark lookalike from the hotel. Petrocelli made a fair point. I was stressed and slightly crazed, but I knew what I saw. Since that hotel would be the scene of tomorrow's party, it'd make sense that Stark would be there. After all, he approached Sinclair about the party and he connected to whoever was running the syndicate.

"Why won't he take me seriously?" I asked.

Jane looked up. "Who?"

"Petrocelli. I swear I saw Stark at the hotel tonight. I reported it, but everyone acts like I'm crazy."

"Do you think he's gaslighting you?"

"Not intentionally. He checked surveillance footage, the hotel's guest registry, everything short of knocking on doors to perform a bed check."

"Isn't Stark under surveillance?"

"He was, but—"

"You think he gave us the slip."

"A guy like that must have his ways."

"What do you want to do? We could get the surveillance team's location and check it out ourselves."

"I can't afford to let him see me."

"Do you want me to go?"

The look on her face told me the correct answer was no, so that's what I said.

"All right, let's say Stark was at the hotel tonight.

Wouldn't that be a good thing? He connects to all this. The entire point of you getting hired on by an escort service and getting hired to work this event was to put you on a collision course with Stark."

"I don't want him to see me. I'm supposed to be gathering intel on how people are being trafficked or bought and sold. I'm investigating the import/export side of things."

Jane snorted. "That's one way of putting it." She glanced back at the conference room where Petrocelli remained. "Do you think he didn't want to tell you Stark was there so you wouldn't freak out?"

"I'm a cop. We aren't allowed to freak out."

"I hate to break it to you, but you're kind of freaking out right now."

I took a calming breath and slowly released it. "Lightman would be straight with me."

She gestured to the double doors which led to the stairwell. "Go ask him. I'll be here when you get back."

I checked the time. "He's gone home by now."

"That's what I'd like to do too."

I picked up my pen. "All right. Let's knock these reports out. I can worry about Stark on my own time."

Jane and I spent the rest of the night working out the finer details of our assignment. The brass never expected us to score such a wonderful opportunity on the first day of phase three. We were under strict orders not to botch it. So far, we had done an exemplary job, but I was convinced our perceived progress would come to a screeching halt, particularly if Stark was around to throw a wrench in the works. Did he think I was the reason he was arrested? Or did he really believe I was a sex worker?

Only time would tell. When I left the station, I was careful to make sure no one was watching me and I wasn't followed home. Memories flooded me. This time, Michael wouldn't be coming to the rescue if someone was waiting at my place to kill me.

I rubbed the scar on my arm, which itched a little from the caked-on makeup. I knew one thing for certain. Jeff Stark was at that hotel, and he wasn't there for the pillow mints. He was there to conduct business.

More than anything, I wanted to talk to Michael. Preston was right. We worked better together, and since our assignments overlapped, we'd be able to figure this out much faster. Instead, we couldn't talk or communicate. I wondered if Preston or Lightman had gotten word to him that I was assisting. Surely, after our two close encounters, he had to know I was part of this. Since the intelligence unit put this in motion, Michael would have been privy to the details concerning vice's role.

As I let myself into my apartment, I couldn't help but wonder just how much Michael knew and how much he intentionally kept from me.

TWENTY-FOUR

I didn't sleep well again that night. I blamed it on my arm for itching, but it wasn't that. I was worried that I had seen Michael with Antonio Vargas. Heavy duty weapons like that meant trouble. If Vargas was buying them, either for himself or the syndicate, he had plans to use them.

On the bright side, Michael's cover remained intact for now. However, he had infiltrated a dangerous organization whose associates hadn't thought twice before opening fire on police officers. If his cover was compromised, they wouldn't hesitate to blow him away. With that final disconcerting thought, I got out of bed.

As I dressed for my workout, Preston's words played through my mind. Michael didn't want me to know about this. He didn't want me involved. I hadn't heard a word from him since he left my apartment that night. Part of me was so angry with him, and the other part was terrified. And of course, there was the guilt, which kept eating at me every time I had a mean thought.

What if he was dead or in danger? How could I be mad at him? Didn't he have the best intentions by keeping me out of this? He said he wanted to tell me but couldn't. Why didn't I believe that?

Perhaps no news was good news. If something happened to Michael, we would have heard about it by now. Hopefully, he was closing in on identifying whoever was in charge of the syndicate so we could put this to rest. In the meantime,

I'd try my damnedest to get answers on what or who was being moved. That would lead back to the buyer and seller, and that would be just as good.

After pounding out the miles on the treadmill, which unfortunately did nothing to relax me, I filled the tub, pinned my hair on top of my head, and eased into the warm, bubbly water. My thoughts drifted back to Michael—his sexy smirk, his playful grin, and his teasing banter.

I missed him. And I hated it. I didn't want to be dependent on anyone for my physical or emotional well-being, but Michael had wormed his way into my heart. That was something I didn't believe was possible after my last relationship blew up in my face. Maybe that's why I was so mad. I was mad at myself for being so emotionally invested. I loved him more than I ever loved anyone. We clicked, at least I thought we did.

After my bath, I called Amber. My best friend was a hospital administrator. While I couldn't tell her much about the situation, it was nice to have someone who was always around to listen. Except now, when the call went straight to voicemail.

"Seriously?" I thought about leaving her a message but decided against it, put my game face on, dug through my closet for something sexy and elegant for a black-tie affair, and hoped the op wouldn't end in a firefight.

On my way to work, I studied my reflection in the rearview mirror. The lack of a follow car reminded me the brass didn't believe Jeff Stark posed a danger to me. However, I couldn't help but wonder how Stark fit into Michael's undercover assignment. How did Stark cross paths with local organized crime when he had such notoriety? Why did gangs send Michael to infiltrate the syndicate's rank and file? Usually, Detective Devereaux went undercover. Did Michael volunteer?

Dammit, what was I missing?

If Stark was as untouchable as everyone believed, Michael had no business being anywhere near him. "Cool it, Lexie," I said to myself. I'd hate for Michael to tell me I couldn't work a case, so I had no business thinking he shouldn't either. But the secrecy was driving me mad. Of course every scenario I came up with was ten times worse than whatever was going on. Unfortunately, I had no way of knowing that, so I had to assume my imagination was running away with me. But the pessimistic voice in the back of my head wasn't convinced. If anything, she thought I may not be grasping the severity of the situation.

"You look nice," Petrocelli said when he intercepted me on the way to Sgt. Hunter's office.

"Thanks."

He fell into step beside me. "Are you ready for this?"

"I guess we'll see."

"Hey, Lexie." He stopped, which forced me to stop and turn to look at him. "Do you have a plan if you run into Stark at tonight's event?"

"Why would I run into Stark? You told me I was crazy."

"I shouldn't have said that." He scratched at the back of his head. "The intel doesn't indicate he'd have any reason to be there, but it's best to always be prepared."

"Dammit, we are not boy scouts."

"What?"

"Ask Jane." But he was right. I had to be prepared and able to think on my feet. That had never been a problem, but this assignment had thrown me. "I'll come up with something."

Petrocelli held out a folder. "I already did."

I flipped it open. Inside were details on a cover identity he had created for me. Everything from a fabricated name, date of birth, work history, arrest record, and known associates, family, and friends. "When did you have time to do this?"

He shrugged. "Who needs to sleep?"

"Thanks."

"I figured I owed you." He took a step back. "Find me after you speak to the sergeant if you want someone to help you go over the details."

"Shouldn't I go over this with Jane? She's going undercover with me."

"You're probably right, but the offer stands." He headed back to the conference room. I wasn't sure what his deal was, but his mood swings were bound to give me whiplash.

~*~

After Jane and I exhausted ourselves with the minute details, we headed to the hotel. The large banquet hall was decked out in glitz and glamour. Surely, this was something out of a Hollywood A-list event.

Two dozen women outfitted in extravagant gowns were positioned throughout the room. Caterers, butlers, and various security personnel were inside, but the guests of honor hadn't arrived yet.

Olivia, our recruiter, greeted us immediately, assessing our clothing choices and instructing us to relax. "This will be fun. Have a drink. Enjoy yourselves. But don't make an approach. If someone is interested in you, they will speak to you. This isn't like the bars and clubs you usually work."

"So no advertising?" Jane asked.

"No reason. The guests know why you're here." Olivia glanced around. "Well, that is whenever they show up."

"Who's showing up?" I asked.

"Some businessmen. They had a convention earlier." The way she said it sounded like a lie. "You are the entertainment. An ear to listen. A shoulder to cry on. A beautiful accessory to hang off their arms. A special treat to celebrate. You are whatever they want you to be."

"So just another day in the salt mines," Jane said.

Olivia gave us another look. "I'll be around if there are any problems."

"Great." The biggest problem I could see was not gaining any intel from this venture. The next biggest problem would be running into Jeff Stark. I hadn't been able to shake the thought since Petrocelli brought it up. Deep down, I knew he'd show. Hopefully, he wouldn't start screaming entrapment and police brutality again.

"This ought to be fun." Jane gave me a look. "Last night was challenging enough. I'm not sure what tricks we have left to keep from turning tricks."

"We'll figure it out. We always do." Tactical support and backup were close. If this turned into a break glass situation, the place would be raided. Before that happened, I might pull the fire alarm. That would provide the same benefits without compromising the op. Though, our pals at the fire department might not see it that way.

We found seats at the corner of the bar. Despite all the negatives, this third phase was better than I imagined. We were in a ritzy, posh lounge with comfortable seats, an elegant bar, and the crème de la crème of potential suspects.

"What happens if we find the mayor or some other highly ranked government official in a compromising position with an equally high-end call girl?" I asked.

"We make sure to arrest his ass. That'll teach him for instituting this ridiculous crackdown initiative," Jane whispered before letting out a giggle and crossing her legs. "You know what will suck balls?" She sipped her seltzer. "If there's a gorgeous mogul who actually wants a real date and not one he has to pay for by the hour."

"If he's that gorgeous and rich, he wouldn't be here."

"You mean this so-called convention isn't a meeting of rich, handsome, ambitious men?"

"I doubt it, but if that's the case, I'll pass the handsome, desperate ones off to you."

She grinned, keeping her voice down. "Goodbye, gun and badge. Hello, Dolce and Gabana."

I laughed like any paid party girl. The more fun it looked like we were having, the more someone would want to join in. Of course, our conversation wasn't appropriate and could compromise everything, so I dug into the fabricated profile and changed topics to the best places to get knock-off designer stilettos.

A few minutes later, the doors opened and more than twenty men entered. They didn't dawdle, moving around the room as if they'd done this before, which they probably had. This was worse than I imagined. We were like livestock being sold at market.

I studied each of them, making flirty bedroom eyes while I committed their faces to memory. By the end of this, I hoped to put all of them behind bars.

"Make sure to pass the hot ones off to me," Jane said. "While you're at it, make sure they don't have wedding rings either."

"You really want a lot," I teased, aware she was sizing up our suspects too.

The staticky voice in my ear told us to stop yapping and pay attention. At least our radio communications were up and running. We remained at the bar, watching and waiting for something to happen. Gradually, men would strike up conversations or disappear with Sinclair's escorts.

Since we were inside a hotel, disappearing with a date wasn't suspicious, particularly when the girls weren't dressed like hookers. Other teams would maintain eyes on them and see what happened. With any luck, no one would be trafficked or disappeared on my watch without us noticing. We needed to find out who was behind this, where the women were being taken, and how they were being moved.

"Evening," a gentleman said, plucking a champagne flute from a nearby tray, "you ladies appear shy. I don't recall seeing either of you before."

"We're new," Jane said.

"You're virgins, so to speak." He studied the two of us for a few moments. "I'll take you both." With a flick of his wrist, he made a gesture that caused Olivia to appear out of thin air. They exchanged a few quiet whispers. Then she gave us a knowing look and practically shoved us out of the room after the man who purchased our companionship. "I'm staying in the executive suite." He led us to a private elevator.

"Nice," Jane muttered. "We value privacy."

"As do I," he replied. "You may address me as Ace. No real names. No personal information. I value discretion."

"Sure," I said. "Why else would you have the executive suite?"

At least now information was being relayed to our team concerning our whereabouts. They'd want to bust the banquet hall and whatever escapees they could find with their pants down in the distant future. In the meantime, Jane and I were supposed to get as much information as we could concerning Ace's arrangement with Madam Sinclair and anything else he could tell us about what really went on at these events.

"So, sugar," Jane cooed in his ear, taking the lead like any professional would, "what did you have in mind? I'm usually a solo act. Are you sure you're up to handling both of us?"

"I'll choose not to view that as an insult," he said, "and you aren't here for my entertainment. You're to cater to my business partners. I thought a nice bonus would ensure we close the deal, so don't disappoint me."

"Of course not," I replied, following him down the corridor to the suite with Jane hanging on his shoulder.

"Any reason you picked us?" Jane blew in his ear. "Maybe you want a taste before your friends get here."

"My associate likes fresh blood. He never does the same girl twice." He unlocked the door and let us inside. "Olivia said she picked the two of you out yesterday for this exact reason. You were chosen for him."

"Wonderful." I examined the room for escape routes and contraband. "I'll powder my nose in the meantime." I went into the bathroom and updated our support team while Jane kept Ace distracted.

Before I exited, a new voice boomed from the next room. It didn't sound like Ace's business associate was thrilled by his special bonus gift. Carefully, I opened the door.

"What about her?" the man asked, pointing at me. "Will she do?"

Jeff Stark stood near the door. The man beside him had the scruffy start of a beard with uncharacteristically long hair and undeniable piercing blue eyes.

"You've got to be kidding me." Stark stared at me. "Who the hell are you?"

"What?" I asked, playing dumb.

"Your name, sweetheart," Stark hissed. "What is it?"

"Jessica Evans."

"And you?" Stark turned to Jane.

"Janet Greene," she said.

"Are you working with the cops?"

I let my jaw drop. "You. You're the reason I got arrested the other day. That was your fault."

"My fault?" Stark stared at me. "You're a fucking cock tease." He sneered. "I'm leaving. She's probably a cop. We're all gonna get busted again, aren't we?"

"She works for Sinclair," the man who selected us from downstairs said.

Stark turned to him. "Are you sure about that?"

"I'm positive."

Michael glanced up from the bar where he was studying the bottles of liquor. "What do you want to do?"

When Stark glanced in Michael's direction, I pulled the earpiece out, fearing he may want to search me, and dropped it behind the couch cushion. My pulse pounded in my ears. A part of me wanted to call it. Support teams would burst through the door. They'd pull me and Jane out, and Michael would be brought in, except we didn't have whatever we needed on the syndicate to close the case. So I had to play it cool.

"They're paid for," the man said. "If you're not interested in Jessica, maybe you'd be okay with Janet."

"What do you say, handsome?" Jane asked. "You look like you could use some stress management."

Stark looked around. "This doesn't feel right."

"All right." Michael put down the drink he had poured. "Let's get out of here."

"Good riddance," I said.

Stark stormed toward me. Michael tensed behind him but didn't make a move. However, I could read my boyfriend's thoughts loud and clear. *What the fuck are you doing, Lexie?*

Stark shoved me against the wall, like he had in the motel. He put his hands all over me, presumably searching for a wire, but with the thin, skintight material of my gown, he would have seen one if it was there.

Michael stared into my eyes while I waited for Stark to finish.

"I'd say groping costs extra, but I've already gotten paid." I tore my gaze away from Michael and looked into Stark's eyes. "Have you changed your mind?"

He scrutinized the costume jewelry I wore, searching for a camera or microphone, but that's not where we hid such things. We weren't spies or Feds. Vice didn't get to use that kind of equipment usually.

"I'm feeling left out over here," Jane said, her tone

indicating she didn't like this situation any better than Michael did.

Stark grabbed my chin and forced me to look at him.

Michael took a step forward. "If you're worried what will happen, I'd be willing to risk my luck with her."

Stark stared at me for a long moment before letting go. "I'm leaving. Do what you want."

"Sir, please," the man who selected us followed Stark out of the room and down the hallway.

"Are you okay?" Michael asked.

I nodded.

"I have to go." He gave me a look that was a cross between my Michael and the asshole he was pretending to be. "Until next time."

"Yep."

The sound of the door slamming made me jump. We didn't have long. Either the man from downstairs would return or Olivia would. I shoved the couch cushions out of the way until I found the earpiece and tucked it back into my ear and made sure my hair covered it.

Jane kept an eye on the door. "That didn't go as planned."

"No, it didn't."

She went to the bar, poured a few drinks, and pressed the glass against her lips, leaving a half moon red smear on the rim before repeating the process on another glass. Then she poured a good portion of the bottle down the drain and swished some of the liquor in her mouth before spitting it out.

By the time Olivia showed up, it looked like Jane and I were having our own private party. "What's going on here?" Olivia asked.

"The guys left. They thought it was a setup," I said.

After I explained my version of the situation, she nodded a few times. "Things happen. It's fine. We'll find someone else for you to entertain. Let's go back to the banquet hall."

The three of us went out the door but only made it halfway down the corridor when Det. Petrocelli came out of the elevator dressed to the nines. "Are they available?" he asked. "I arrived a little late and no one downstairs is doing it for me."

"Which do you want?" Olivia asked.

"Both."

She gave him an inquisitive look, as if realizing she didn't know who he was, but Petrocelli pulled out a card and what looked like a crypto wallet and handed it to her. "That should cover it. I'll return them by the morning."

"Very good, sir." She looked at the two of us. "Have fun."

Petrocelli led us to one of the rooms, slid a card, and urged us inside.

"What's going on?" I asked.

"You might have been right, Lexie. There's a reason Jeff Stark keeps popping up everywhere you go."

TWENTY-FIVE

"We received some new intel." Petrocelli had swept the room. No one was eavesdropping on us. It was secure, even if the rest of the hotel wasn't. "It turns out the syndicate is hoping to strike a deal with Stark. We don't have a firm grasp on exactly what our Procurer is trying to procure, but it's big and bad."

"Like the world's largest dildo?" Jane asked.

"No, like something that will go boom."

"The weapons deal," I said. "Vargas was buying, not selling. He wants artillery. Do we know why?"

"Intel's fuzzy," Petrocelli said.

"How did we get this intel?" I asked. Michael had been in the room with Stark. I didn't think he detoured to make a drop or have a debrief. Then again, maybe he left a note for one of the undercovers to pick up. I had no way of knowing. All I knew was he didn't say anything to me. I played the encounter over again in my head, but the only thing I got from Michael was he wanted me to be careful and he didn't like Stark touching me. In fact, he didn't like Stark anywhere near me.

"A few sources. A couple of informants had half-stories that coincided." Petrocelli gave the king size bed a look before opening the closet and pulling out the spare pillow and blanket.

"What about word from our inside man?" I asked.

"You'd know better than I would."

Jane looked from Petrocelli to me. "Who's working for us?"

I didn't want to say, so I stared at Petrocelli. He knew a lot more than I did. He could make the call.

"It doesn't matter," he said.

Jane stared at me. "After everything, you don't trust me, Lex?"

I had said the same thing to Michael. "It's not that." And he had said that to me. Wow, how quickly I had fallen off that high horse of mine.

"It could compromise the op." Petrocelli looked around. "But you're just as much a part of this now as anyone else. Welcome aboard, Officer Reeve."

"Jane," she said, waiting for an answer.

Petrocelli turned, giving me the go-ahead.

"Stark's accomplice. The other man—"

"The one who looked like he'd rip Stark's head off if he tried to do something to you?" Jane asked.

"Yeah."

She snorted. "I figured as much with the way you hid the earpiece and retrieved it. You've worked together before, I take it."

"Uh-huh."

Jane gave me a look which meant I'd have to tell her the rest of the story one of these days, but that wasn't today. "Okay, so we have someone planted close to Stark. We know he's hoping to get weapons to Antonio Vargas. How does that explain Stark stalking Lexie?"

That's what I wanted to know too. "This isn't about supply lines, is it?" I asked.

Petrocelli shook his head as he spread the sheet and blanket out on the couch. "The Feds have been hearing whispers that an overseas dealer is about to move something very large and very scary."

"Again with the dildo," Jane said.

The look on Petrocelli's face made me want to laugh, but now wasn't the time. Though, if I had my camera handy, a snapshot of that would have been priceless.

"The intel suggests whatever the dealer is hoping to sell is what Stark is planning to buy, but to close the deal, Stark has to deliver a lot of cash and something far more valuable." Petrocelli didn't say it, but I could read between the lines and see the utter disgust on his face.

"How many sex slaves does he want?" I asked.

"I don't know the exact number, but it was described to me as a smorgasbord. This asshole dealer is building a harem and wants to sample a little of everything."

Jane shivered. "That's fucking sick."

"All of this is fucking sick," I said. The man who had selected Jane and me from the banquet hall had said we were chosen for a reason. "Stark went to Madam Sinclair to help him procure the items necessary to make the trade."

"That's what we think." Petrocelli finished making up the couch and sat down.

"Why me?" I asked.

"You're the classic Mediterranean beauty." He turned to Jane. "And you're America's sweetheart. The girl next door."

"How many women has this guy already collected?" Jane asked.

"We don't know."

She let out a string of expletives. "We have to stop him. We can't let him do this. I don't want to see anyone get trafficked or sold. Not on my watch. Not when we're this fucking close. What's the plan?"

"The same as before," I said, "we get taken. We get on the inside, and we stop it from happening."

"With the added bonus of figuring out what the syndicate is hoping to get its hands on," Petrocelli said. "Just remember, support teams are on standby. If it gets too hot, say the word and we will pull you out."

This was a bad plan, but the stakes were too high. We had to see it through. No wonder I hated working vice. "Any reason you're making up the couch?" I asked.

"Madam Sinclair's event will be going on all night. Olivia will remain to keep an eye on things. We can't make any busts, not with Stark here. If he experiences another close call, we may lose him, and if we do, we'll lose whatever lead we have on stopping the syndicate from obtaining," he quirked an eyebrow at Jane, "the alleged giant dildo."

She snickered.

"I thought you questioned Stark when he was being held in interrogation," I said. "Won't he recognize you?"

"I didn't question him," Petrocelli said. "I observed the interrogation from the observation room. And Olivia has no reason to question my identity. I handed her a crypto wallet with five figures."

"Where did you get that?"

"Patrol busted one of the late comers to the party, someone Olivia had never met. It was easy for me to become him."

"Is any of that legal?" Jane asked.

Petrocelli ran a hand through his hair before putting his feet on the coffee table. "I was just following orders." He settled into the cushions. "You ladies should get comfortable. We're going to be here all night."

~*~

The next morning, the three of us left our room. Petrocelli did his best to look like he had a wild night. He hadn't slept much. Neither had I. Jane, on the other hand, had conked out. She could sleep just about anywhere, which I never understood. What I wouldn't give to compartmentalize the things we saw and dealt with with such ease.

The hotel lobby remained crowded. Olivia waited near the elevator, speaking to each of the guests as they left, collecting any final payments, and making sure Sinclair's escorts had been treated appropriately.

Jane and I hung off Petrocelli's shoulders as the doors opened. He had his arms around our waists, a dumb smile on his face while he whispered something in her ear that made her laugh. She pointed to her cheek for a final kiss before breaking free.

I tried to do the same, but Petrocelli kept a firm grip on my waist. He turned to me, brushing my hair out of my face. He moved in close, my breath hitching. He better not kiss me again.

"What are you doing?" I asked.

Before he could say anything, Olivia tapped him on the shoulder. "Do you want to pay for another day?" she asked.

"You look smitten."

He took a step back. "I had a really good time, but I have other appointments this afternoon. However, I wouldn't mind making this a regular thing."

"I wouldn't mind either," I said.

Olivia nodded. "All right. Jessica," she said my cover name as if she wasn't convinced it was real, "it looks like you may have earned your keep."

"Keep?" Petrocelli cocked an eyebrow. "What does that mean?"

"Don't worry about it, Mr. Armanti." She handed him a card. "Call that number to update your preferences and let us know when you'll be in need of an escort again. We'd love to be of service."

"A kiss for the road?" he asked.

Olivia turned to me. "Physical contact isn't part of the contract. That's entirely up to Jessica." But those words felt like a test. Petrocelli arranged it that way.

"Sure. Why not?" I moved closer, expecting the same peck he gave Jane. Instead, he grasped my chin and kissed me on the mouth. It wasn't X-rated, but it wasn't innocent either. It put a sick feeling in my stomach. But this was an act. None of it was real. It didn't mean anything. However, it made me feel like a cheater, and it made me wonder what kinds of things Michael had to do to keep his cover intact.

"Until next time." Petrocelli nodded to Olivia and excused himself.

Jane had made herself comfortable nearby, but this was my show. I hadn't realized everything being a detective would entail. Not once did I ever think I'd get thrown into the deep end, but here I was, doing my best to tread water.

"Come on." Olivia led me to the couches and took a seat. Beside her cup were two other coffees. Jane had already helped herself to one. I picked up the other, examining the creamer and sugar packets before popping off the lid and giving it a sniff. "How was your night?"

"Not bad," Jane said. "A little better than usual."

"A lot better," I said. "What's our cut?"

"Oh, you think you're getting paid?" Olivia asked.

"Aren't we?"

She chuckled. "I told you this was a job interview."

"Well? Did we pass? You heard Mr. Armanti. He's looking to make this a regular thing," I said.

"I heard." Olivia sipped her coffee, her gaze coming to rest on someone across the room. Resisting the urge to look, I waited for her to give a small nod and collect her belongings before cautioning a glance in that direction.

From the darkened corner beside the entrance to the hotel bar, Stark and Michael were waiting. The sick feeling in the pit of my stomach got worse. *How long had he been watching us?*

Olivia stood. "I'll speak to Ms. Sinclair and get back to you." She held her hand out to Jane. "Your phone."

Confused, Jane held out the device, enough of a pro to have everything locked and protected. Olivia tapped hers against it, causing a familiar chime to sound. "That's payment for last night." She turned to me. "Your turn."

I followed suit. "When do you think we'll hear back?"

"Soon." Olivia jerked her chin toward the door. "Good day, ladies."

TWENTY-SIX

After that encounter, Jane and I had taken a cab to a sketchier neighborhood. I didn't think we'd been followed, but I didn't want to take any chances. The support team who'd been keeping an eye on us didn't notice anyone either, but out of an abundance of caution, we waited to make sure before getting a ride back to the station.

Petrocelli had already briefed everyone by the time we arrived. Jane took a seat, but my old partner was being uncharacteristically quiet.

When Lightman finished summarizing everything Petrocelli had told him about the previous night, the head of my new unit turned his attention to Jane. "Is there anything you'd like to add, Officer Reeve?"

"No, sir."

Lightman gave her a look before turning to me. "What about you, Detective?"

I glanced at Jane, but she'd been read in, despite everyone's insistence that officers were not made privy to the undercover operation. "I spotted Riley this morning. He and Stark were still at the hotel." I told them about the head nod.

"Stark doesn't like you," Lightman said. "He doesn't like having unfinished business."

"You left him with a raging case of blue balls," Petrocelli said. "That may be why he's decided you'd make a great addition to his buyer's harem."

Preston rolled her eyes. "Stark chose you the day we busted him. It'd be easy enough for him to find a replacement, but like Dean said, part of this is about revenge."

"Stark has a reputation to uphold. He's the best. He can't let some nobody off the street get the upper hand," Lightman added.

"I didn't do anything. I was a decoy. I followed—"

Lightman held up his hand. "I know, Sarconi. You're not being reprimanded. I'm stating a fact. You need to get into this guy's head the same way Riley has. You need to calculate his next move, or you won't stand a chance."

Thanks, I thought sarcastically. "What is the plan?"

"We wait for Olivia to call and hope whatever your next job is will lead you directly to Stark. There isn't much we can do other than that. Petrocelli made sure Madam Sinclair would view you as an asset. That solidified your cover. In the unlikely event Stark changes his mind, you may be able to get something from inside the escort service. Surely, at least one of her other escorts has been selected."

Jane held up her hand. "Question." She waited for Lightman to look at her. "Madam Sinclair makes money off her escorts. It's how her business functions. It's how she stays afloat. Why would she allow any of her people to be trafficked? That would destroy the foundation of her business. No one would want to work for her and she'd lose clients on top of that."

"She's not getting rid of regulars," Lightman said.

"That's why she's been hiring new blood. Besides Olivia, we don't believe anyone else in her employ knows what's going on," Preston said.

"Right." Jane studied the corkboard. "Sinclair's done this before. I remember vice tried to catch her, but there were no witnesses. Hell, we didn't even know who the victims were. We just got a tip that women were being moved, and missing persons had maybe one or two reports that could have fit."

"She does it to boost her income," Petrocelli said. "I also think she uses it as a way to get rid of any squeaky wheels and potential problems. If an escort gets roughed up too badly or does something she doesn't approve, like attack a client, she makes them disappear."

"She doesn't kill them?" I asked.

Petrocelli snorted. "No, but circumstances have led to several RHD investigations. Unfortunately, no body, no crime."

"That doesn't mean they weren't murdered."

"Financials suggest otherwise," he said. I wasn't in a position to argue. He was RHD. He should know what constituted murder. "Stark, however, is a killer or has people killed. I don't doubt that. This man is unbelievable. He will do whatever it takes to deliver on his promises. That includes taking whatever he wants through any means necessary and killing whoever stands in his way."

"Which is worrisome since the syndicate has tasked him with delivering a massive weapon," Lightman said.

Jane whispered, "Giant dildo."

Luckily, she said it so quietly, no one let on that they heard her. Maybe she hadn't even said it. Maybe I had read her mind. When we worked together, she used to joke we had a telepathic connection. Shaking away the wayward thoughts, I realized I was starting to lose it on account of no sleep.

I held up my hand, like Jane had earlier. We weren't in school, but for some reason, she and I felt the need to raise our hands. Damn telepathy. "What kind of weapon is it? And you keep saying the syndicate. I thought Vargas was behind this?"

"Vargas set the last exchange in motion, but he was acting on someone else's orders. That's what Riley said. We still don't know who is pulling the strings or exactly what this person wants. The FBI is looking into the matter, but the possibilities as to what this weapon is will send chills through you." Lightman glanced at Jane. "That does not get mentioned outside of this room. Do you understand?"

"Yes, sir." She rocked a little in her chair. "Shouldn't someone else be handling this?"

"You don't think we're capable?"

"Not if we're talking dirty bomb," she said.

"No one said that."

"Not in those words, but that would send chills through

me."

Me too, but I didn't jump to her defense. "What did Ray have to say about the matter?" I asked.

"Not much." Lightman stared at the board.

"Jack," Preston said, "you might as well tell them. This is our team now. Like it or not."

Lightman gave her a look. "My team. Not our team."

Preston laughed. "Whatever you say, Jack. But be that as it may, Ray said Antonio Vargas was hoping to get his hands on something that would take out a building. We know Vargas isn't calling the shots, so we have to figure the syndicate has a place in mind. We assume he's looking for some sort of explosive, but we can't be sure."

"Does Riley have any additional details?" I asked.

"He doesn't know, but he's hoping to come up with potential targets. The syndicate is nothing but an overgrown gang. We assume they want to take out their rivals, but they wouldn't need that kind of device for something like that." Preston played with the edge of her notepad. "This situation doesn't read well."

"But Vargas wanted guns. The syndicate wanted guns and grenades and whatever else Ray had stockpiled."

Lightman turned away from the board. "They have something in mind. Someplace they want to breach. Something that will put them on the map." He headed for the door. "I'm gonna check on some things. Let me know when Olivia reaches out to you, Sarconi." He glanced at Jane. "Not a word, Officer Reeve. Remember that."

"No, sir. Not a word." She waited for Lightman to leave before asking, "Is he always like that?"

"No, he's usually worse," I said.

Preston snickered. "Look, go home. Get some sleep. Until Olivia or Stark reach out, there's not much you can do. Stick with the cover vice has for you. Continue to work phase three, and hopefully, Michael will get in contact with more intel."

"Maybe the FBI will come through first," Petrocelli said.

I could sense they were about to have another of their arguments. "All right. Call if you need us."

Jane followed me out of the room. "You left me for

them?"

"I didn't want to work vice."

"Are you sure this is better?"

"No." And now we had to figure out what the syndicate had planned and stop Stark from getting his hands on it. This job was too important to walk away, but with the stakes this high, a seasoned investigator should have been on the case, not me. Maybe that's why Michael volunteered.

~*~

"Did you meet Prince Charming?" I asked.

It had been three days since I'd seen Stark or Michael, but I couldn't shake the feeling they were close, watching and waiting. Stark was paranoid enough that he'd be hoping to find proof I was a cop. Hopefully, that would distract him from realizing there was a detective standing right beside him.

"No." Jane sounded annoyed. "Thankfully, someone arrested the frogs before they could kiss me. The rest couldn't afford me. And that's all she wrote." She sipped her drink, which looked like a cosmopolitan but was actually a much tastier mocktail.

We'd had enough dates with other decoys to appear to be doing an okay business. Not too busy. Most were duds, just like regular dating, but we'd been careful about the men we propositioned and who we let approach us. Any one of them could have been a plant sent by Olivia or Stark.

It was a slow night. We'd gone back to the hotel where we'd encountered Olivia, but it was early. Either she wasn't going to show, or she had no interest in us. To raise the stakes, Petrocelli had called the number she gave him to make some requests, but he didn't want to be too demanding or Sinclair could decide to hire me on permanently instead of letting Stark do with me as he liked.

After all, this business was nothing but an exercise in capitalism. If I was worth more working for Sinclair, she'd hire me. But Stark wanted to prove he was on top. He'd overpay just to say he won. And with what I could only imagine were unlimited assets, given his reputation, fake identities, and legal team, Sinclair would have no choice but to give in. Her pocketbook made the decisions for her.

"Incoming," Jane whispered.

I clocked the men entering through their reflections in the windows. When a familiar presence pushed up against the bar beside me, I wanted to turn and look into those piercing blue eyes. But I didn't. Instead, I studied Stark who stood on the other side of Jane.

"You're like a bad habit I can't kick," I said.

Jane spun, the phony smile painted on her face as she remained in character. "Hey, handsome. Looking to have some fun?"

He put cash on the bar in front of her. "Will that cover it?"

She fanned out the money. "What do you have in mind?"

"Get lost."

"Excuse me?"

Stark jerked his thumb behind him. "Take a break. I want to speak to your friend."

"Jessica?" she asked.

"It's okay. You said you were going to call it a night anyway," I said.

"All right, but text me in an hour." She gave Stark another look. "Don't I know you from somewhere?"

"He didn't like us," I said. "In the hotel room, he walked out."

"Oh." She gave him another look. "Ooohhh. Yeah." She made a face and slid off the stool. "Asshole."

Stark slid onto the stool she vacated, not bothering to see if she had walked away. "Jessica, huh? We never got to names the night we met."

"Blame the cops for that."

"How about I give you another shot?"

"It may be a slow night, but I'm not that desperate." I glanced at his lap. "Maybe you are, but that's not my problem."

"For a sex worker, you're rather choosy. You said anything was on the table, and then you said stop. Is this what you do? Antics like that are a death wish."

"I didn't say stop. I wanted you to wait. I was still

negotiating."

"The deal was done."

Before I could open my mouth to say something else, Michael moved closer. He put his hand on my shoulder. "Come with me."

I jumped, spinning as if I hadn't realized he was there. "What the hell is this?"

"I paid you. You owe me," Stark said. "And since I don't want to collect," he eyed me up and down, a look of mistrust on his face, "my buddy will do the honors."

"He will not. I didn't get the cash. The police confiscated that as evidence."

"Not my problem," Stark said. He stared at Michael, his eyes soulless and deadly. "You want Madam Sinclair to give you a job, you have to prove you can hold up your end of the deal."

"What do you have to do with Madam Sinclair's business?" I asked.

"Let's just say I have her ear."

"You're full of shit."

"Come with me," Michael said, his voice hard as nails. A moment later, something poked against my ribs. He had a gun concealed beneath his jacket.

"Yeah, okay. Take it easy." I held up my hands.

Stark laughed. "I'll have to remember that trick for next time." He blew a kiss in my direction. "The two of you have fun. I'll be waiting."

TWENTY-SEVEN

Michael unlocked the door to a guest room on the first floor. "Strip and get in the shower. I don't want to make a mess."

"Are you going to kill me?"

"I will if you don't give me a choice." He communicated with his eyes that I should listen.

"All right, take it easy. No one wants that. Like I said, my arrangement with your friend got interrupted. I was only—"

"Enough chatting. Take off your clothes."

I raised an eyebrow, unsure if he was serious. In fact, I had no idea what was going on or why he was acting like this. Stark must have had surveillance set up inside the room. That was the only reason Michael would be acting like this if we were alone. "Fine. Help me with my zipper."

Michael pulled his shirt over his head and tossed it onto one of the beds before undoing his belt. He left it attached to his pants, but let the two ends hang as he approached, roughly spun me around, and tugged the zipper down. He let the dress fall to the floor, remaining so close I could feel his body heat against my back.

He pushed me into the bathroom and kicked the door closed behind him. Pressing a finger to his lips, he put the gun on top of the toilet tank, carefully peered around the room, and pulled the door open to the shower.

Unsure what to think, I stepped inside. Michael shed his pants, leaving his boxer briefs on as he stepped into the oversized stall to join me. Without a word, he turned on the water and backed me against the rear wall, away from the spray.

Pressing against me, he wrapped his arms around me and buried his face in my neck. A tremble traveled through him, and I hugged him. An unexpected wave of emotion hitting me.

"I'm sorry," Michael whispered. "Are you okay?"

I nodded against him, afraid my voice would crack if I answered. After giving him another squeeze, I said, "I missed you."

He chuckled. "I had a better reunion planned than this."

"I'd hope so." I forced the lump down my throat. "What's going on?"

"I was hoping you could tell me."

"What's with the shower?"

"Stark's paranoid. I think the room may be under surveillance. I'm not sure, but we can't take any chances. With the frosted glass and running water, we should be okay to talk in here. Just keep your voice down." He stepped back a little, coming to his full height. He ran the back of his hand against the side of my face before gently kissing me. "You shouldn't be here. I didn't want you anywhere near this."

"They sent me to assist vice."

"I know. Well, I suspected." Something dark crossed behind his eyes. "You shouldn't be here. You haven't gone through undercover training yet. This is dangerous. Too dangerous."

"Michael, now's not the time. Whether you like it or not, I'm all you've got."

He gave me a reassuring smile. "All right. What's the plan?"

"I let Stark trade me for whatever weapon he's attempting to obtain."

"No way. That's insane. Who the hell came up with that?"

"I'm not sure. It was a group effort. Do you know anything about Stark's connection to Madam Sinclair? We need to find out who the dealer is or where he's sending these women."

Michael shook his head.

"What about who's in charge of the syndicate or what

they hope to obtain?"

"I'm getting closer. Stark has a meeting set three days from now." Michael gave me the location of a condemned packing facility. "Stark will only deliver to the man in charge. He wants the exchange to be face-to-face. As soon as that happens, we'll know who's behind this, who's hoping to buy weapons, and be able to move in. Tell Jack not to make a move until Stark concludes his business. We have to get them both."

"That means before now and then, Stark has to arrange shipment and collect his payment. Any idea what kind of weapon it is?"

The look on Michael's face chilled me to the bone. "Chemical, I think."

"What do they—"

"I don't know, Lex. I don't know the target. I'm hoping Stark will open up to me. I'm hoping after this," he gestured at the shower around us, "he'll decide he trusts me enough to confide in me."

"His profile doesn't support that. Stark's a lone wolf. He functions on his own. He's never been caught. He wouldn't risk something like that. How do you know he won't kill you once the deal is done?"

"I don't." Michael smirked. "But I have no intention of letting that happen."

I let my hands tangle in his hair and kissed him. I missed him so much, and now I wondered if this would be the last time we ever saw one another again. When we broke for air, I played it off as best I could. "You could use a haircut."

"As soon as I get home."

"There's something else you need to do as soon as you get home."

He rubbed his thumb against my cheek to wipe off a droplet of water, hopefully from the shower and not from my eyes. "You?"

"Well, Stark expects it. You wouldn't want to disappoint him."

The darkness returned to Michael's eyes. "You have to be careful, Lex. What you're doing is dangerous."

"And what you're doing isn't?" I sighed. "Now's not the

time for this conversation."

"You're right. It isn't." He gripped my waist and pulled me closer. "We need to focus on what's about to happen."

"Which is?"

"When we get out of here, Stark will be waiting. You've already established your cover with him. Stay in character. Do your best to follow my lead. I expect he'll want a play-by-play."

"Are you really going to give him one?"

"We don't have a choice," Michael said. "I was thinking our last date night, when we came back from the movies. You remember how that went, right?"

"You want to tell him about that?"

"The setting's the same. Shower. Clothes everywhere. Me not wanting to take my hands off you."

The last thing I wanted to do was share intimate details of my sex life with a psychopath. "Michael—"

"I know, but it's the easiest way to make sure we keep our stories straight."

"You don't think he trusts you?"

"I already told you I'm working on it." He kissed me one final time. "I hate this as much as you do, but I don't think we have a choice."

"We could pull the plug, have Stark arrested—"

"We have to stop the syndicate. That's where all the unknowns are. A chemical weapon could kill hundreds, maybe thousands. If Stark doesn't supply it, someone else will. And we need to stop this human trafficking ring while we're at it. Whoever's offered to make a trade with Stark must have done this before."

I shivered. "All right. We stay the course. You become his BFF and figure that out, and I'll figure out how to stop the human trafficking and prevent the weapon from being delivered."

"That's the plan?"

"Yeah." I shrugged. "Lightman said we work better together. Obviously, the reason this was taking so long was because you needed my help. Now that I'm here, we can wrap this up and get back to our lives."

He gave me a final kiss and shut off the water.

~*~

"Is that everything Riley said?" Lightman asked.

"That's all he knows."

"And you're positive his cover and yours are intact."

"Yeah." The questions Stark asked, the way he watched us, the way he looked, the bastard had wanted to humiliate me, and there was a good chance he'd get off on those details later. There was also a chance he may have changed his mind about wanting to keep his distance from me, which is why Michael had said some of the things he did. But with sickos like Stark, there was never any way to know what they'd do.

Lightman pointed to my phone. "Olivia should be calling with an offer. That's how you'll know he bought it. We'll need that verification to ensure the op isn't blown."

"It isn't," I said through gritted teeth.

"How'd you convince him?"

"You know how," I spat. "Is that the reason you sent me in? You knew Michael and I would be convincing enough to pull this off?"

Lightman gawked at me from the other side of his desk. Luckily, we were having this conversation in private, unlike the earlier debrief in the conference room. Downstairs, no one asked such prying questions. The details didn't matter, only the intel did. "I didn't send you in, Sarconi. Stark picked you. I simply made lemonade from the lemons we were served." A thought crossed behind his eyes.

"You've never seemed pleased when Michael and I work together."

"His feelings could get in the way. I guess this will be the ultimate test to see if the two of you can work together in my unit without sacrificing the case or your own safety. Dismissed."

A part of me wanted to stay and argue. But that wouldn't be the best way to make a good impression on my new boss. "What about the chemical weapon?"

"We're working on it. You'll be briefed once we have a plan. Until—"

My phone rang. "It's Olivia."

"We knew she'd be making contact. Put it on speaker."

I did as Lightman instructed and put the device down on his desk. "Hello?"

"Ms. Sinclair was pleased with the glowing reviews she received."

"Reviews? I thought Mr. Armanti was the only client I dated," I said.

"Not exactly," Olivia said. "Don't worry about it. All that matters is you passed. We have a job lined up, if you're interested. He's a high-roller. You're looking to make a thousand dollars for the night. How does that sound?"

Lightman gave me the thumbs up.

"Fantastic," I said. "When and where?"

"He's hosting a party on his private yacht. Pier twenty-seven. Get there by 8 p.m. tomorrow."

"Black-tie?" I asked.

"No. It's more of a party. Think cocktail attire."

"Got it." I made sure Lightman had a pen. If not, I'd grab one. "What's the client's name?"

"Jason."

"Jason what?"

"Just Jason."

"Like the horror film killer?"

She let out an ugly laugh.

"How will I know him?" I asked. "Will he be wearing a hockey mask?"

"He'll find you. Just provide your name. The rest will be taken care of."

"All right."

She disconnected before I could ask any other questions.

"Find out if Reeve also got a call," Lightman said. "I'll convene the task force and call the Feds and Customs and see what I can find out about this yacht and the owner."

"A private ship would be a great way to traffic unsuspecting victims. Drug them, sail into international waters, meet with a larger ship or helicopter, whatever, and have the victims transported elsewhere."

"We'll stop them." Lightman jerked his chin toward the door. "Get going."

TWENTY-EIGHT

"Listen up," Petrocelli said from the head of the makeshift table someone had set up using plywood and sawhorses, "our priorities have shifted. Originally, this was a phased attack, focused on stopping prostitution. Now it's about to become a straight-up assault." He stared at the two tactical units wearing military-grade Kevlar. "We have reason to believe this party is a front for human trafficking. We don't know precisely how that will happen, but we speculate some of the guests on board will be kept on board after the party ends. When the yacht sets sail, they will be moving human cargo. Once they hit international waters, our hands will be tied, so we want to stop them before that. However, we need to do it quietly."

Petrocelli turned his attention to Lieutenant Peterson who had just arrived. The lieutenant nodded, and Petrocelli continued.

"What most of you don't know is a large cache of illegal firearms and possibly a chemical weapon are being moved into the area. The exchange isn't supposed to happen aboard the ship, which means if we stop payment from being received, we may botch that."

"Payment being what?" a member of SWAT asked.

"The women," I said.

He looked at me. "How do you know that?"

The lieutenant fielded the question for me. "Detective Sarconi, step up here. Front and center." He indicated the spot near the table. "This is one of two undercovers who will be on board the ship. We have every reason to believe they were lured here to serve as payment, along with an unknown number of potential victims. Pay attention to how Sarconi is dressed. She's one of ours." The lieutenant pointed to Jane. "That's Officer Reeve. She'll also be undercover. Again, let's not confuse our own with anyone else at the party. We need their covers to remain intact. We don't want anyone to think they're involved in this. Countless lives are on the line." He nodded to Petrocelli to continue the briefing.

"As I was saying, this is serious. A chemical weapon is suspected to be in play. We don't know how that's arriving. It could be on the yacht or anywhere else. Until that's been secured, we can't let the parties involved know we are on to them."

"How do we do that when you want us to stop this ship from disappearing?" another member of SWAT asked.

"We do the best we can," Lt. Peterson said. "We'll wait for the guests to clear out. Surveillance will be working overtime to make sure we ID every person who steps foot in the area. Any one of them could be involved. But the fewer witnesses, the better. Once things have calmed down, you'll utilize every advanced tactic you've been taught. We'll have jammers to prevent cell and radio signals from getting out. We'll make sure everyone on the yacht is silent. No outside communication. We conduct the takedown as quickly and quietly as possible. And we'll hold everyone. No one outside of that bubble will have any idea what happened."

Given the timing of Michael's meet, it could be done. We had to buy twenty-four hours, but that was doable. The law allowed a little bit of wiggle room. If we dragged our heels processing everyone, we'd stay on the right side of things.

"We have someone on the inside monitoring the situation, but it's been difficult to maintain communication with him. The last we heard, our undercover has infiltrated Antonio Vargas's crew. Vargas is running with a gang referred to as the syndicate. We don't know who's in charge. It's possible a guest on the ship could be part of the syndicate. All we know for certain is the syndicate wants the weapon, and someone on board is selling it in exchange for literal pounds of flesh. Keep your eyes and ears open. Pay attention to everything. If anything sounds suspicious or hinky, bring it to our attention," Petrocelli said.

Peterson took over the briefing. "If circumstances weren't dire, we'd wait to see what happens. Prioritizing the chemical weapon makes the most sense. Stopping it from getting into the wrong hands will save the most lives. However, we can't allow anyone to be abducted. We have to stop the human trafficking ring also."

"There are other risks," Petrocelli said. "We don't know what kind of security is on the yacht or if we'll meet resistance. Furthermore, undercovers are involved. They'll be unarmed. No IDs. No guns. We don't want any of our people caught in the crossfire or taking friendly fire. There's also a chance another detective might be on the scene. He should be able to handle himself, but if you recognize him or if he's arrested, do not blow his cover either. We don't anticipate him being there, but we can't say for certain." Petrocelli pointed to a photo of Michael which had been plastered to the board behind him. "This is our guy. Don't shoot him. Is that understood?"

When the conversation turned to blueprints, possible chokepoints, and areas to breach, I left to get ready. I was already dressed for an evening of undercover work, but I needed to put on my makeup and make sure my hair was behaving. Jessica couldn't afford to make a bad impression.

Jane met me in the locker room where Terri was waiting.

"You guys get to have all the fun," Terri said. "How come I got left out?"

"Be thankful," I said.

"Seriously." Jane sighed. "We drew the short straws on this one."

"I got you guys something." Terri put two small, triangular blades down on the counter beside me. "In case things get rough."

"Push daggers are against regulations," I said.

Jane picked hers up. "I'd rather have this than step foot on that boat unarmed." She tucked it into the side of her garter. "Come on, Lex, don't be stupid."

"I'm not." I picked it up, hating to think how close

someone would have to be for this to be of use. "Let's hope it doesn't come down to this."

"Agreed." Jane nodded to Terri. "Thanks."

"Hey, I have to watch out for my partner somehow since you ditched me for a fabulous yacht party." Terri gave Jane a pat on the back. "You better come back in one piece."

"Always."

A knock sounded against the door before it creaked open. Petrocelli stood in the doorway. "Are you ladies ready to saddle up?" He wore a vest with the velcro strip that said 'police' missing from the front. He smiled at Terri. "It's nice to know you're watching out for your friends."

"You heard that conversation?" she asked.

"The locker room isn't exactly soundproofed."

"I'll have to keep that in mind." Terri gave us one last look. "Knock 'em dead."

"Yeah," I said.

"Please don't." Petrocelli waited until we were alone. "I thought about trying to get an invite as Mr. Armanti, but since we don't know who's on the guest list, I couldn't get approval."

"This isn't a Sinclair party," I said. "This is whatever ridiculous cover Stark and his mystery dealer concocted."

"No shit, but I thought you could use backup," Petrocelli said.

"We'll be fine," Jane said.

"Yeah. We got this," I added.

"Once the place clears out and we're positive the exchange is happening, alpha team will move in. Keep your heads down, and you should be fine. If something changes, if they try to transport the escorts another way, let us know immediately. The area will be under surveillance, so we should notice any suspicious activity," he tugged on the collar of his vest, "but it's best to be safe than sorry."

"Agreed," I said.

"I'll be nearby. So will Detective Devereaux. We'll let tactical lead the forward assault, but we'll be right behind them. Stay on your toes. It may look like a big boat, but if this turns into a firefight or worse, it'll be close quarters with a lot of unknowns. Things might get dicey. Do the two of you know how to swim?"

"Are you serious?" Jane asked.

Petrocelli shrugged. "If it comes down to it, take to the water. We'll have the Coast Guard fish you out."

"It better not come down to it," I said.

TWENTY-NINE

Security to get onto the yacht was tight. I gave my name to the man working the gate. When he radioed for verification that Jessica and Janet should be allowed entry, I noticed the weapon concealed beneath his jacket. I exchanged a look with Jane to make sure she noticed it too.

"Madam Sinclair sent us," she said. "I would hate for our dates to get lonely while they waited for us to enter."

I wasn't sure we should push that hard, but Jane had more experience as a decoy. Still, impersonating a sex worker on Sunset was a little different from pretending to be a high-end escort. However, Olivia knew what we were when she selected us. Maybe Jane's pushiness was called for.

Dammit, stop overthinking, the voice in my head reminded me.

"Is there a problem?" I asked. "Jason's expecting me. Unfortunately, I don't know his last name."

At that mention, the security guard straightened and offered his hand. "Watch your step, ladies."

"That's more like it." Jane smiled at him. "Too bad you'll be working all night. I hope my date is as handsome as you."

"Right through there." He pointed to a walkway that led to the front of the ship. *Aft, starboard, port.* My limited nautical knowledge left a lot to be desired. I'd heard all those terms but had no idea what any of them meant. Hopefully, that wouldn't be important.

Jane and I made our way around the side, passing several

people in nice suits and fancy dresses. Most appeared to be having the time of their lives. Others looked like the corporate types who'd spend hours discussing business instead of ever looking up to see what was going on around them.

"Strange mix," Jane said.

"That's what I was thinking."

When we emerged on the other side, another member of the security team was waiting for us. This one wore a double-shoulder holster. Given how far the barrels extended beyond the opening, I assumed he had suppressors screwed on to the handguns. Did this guy get his fashion sense from *Hitman?* It would explain the shaved head.

"Ladies, Jason asked that I bring you to him."

Jane eyed the bar while we assessed the situation and performed a headcount. "Can't we get a drink first? The champagne tower looks rather impressive."

"And it's pink," I said. "I love pink champagne."

"You love the bubbles," Jane said.

"I'm telling you the carbonation gets me buzzed."

Our conversation delayed the security guard long enough for us to finish scoping out the area. "Jason has drinks waiting for you." He gestured to a doorway that led to the lower level. "Right this way."

"After you," I said to Jane.

"No, after you," she retorted.

"Ladies, please." The security guard was becoming exasperated.

Two other men in similar suits caught my eye. More armed security. So far, that was four.

Jane went ahead of me. I followed, aware of the guard behind me. While we'd been on the main deck, I hadn't seen any familiar faces. Of course, the only mugshots I'd checked out before our arrival were Antonio Vargas's known associates, and of course, they wouldn't be here. If they were, the syndicate wouldn't need to hire a middleman like Stark to procure the weapon.

"It's the cabin to your left," the security guard said.

We stepped inside. The cabin was large, unlike the narrow staircase and hallway. It had several windows on the side, not the usual portholes but actual windows. A sectional sofa appeared to be built into the side, taking up the corner of the room. A nice coffee table and several other seats were nearby, making a cozy seating area.

"This room is nicer than my apartment," Jane said. "Bigger too."

"Why thank you," a man said, emerging from the attached ensuite. "I've always had a fascination with cruise ships. This is much smaller. A personal vehicle. Barely big enough to host a small gathering, but I wanted to maintain some of the elegance and charm."

Small gathering, I thought, *there must be fifty people out there.*

"Mission accomplished." Jane made herself comfortable on the couch, crossing her legs suggestively. "I guess we're here to entertain you."

Jason dismissed the security guard, who closed the door behind him. He gave Jane a polite smile, but it was out of courtesy more than desire or intrigue. "You're Janet, right?"

"Guilty," she said.

His gaze burned into me. "That makes you Jessica."

"Seems the three of us have the J thing down," I said.

"J thing?" he asked. "I'm unfamiliar with the term. Is that slang for something sexual?"

"No. Our names. Jason, Janet, Jessica."

He smiled wolfishly. "Oh, I see. I guess that means we were meant to be."

"I guess so." I visually searched him, but I didn't believe he was armed.

"You're stunning," he said. "Both of you." But his eyes remained on me. "Where are my manners? Let me pour you a glass of champagne. After all, this is a party." He kept his back to me as he popped the cork and poured. As he picked up the glasses, he gave them each a little swirl with his wrist. He handed one to me and the other to Jane. "Enjoy."

"Where's yours?" I asked, hoping Jane wouldn't take a sip since I was pretty sure he'd roofied them. "I'd love to make a toast to the man of the hour. Speaking of, shouldn't we be upstairs with your guests?"

He went back to the bar, picked up a flipped over lowball

glass, and poured a splash of scotch into it. "I thought we'd have our own little party down here first. Is that a problem?"

"Not at all," I said. "You asked for a date. That's why we're here. It's up to you what we do."

"Is it?" The way he said it reminded me of Stark.

"To a point." Jane climbed onto her knees and propped her elbows up on the arm of the couch as she stared at him seductively. "I'm sure Madam Sinclair briefed you on the rules."

"Rules are made to be broken," he said.

"For a price," she said.

Jason fought to keep his face neutral, but a dark look smoldered in his eyes. He wanted to punish her for her insolence, which led to a visceral response in me. But I fought to shake it off. "Ah, a real businesswoman. I see I may have met my match."

"What is it you do?" I asked. "Am I detecting a hint of an accent?"

"I'm in the travel industry. I'm from all over." He snaked an arm around my waist and forced me toward the couch. Once I was seated, he sat beside me and held out his glass. "Cheers."

"Salute," I said.

"L'chaim." Jane clinked her glass with his.

Jason looked increasingly uncomfortable. He sipped his scotch, watching to make sure we drank our champagne.

Jane brought her glass to her lips. She was ready to drink when I bumped my elbow against her, forcing her to spill.

"Sorry." I put mine down on the table and reached for a cocktail napkin. I blotted the spot on her dress. "I was about to ask if you saw that painting. Isn't it fabulous? Is that a print of a Matisse?"

"It's the original." Jason put his scotch down, picked up my champagne flute, and practically crawled on top of me. "I have some other works I'd love to show you. Here," he forced the glass into my hand, "let me take you on a tour."

"Whatever you want, handsome." I brushed a hand through his hair, finding it sticky from too much product. This guy was all kinds of greasy.

He took that as a good sign, leaning in and stealing a kiss.

Even though he didn't use a lot of force, his actions were aggressive. He left the taste of clove, smoke, and scotch on my lips.

"Kissing's extra," Jane said.

"Cool it," I hissed. "Mr. Jason isn't our normal client."

He smiled at me. "Mr. Jason. I like that."

"And I like you." I brought the glass to my lips, pressed them firmly together, letting the liquid wet them before swallowing, so he'd think I had taken a sip. "This is also fabulous. It has a hint of something I can't quite place. Something I'm not familiar with."

"A splash of rose water," he said.

I knew it wasn't that. Who would even put that in champagne?

"Come along. I have more art for you to enjoy." He offered me his arm, and Jane brought up the rear.

At the first opportunity, I poured some of my champagne into a potted plant. Jane did the same. I wasn't sure what was supposed to be in the glass, but he wouldn't kill us. Given how this tour was leading us deeper into the bowels of the ship, boat, whatever, I had to assume it would knock us out or make us pliable to his whims.

"Is it getting warm in here?" Jane asked.

"Yeah, it is," I said, after he finished showing us a mosaic by another famous artist. I fanned myself with my hand. "I think I need to sit down."

He smiled that same wolfish look from before. "Right this way."

After leading us into what must have been crew's quarters, complete with a full-sized bed and dresser, he took our empty glasses and refilled them from another bottle. "Here. This should cool you off."

"The bubbles went straight to my head," I said, spilling some of it, while he steered Jane into an attached room and shut the door. Then he pushed me toward the bed.

"Make yourself comfortable."

"Is the room spinning?" I pretended to stumble. My heart pounded in my chest. I'd faked things up to this point, but now I wasn't sure what to do. This was far from an ideal situation. Backup couldn't breach. The radio in my ear should still be working. SWAT wouldn't have activated the jammers yet, but I couldn't call this in. I had to wait. I had to let it play. If they busted in here, there was no guarantee we'd find the weapon or discover the target or even who intended to use it.

Jason forced me onto my back.

"I think I'm gonna be sick," I said. Worst case, I'd have to knock him out and make it look like an accident. Jane was in the next room. She wouldn't stay there for very long, unless he locked the door.

"You're okay," he said.

I'd read enough accounts and seen what date rape drugs could do to people, so I hoped that's all he had slipped into the drinks and did my best to act accordingly, making my movements sluggish and slow. If he left me no choice, I'd stab him with the push dagger, but that wouldn't work out for this op either. I needed better options. More choices.

He kissed me. "You're stunning."

"Thanks." I tried to push his arm away and sit up, but I couldn't be too precise or forceful. Instead, I let my arm swing a little.

He grasped my forearm, pausing when he felt the rough patches from my recent scar. "What's this?"

"Nothing." I tried to pull my arm away, but he held firm.

The thick makeup did a decent job covering the marks, but the change in texture confused him. He rubbed his thumb roughly against it.

"Stop. That hurts." It did, both physically and mentally. But I wasn't in that liquor store. I may have been somewhere worse. But unlike last time, I had my faculties about me and wasn't outnumbered or outgunned, at least not in this room.

He grabbed the edge of the sheet and rubbed the scratchy cloth against my arm. "You've been marked."

"Hazard of the job," I slurred, hoping he was buying the act.

"How could this be? This is not acceptable."

"I agree."

He got up. "Fuck." Without bothering with the charade, he stormed out of the room and slammed the door behind him.

Jane appeared in the doorway to the connected room, the handle of the push dagger secured in her hand, the blade sticking out, ready for use. "Are you okay?"

"For now." I sat up. "He didn't like my scar, so he left." I wasn't sure if we were under surveillance. I wouldn't put it past him to film his victims. But I didn't see any cameras, hidden or otherwise. "We won't learn anything from in here."

"What do you think he slipped in our drinks?" she asked.

"I'm not sure." I tried the handle, but the door wasn't locked. "But he thinks we'll be down for the count."

"Won't he be surprised?"

I tapped the button on the earpiece. "Jason's not happy with his arrangement. I'm not sure what's going on. We've been taken below deck. Please advise."

"Hang tight. We'll maintain eyes up here. Have you found any other victims?" Petrocelli asked.

"Negative, but Jason has kept us isolated since we were taken to him." I described him. "He's foreign. His accent is faint, but I'd say he's Eastern European. Hungarian, maybe? I can't be sure."

"All right. I'll run all of that. Once we get eyes on him, I'll float his picture to the Feds and see what they can tell us. Be careful, Lex."

The way he said it sounded like Michael. "Yeah, no problem."

THIRTY

Jason's angry voice sounded from somewhere above me. Looking up, I spotted a small air vent. He must have been on the other side of it or near one of the other vents.

Pressing my finger to my lips, I indicated with my eyes where the sound was coming from. Jane nodded, signaling that she would continue to check the nearby rooms while I eavesdropped.

"The deal was for five," Jason said. "One is damaged. The others are of little interest." He fumed. "No. You listen. I delivered. As soon as the last two came aboard, I gave you the location. So you're going to fix this. I need replacements. High quality. By tomorrow."

Five. That meant we were looking for three other women.

"Lex," Jane whispered, "over here."

I glanced behind me, making sure no one was about to come down the stairs, before hurrying to her position. The room Jane had entered looked like the one we'd left. A redhead was passed out on the bed. A tipped over champagne flute was on the floor beside her.

"The rest of the room is clear."

"Watch the door." I knelt beside the woman, checking her vitals. "Hey," I said, "can you open your eyes?"

"How is she?" Jane asked.

"I don't know. Her pulse feels steady. She's breathing okay." I lifted one of her eyelids, which caused her to make a noise. "Hey, there you are. I need you to wake up."

The redhead mumbled something incoherent. The last thing I wanted to do was leave her, but we had two other women to find. I radioed in the details and her condition.

"We're going to try to locate the other two." Getting up, I gave the woman one last look. "We'll be back soon. Keep breathing."

"That was grim," Jane mumbled as I took lead.

"Yeah, well, that's life."

"You used to be more upbeat."

"Not in these situations." The next door led to a utility area. I didn't know what half the equipment did, but it was of no consequence. All I cared about was finding the other two women.

I pointed to the doorway to the left while I moved on to the doorway on the right. We didn't have time to waste. Splitting up made the most sense. Pushing open the door, I found another woman passed out. She was half on the couch, half on the floor, as if she'd tried to crawl away and couldn't quite make it.

When I touched her, she made a noise and jerked away.

"Hey," I said, "I'm here to help. I'm gonna get you out of here." I pressed my fingers against her neck. *Strong pulse.*

"Who?" she asked as I turned her over. Her eyes fluttered. Half the champagne remained in her glass.

"I'm Lexie," I said. "What's your name?"

"Del-ee-lah." Her slurring made her hard to understand.

"Delilah?" I asked.

She swallowed, fighting to keep her eyes open. "Where is he?"

"Jason?"

She gave a weak nod. "He—" She tried to swallow a second time, but her throat was dry.

"Do you think you can move?" She struck me as a fighter.

"Numb."

I nodded. "That should wear off soon. You'll be okay." I hoped that was true.

"Lex," Jane hissed from the other room, "I found another one."

"Me too." I turned back to Delilah. "I will be right back. I promise."

"Please." Her eyes begged me not to leave.

"It'll just be a minute. You can trust me."

I darted across the hallway. The final victim was the most coherent of the three.

"This is Penny," Jane said.

From the looks of it, Penny had put up a fight that didn't end in her favor. Her right eyebrow was split, blood dripped down her face. She had a bump to go with it, and her wrists and arms had the beginnings of bruises. I wanted to kill Jason. He'd pay for this. Everyone involved would pay. I'd make it my life's mission.

"Are you ready to get out of here?" I asked.

Penny nodded.

Jane gave me another look. "How do you want to do this? We can't walk them out the front door."

"We could." I wondered if the security guards would open fire or what Jason's actual guests would do if they knew what was happening beneath their feet. However, I had no way of knowing if anyone on this ship was a decent human being. They could all be monsters, like their host.

"Lex," Jane eyed me, "that's playing with fire. We should call for tactical."

I knew why we couldn't. So did Jane. Instead, we'd need a distraction or a plan B. Petrocelli said I should jump overboard and wait for the Coast Guard. Maybe that wasn't such a bad idea.

"Lexie, I know that look. Whatever you're thinking, you should reconsider."

"Look around. I don't think we have any other options."

I tapped the radio in my ear and waited for Petrocelli's, "Go ahead."

"I believe we may have located all three victims." I told him what I overheard. "When we were going over schematics and blueprints, I remember something about a life raft. Right now, we're two decks below. I passed a utility room. Tell me how we get out of here."

"Hang on."

While I waited for a response, I checked the two remaining rooms, but they were empty, possibly belonging to the guards upstairs. All that mattered was we had located the victims.

"There's a second staircase that will lead to the floor

above. That level is above the waterline. There should be an access point you can use to get off the yacht from the stern."

"Stern. Is that at the front or back?"

Petrocelli chuckled. "Back. The party's limited to the bow, so you should be able to sneak away. The yacht left the dock as soon as you got on board. It's circling the bay, so you'll have to be careful not to get spotted."

"What about security? Jason has heavily armed men keeping watch on things."

"Lexie, you should wait. Once the party clears out, SWAT will move in and assist you with the extraction."

"Waiting is not an option, so I'm coming up with a new plan."

"You need to follow orders."

"I'm the highest ranked officer on scene. That means I'm in charge."

"That's not how the command structure works. I'm sure you read up on that when you were studying for the exam and memorizing the rulebook."

"Nope, pretty sure I'm in charge." I returned to Delilah, who had pulled herself onto the couch. She glanced in my direction. "I'm back," I said.

She wiggled her fingers. "Progress."

I smiled. "Yeah, that's good. That's very good."

"Lexie, answer me," Petrocelli said in my ear, even though I'd been ignoring him. "What's the condition of the victims?"

"Have EMTs on standby."

"How are you going to get them out? There's only two of you and three of them."

"We'll find a way," I said. "Unless you have something useful to say, shut up."

He made a humming noise but didn't say a word. Maybe I'd be reprimanded or demoted by the time I made it off this damn boat, but that didn't matter.

Jane appeared in the doorway. Penny had her arm over Jane's shoulder as my partner half-dragged her toward us. "Lex, I hear footsteps upstairs. I think someone's coming. If we're gonna go, we have to go now."

"Dean," I said, hoping Petrocelli wasn't too full of himself to ignore my requests, "I need a distraction. Something loud and attention catching. Something that will divert the security teams."

"Like what?"

"Gunfire usually works."

"You're crazy," he said.

"I know."

Jane left Penny leaning against the doorjamb while she helped me pull Delilah to her feet. Getting her upright was a challenge. Keeping her that way was even harder. We draped Delilah between us while Penny clung to Jane's shoulders and stumbled behind us as we squeezed our way through the narrow hallway. Once we got to the staircase, Penny sunk to the floor.

"I have to go back for the redhead," I said. "We can't leave her."

More footsteps sounded from above.

"Lexie," Jane warned, "there isn't time. Backup—"

"Stay here." I tapped my ear. "Where's that distraction, Dean?"

"Again with Dean?" he asked. "I didn't realize we were that friendly."

"You've been calling me by my first name this entire op. It's only fair."

"That was to protect your identity."

"Sure, it was." I raced down the hallway. Each footstep that sounded from above sent a surge of adrenaline through me. "Where's that gunfire?"

"What do you want me to do?"

"Fire a few shots and get the hell out of there." The staging area wasn't that close. A random shot or two wouldn't give away our operation. Even if it did, no arrests would be made. Nothing would be compromised. At least, I didn't think so. If Jane and I got the women off the boat without police intervention, without the use of jammers or anything else, it'd look like we escaped. The op would remain in play, and once we had the chemical weapon, Stark, and the syndicate's mysterious leader in custody, we could scoop up Jason. I hoped he'd get extradited and rot in a foreign prison. Theirs were worse than ours.

I moved into the bedroom where I'd found the redhead. She remained breathing, but she was out. She was about my size, but that didn't matter. We had to go. Now.

Bending down, I grabbed her arm, threw it over my shoulder and reached for her leg and twisted my arm around it. Once I had her in the proper position for a fireman's carry, I stood. My knees weren't too happy, neither were my quads or glutes. I'd have to remember to do more weighted squats in the future.

As quickly as I could, I scurried down the hallway. To be fair, molasses dripping out of a jar moved faster than I did. Voices were on the staircase behind me.

"Dean," I hissed.

The voices abruptly stopped. Then I heard a very distinct, "What was that?"

"They've been alerted. They'll be looking everywhere. We have a raft waiting for you on the other side. In the dark, they'll be less likely to notice. Go now," he said.

"Okay," I grunted, struggling to pick up the pace.

By the time I reached the other staircase, two men in blackout tactical gear were waiting for me. They took the woman off my back and carried her the rest of the way.

"Reeve?" I asked.

"We got her and the other two victims," a member of SWAT said.

I dropped down the rope ladder and into the waiting raft. We maneuvered around the pier and set out for the other side of the dock. By the time we reached the far end, the command center had packed up. Only surveillance units remained.

"Let's get them to the hospital. No lights or sirens until we're out of range," I said.

"Yes, ma'am." They loaded the redhead into the back of the van, along with Delilah and Penny.

"You'll be okay," I said, climbing in beside them and pulling the doors closed.

Jane nodded to me. "That detective shield suits you."

"I'm not sure Petrocelli feels the same way."

She snickered. "Who asked him?"

THIRTY-ONE

I sat in a private waiting area. The brass decided it'd be best if no one spotted me. Petrocelli was on the phone. Jane sat beside me and poked my thigh.

"What are you thinking?" she asked.

I jerked my chin toward the pacing Petrocelli. "The stakes are so high. What if I made the wrong call?"

"Do you think you did?"

"I don't know. The only thing I know for certain is we had to get them out of there. The longer they were stuck there, the worse it'd be."

"Penny was conscious. They may blame her."

"Maybe." I leaned forward, resting my forearms on my knees. "Our surveillance unit lost sight of Stark days ago, but it sounds like he already picked up the weapon."

"You mean the giant dildo."

I turned, knowing Jane's odd sense of humor was meant to cheer me up, but it didn't. "This is serious."

"I know," she said. "So was the situation we were in."

"I couldn't let them stay there. I just couldn't."

"That was the right call, Lex. No one will blame you for that."

"He might."

She followed my gaze to Petrocelli. "Fuck him."

Petrocelli tucked the phone into his pocket and took a seat beside me. "That was Lt. Peterson."

"Are you asking for my badge and gun?"

Petrocelli gave me a confused look. "Why would I? If anything, you may get a commendation for your heroic behavior. Not only did you get the victims to safety, but you made sure the op remained in play. The five of you slipped away. No tactical intervention. No arrests. Even if the yacht had security cameras, the two SWAT members who came on board had jammers. They weren't seen, and even if they were, they wore no insignias, no nothing. Jason won't know who they are. He may even think they're private security for Madam Sinclair."

"Why would Sinclair renege on the deal?"

"Why wouldn't she?" Petrocelli asked. "She gets paid and gets the merchandise back. That'd be a win-win."

"They're people," I snapped.

He held up his palms. "I didn't mean to suggest otherwise."

"It sounded like it."

"I apologize."

I sighed, hating that I was questioning my instincts and the rescue. "Do we have any idea who Jason called?"

"Our best guess is Stark or Sinclair, but we don't know. We still haven't gotten an ID on Jason yet."

"What's taking so long?"

"The yacht is registered to a foreign corporation. It'll take some time to get a name."

"I doubt Jason's even his name," Jane said.

"Probably not," I agreed. Waiting for the doctors was making me crazy. Getting up, I pulled out my phone and dialed my best friend. Unlike the last time I called, she answered. "Hey, Amber, I need a favor. Three women were brought into the ER. They have police protection assigned to them. They were drugged, at least one was assaulted. Is there any way you can fast-track us as to their conditions and the type of drugs used?"

"Where are you?" she asked.

I gave her the room number.

"Lexie," I could hear the frustration and concern in her voice, "let me see what the hold-up is with the lab. I'll talk to you in a minute."

Twenty-five minutes and a cup of coffee later, Amber

joined us. She raised an eyebrow at my cocktail dress. "You were there?" She moved toward me, checking my eyes before lifting my wrist and examining the inside of my forearm which was a little red from Jason's attempts to remove the makeup. "Did they drug you too?"

"No, I'm fine."

Amber handed me the report before turning to Jane. "I thought you and Lex broke up."

"You know how break-ups go," Jane said. "Someone always makes a two a.m. booty call."

Amber turned back to me. "We are going to talk about this later."

"I tried calling, but you didn't answer."

"Leave a text or voicemail next time."

"Every time I leave you a voicemail you tease me and make grandma jokes."

Amber growled at me. "Leave a voicemail. What does Ri—"

I gave her a sharp look, barely resisting the urge to slap my hand over her mouth. "They don't know," I hissed.

She looked over my shoulder, noticing Detective Petrocelli for the first time. Leaving me with the report, she strode up to him and held out her hand. "Hi, I'm Amber. This is my hospital. That," she pointed at me, "is my best friend. So you're gonna tell me what the hell is going on."

I skimmed the reports while Petrocelli did his usual answering questions with questions bit. The man wouldn't give an inch if he didn't want to. After I was finished reading, I cut in, saving both of them from what would turn into an unending staring contest.

"They were drugged with a GHB, ketamine concoction. This looks pretty standard and not hard to come by," I said.

Petrocelli took the toxicology reports from me. He scanned the details before turning to Amber. "Can I question the patients?"

"Go ahead."

Petrocelli jerked his chin toward the door. "Let's go, Detective."

"I thought I had to stay here," I said.

"Do you plan on living here now?" he asked.

"No."

"Then come on. We've locked down this place. No one who isn't supposed to be here is allowed anywhere on the premises. You don't have to worry about being spotted, at least not here."

Detective, Amber mouthed as I followed Petrocelli out the door. Before it shut behind me, I could hear her asking Jane what was going on.

"I'm sorry about that," I said.

"It's fine. Friends are supposed to act like that," he said. "They should always have your back."

"Are you and your pals like that?"

He stared straight ahead.

"Come on, you must have friends."

"Who has time?" He glanced at me. "No offense."

"I feel sorry for you."

"Don't."

It didn't take long to question the two victims who were conscious. The redhead was stable, but she had yet to wake up. Unlike the others, she had consumed two glasses of champagne before the drugs hit her, and then they hit hard. Penny hadn't touched the stuff. She was clean and sober and didn't want to get derailed, despite Jason's best attempts.

"That's when he tried to force me to drink," she said. "I knew I was in trouble. I had to get out of there. I came up with an excuse that I thought would have worked, but he didn't buy it. That's when he attacked me. He tried to force himself on me. I fought hard. I did the best I could." She sneered. "This isn't the first time something like this has happened. I wouldn't make it easy for him. He didn't like that. He said he'd train me, and then he locked me in that room."

"But he didn't—" Petrocelli started to ask.

"No," she said.

I gave her hand a squeeze. "Good."

"What about the others?" she asked.

"As far as we know, he knocked them out and left them alone."

"Do you know what he wanted? Was he going to kill us?" she asked.

Petrocelli stopped me from answering. "We're still investigating."

A bitterness came over her. "I know what that means. He walks and we get blamed."

"No," I said. "You have my word. He will be locked up for a very long time."

She studied me closely. "Okay."

After we concluded the interview and spoke to Delilah, who didn't remember much of anything except arriving at the party, taking a sip, and realizing she was in peril, Petrocelli drove Jane and me back to the station. None of us had much to say. The circumstances were too bleak.

After he parked, I waited for Jane to open the back door and let me out. Once inside, we returned the equipment to the AV department, changed in the locker room, and returned our wardrobe to vice.

My thoughts drifted to Michael. What was he doing with Stark? Was he safe? Did they have the weapon? Were any of us safe? Deciding not knowing would drive me crazy, I went in search of answers.

As I pushed open the door labeled *Gangs*, I spotted Kemper and Hawking. All the detectives were gone for the night.

"What's going on?" I asked. "What are you two doing here?"

"Filling in. Warming seats," Kemper said.

"Where is everyone?"

"There was an incident downtown. We don't know the details, but something happened. Lightman and Preston were the only two here, and they took off. They asked us to man the phones and notify them if any intel came in." Hawking flipped through the sticky notes. "We haven't heard a peep."

"Any idea what's going on?" Kemper asked.

I shook my head. "Do me a favor, call me with those updates too."

"I guess we don't have a choice, since you're a gangs detective now and all." He nodded at my badge.

"Yeah." But I wasn't in the mood to celebrate. "I'll see you guys later."

THIRTY-TWO

When I unlocked my apartment, I knew something was wrong. A trail of dirt had been tracked from my front door to my bathroom. Someone was here.

Drawing my gun, I took a steadying breath and tiptoed toward the bathroom. The lights were on inside. Whoever it was had made himself comfortable. For a moment, I wondered if it could be Amber or one of my relatives, but no one would show up at my place uninvited, not if they wanted to live.

Bracing myself, I pressed my back against the wall and leaned around the doorjamb. "Police," I announced, drawing on the large figure in front of my vanity. "Put your hands in the air."

The man did as I said. "Take it easy, Lex. It's only me." Michael's voice was barely a whisper.

"Michael?" I tucked the gun at the small of my back. "What are you doing here? What's going on?" As soon as I got closer, I could see what had brought him here.

Michael had been beaten. Blood dripped from a gash above his eyebrow. His other eye was swollen shut. His lip was split, and his face was bruised. "I thought you were in the middle of an op. You weren't supposed to be back for several more hours. What happened? Did something go wrong?"

"Obviously, something went wrong." I was afraid to touch him and terrified not to. "Did Stark do this?"

"No."

"Come on. Let's get you checked out." I offered him a hand up, but he just stared at it.

"No, Lexie. I can't go to the hospital or the station. I'm still in the middle of this."

"This," I gestured at his face, "tells me you were made."

"I wasn't, I don't think. I don't know." He tried to stand but didn't quite make it. I offered him my hand again, but he was too proud to accept it.

"I'm getting really sick of your undercover persona," I said.

"Tell me what happened. Did you identify the weapons dealer? Is he in custody? Is that why you're home early?"

"No arrests were made. We don't even think he knows police were on his yacht. We're working on getting his identity," I said. "He told me his name is Jason, but I'm sure that's not true. Petrocelli's running down the..." I stopped, my thoughts derailing. "This happened to you because of me."

"No, it didn't."

"I'd think you'd be a better liar."

"Lexie, it isn't your fault," he said more forcefully.

"Then tell me what happened." Thoughts of my conversation with Kemper and Hawking came to mind. "Is this why Preston and Lightman left so abruptly?"

"I called them when we made the pickup. I was with Stark, but I managed to sneak away for a few minutes. Maybe that's why this happened. I don't really know. All I know is we went to some abandoned building. Stark told me to stay outside and keep an eye out. When he returned, he had a box, metal, about this big." Michael held up his hands to show me, and I noticed the growing bloodstain on his shirt.

"Michael." My worried tone made him snicker.

"I know. It's okay. It's just a nick."

"A nick?" I stared at him, perplexed. "Like someone stabbed you?"

"They tried."

I grabbed a washcloth and lifted Michael's shirt to examine the wound. He had several bruises and cuts, but this so-called nick was the only one that looked deep. I pressed the washcloth against it. "You need stitches, probably x-rays. What else hurts?"

"It's not that bad. I'll be fine."

"Who did this?"

"I'm not sure. After Stark retrieved the box, we went to put it somewhere for safe keeping. He didn't trust me to go with him, so he left me outside to keep watch again. That's when I got jumped by three guys. It was dark. They had on suits. I guess they thought they were reenacting a scene from *John Wick*. After all, we were outside a hotel."

"That's not funny." I had my suspicions about who attacked him. "Would you recognize them if you saw them again?"

"Maybe. It was dark. It happened fast."

"Hold this." I waited for him to take over holding the cloth to his side before I pulled out my phone and sent a request for surveillance photos of Jason's security team. Thankfully, I didn't have to explain why I needed them. "Are these the men who jumped you?" I turned the screen to face him.

Michael studied the photos. "No."

For the first time since we started dating, I wasn't sure I believed him. "Are you sure?"

"Positive. It's not them." He leaned his head back, wincing. "Who are those guys?"

"They work for Jason."

"Why would they attack me? Stark made the pickup. Their deal was done."

"I ruined that when I made sure the payment walked away. I heard Jason on the phone. I assume he called Stark. He said he expected replacements. That was before we left. I'm sure it'll only get worse. I'm sorry, Michael. I couldn't leave them there. I did this to you."

"Hey, no. Look at me. You did what you had to. I would have done the same thing." He reached for me, cupping my cheek in his hand. "That would explain why Stark was nervous. He knew they'd retaliate. But they didn't want to kill me. They wanted to send a message. This," Michael gestured at his torso, "was the message."

"Jason must have more guys who work for him," I said.

"Update the task force." Michael winced as he reached into the cabinet with one hand to look for medical supplies.

"Let me take you to the hospital," I said.

"No, I can't. We're so close. The weapon is in play now. We can't take any chances."

"When's Stark delivering it to the syndicate?"

"Tomorrow morning. Once that's done, it'll be over. I left a note for Jack and Sam and planted a tracker on the case. Even if I don't make it, they'll stop this." He gave me a weak smile. "You'll stop this."

"Michael," I whispered, fighting back tears, "it's not worth it."

"Yes, it is." He grabbed my hand. "I'm sorry to show up like this and scare you. I had to be sure no one was coming for you, that I wasn't compromised. I made sure I wasn't followed, but this was a risk. A mistake. I shouldn't be here."

"Well, you are, so let me help you." I grabbed another washcloth, soaked it in hot water, and cleaned the gash above his eyebrow. After putting a bandage over it, I grabbed another washcloth, soaked it in cold, and pressed it against his swollen eye. "I'll get you ice as soon as I make sure you aren't going to bleed to death."

"I won't." He leaned forward a little, until the tip of his nose brushed against mine. With his split lip, he resisted the urge to kiss me, but I knew that's what he wanted. "I didn't mean to scare you, Detective Sarconi."

"Now's not the time for that."

He grasped the back of my neck to keep me from pulling away while he nuzzled against me. "I love you, Lexie. I'm sorry I haven't been around. None of this was supposed to turn out like this."

"It's okay." I fought not to cry. "We have more time, right?"

"Right."

I rinsed the cloth and started again on his torso. "What's the other guy look like?" I joked, hoping it would break the tension.

He shuddered as I ran my fingers along his ribs to determine if they were broken. "I think one of them might walk with a limp from here on out. The other two sustained broken noses, maybe a broken arm and cracked ribs. If there hadn't been so many, they would have ended up flat on the pavement instead of me."

"I'm glad you made it out alive."

"Yeah. Me too." He took my hand in his and pressed my knuckles to his lips. The action left a small red stain on my skin. "But I'm okay. I've had worse."

"I'll get that ice."

"Lexie—"

"I'll be right back." I left the bathroom and grabbed a fistful of ice from the freezer. "Here," I placed the cubes into a washcloth, "hold this on your eye while I figure out what to do with that knife wound."

"It's a nick."

"You were slashed."

Michael pressed the ice to his eye. "Y'know, you should ask Amber to give you a job at the hospital. Nurse. Doctor. You'd be great at that."

"I'd prefer not to practice on you. I also didn't work my ass off to make detective to change my mind."

"No?" Despite everything, he couldn't hide the satisfaction on his face, nor did he want to.

"Stop that. I said we'd discuss this later. Right now, I'm a bit overwhelmed with everything."

"Forgive me?"

"For what?" Despite the situation, my mind flashed to Preston hugging him outside that shitty motel room. I knew what Michael and I had to pretend to do to satisfy Stark. Did he have a similar experience with Preston?

"For taking this assignment. For our lack of communication. For scaring the shit out of you tonight."

"Do I look like a priest, Detective? I'm not here to listen to your confession or absolve you of your sins." I finished taping the cuts on his torso. Thankfully, most were minor. He would be fine. Well, if I didn't kill him, he'd be fine, I hoped.

"Maybe not, but the last time I saw you, you looked like a hooker." He smiled, and his split lip began to bleed again.

I ran my hands gingerly over his abdomen and chest, watching for a reaction, but he remained still, staring into my eyes. That look was breaking my heart.

"Did you change careers while I was gone?" he teased.

"You know how much I hate working vice." I stood, rummaging in the vanity for the ibuprofen. While I searched for the pill bottle, Michael got to his feet and scrubbed his hands in the sink. His knuckles were swollen and cut, but that was from the punches he'd returned. "I think it's in the kitchen," I muttered, planning another retreat. Before I could leave, he grabbed my forearm and pulled me against him. He let out a groan of discomfort but held me tightly. I hugged him back. "Thanks for solidifying my cover with Stark. If you hadn't, I hate to think what may have happened to those women tonight." Even if I hated what happened to Michael because of it.

"I'm glad I was there," he mumbled against my hair.

As we stood in that embrace, he began to weigh more heavily against me. I barely managed to cushion his descent as he sunk to the floor.

"You need a doctor," I said.

"I just need some time to recover. I'll be right as rain in a couple of hours." He wouldn't budge, at least not until the assignment was over.

I went into the kitchen, found the bottle of ibuprofen, and filled a glass with water. I brought the items back into the bathroom. Then I went into the bedroom and grabbed the pillow and blankets from my bed. By the time I returned, he had taken a few pain relievers. Hopefully, that would help.

"Y'know, we're not evenly matched." I covered him with the blanket. "When I was injured, you carried me up the stairs like I was a rag doll, but I can't even lift you off the floor." Trying to make him as comfortable as possible, I sat on the cold tile and put his head in my lap.

"It's fine, Lex." He looked up with his one good eye. "Eight a.m. is the meet. Tactical will move in after the tradeoff, and then it'll be over." He sighed and gritted his teeth as he folded part of the blanket underneath his body to cushion himself from the hard tile. "Promise you'll make sure I'm out of here by six."

"Okay."

His one open eyelid began to droop.

"Go to sleep. You're safe now. I'm right here," I said.

"You have no idea how much I miss sleeping beside you."

"Me too." Gently, I held the ice against his swollen eye and stroked his hair.

As the hours ticked by, I leaned my head against the wall, trying to hide the silent cascade of tears that hadn't stopped since he fell asleep. He would moan and let out little gasps, but other than that, he slept. Michael Riley was strong—a fighter. To see him this broken tore at my heart. There was nothing I could do except pray he'd be safe.

It was a little after four when Michael shifted on my lap. I removed my fingers from his hair and wiped my tears away. He opened his eyes, both of them, and even though one of those brilliant blues was surrounded by a sea of red, his strength and defiance had returned. He sat up and stretched.

"You've been crying," he said matter-of-factly, his cover identity sliding back into place and replacing the Michael I knew. It meant he was feeling better. He got to his feet and checked his reflection in the mirror. "See, I'm okay. I said I'd be okay."

He was far from okay, but he'd function long enough to finish the assignment. He was too stubborn not to.

I got off the floor on stiff legs and ran my palms against the muscles along his back. There were half a dozen bruises, all round in nature, likely from some asshole's fist or the toe of a shoe. Michael didn't flinch.

I placed my lips softly on his shoulder blade and rested my cheek against his spine. He found my hands and pulled them around his waist, running his fingertips along my arms. Our breathing synchronized, and this time, the silence between us was reassuring.

He turned in my arms and held me against his chest, tucking my head underneath his chin. He took a few deep breaths, kissed my hair, and released me. He was mentally preparing himself for today, which meant he had to compartmentalize for the next several hours.

"I'll get you some clean clothes," I offered.

He always left a few things at my place in case he got called to work, but since his undercover persona didn't need a dress shirt and slacks, I grabbed the t-shirt and jeans from my dresser drawer and brought them to him. I studied him as he shrugged into his clothing. He was sore, but he had almost a full range of motion. It was a miracle his assessment of his own condition had been so accurate. I wondered how many times he'd been in a similar condition or worse. My internal voice fretted over the likelihood, and I cringed.

He popped a couple more pills and met my eyes. "Thanks." I saw the crack in his exterior. Hopefully, no one else would. He had to remain in character if he wanted to survive. "Can you pass a message to Lightman before the meet?"

"No problem."

"Okay." He handed me a crumpled sheet of paper. "Make sure he gets that."

"I will."

He grabbed me in a one-armed hug. After a few seconds, he brushed past and went out the door before I had time to say anything else.

I surveyed the mess of bloodied rags and bedding littering my bathroom floor and gulped down air, suddenly dizzy. Sinking to the ground, I hugged the blanket and sobbed. Michael could have died, and I wouldn't have known until it was too late.

Relationships were hard, but these last two months were unbearable. First, there had been my close call and now his. Maybe I should have gone with him as backup.

I looked at my phone and called Lightman.

THIRTY-THREE

Stark was making the exchange at an abandoned warehouse not far from Antonio Vargas's old neighborhood. Vargas would be there, along with several other syndicate members and the man in charge.

Stark had his own security measures. Michael being one of them, but Stark was a professional. He'd made a lot of deals with a lot of unsavory people. He had other protections in place. However, Michael didn't know exactly what those were. From what little I knew of Stark, he must have had an insurance policy, some kind of assured mutual destruction should things take a turn.

However, with a chemical weapon in play, the stakes were even higher. A lot more risk was involved. The one thing we wanted to avoid was a shootout.

By the time I phoned, Lightman had already sent snipers to secure the area. The hardest part was setting up in advance without being spotted. That would be just as bad, and it would put Michael's life in even greater danger. But Lightman assured me no one would spot our teams. They knew what they were doing. That made one of us.

Since I was officially part of this, I was allowed to tag along. To avoid drawing too much attention to ourselves, we went over the details at the station.

Surveillance teams had taken as many photos as they could of the meeting place. But snapping shots through broken windows and half-opened doors wasn't the most helpful. However, we had the basic layout, thanks to the blueprints. We just didn't know what kinds of obstacles or booby-traps may be in the way.

"Our main priority is securing the weapon. According to our UC, it's in a metal case." Lightman pointed to a photo Michael had taken. "The tracker he planted shows the case is here." It connected to a hotel where Stark had stashed it. "Surveillance is keeping an eye on it."

"Why don't we take it now?" someone asked.

"We could, but I want the man who's looking to acquire it. Even if we take this weapon off the board, he'll find another one. I don't want to be responsible for that. Do you?"

"No, sir." The officer fell silent.

"Once the case is picked up, surveillance will keep an eye on it, and we will keep an eye on the tracker. In the meantime, our primary teams are already set up around the agreed upon meeting place. If anything changes, we'll know about it and roll with the punches." Lightman nodded to me. "Detective Sarconi was made aware that the arms dealer is not happy with the deal he struck with Stark. If his people show up, they may pose problems. We don't know how real the threat is, but based on events that occurred late last night, make sure you keep your eyes peeled."

The next forty something minutes were interminable while we did nothing but wait and prepare. It was like packing for a vacation two weeks early, except this was no vacation.

"We have movement," someone called, listening to the radio. "Two SUVs just pulled up. Our team counted six men." There was a pause. "Correction, seven. They appear to be armed. They are moving into the warehouse."

"Any visible contraband?" Detective Devereaux asked.

"No, sir."

"What about containers or duffel bags? Is anyone remaining inside the vehicles?" Petrocelli asked.

"Not that we can tell. The windows are blacked out, but," the officer shrugged, relaying the questions and answers from our team to the snipers stationed near the warehouse, "it is possible."

Lightman cleared his throat, drawing everyone's attention. "The case is in motion. Our team spotted Stark at the hotel." He studied the screen in front of him. "They appear to be heading to the warehouse. They aren't deviating." He picked up the radio. "Make sure you don't spook them." He scanned the room for a minute. "Let's head out. In the meantime, I want IDs for the seven men who entered the warehouse. Let's make sure they work for the syndicate. We don't want any surprises."

"Yes, sir."

We were halfway to the warehouse when verification came over the radio. Antonio Vargas, two of his close associates, and three men who used to run in the gang with him were positively IDed. The syndicate was there.

"Is lucky number seven the leader?" I asked.

"Wouldn't that be nice?" Lightman keyed the radio. "We need that last ID."

Five minutes later, an update came over the radio that Stark and the case had arrived at the warehouse.

"Where's Riley?" I asked.

Lightman held the radio to his lips. "How many were in the SUV with Stark?"

"No one. He was alone."

"Detective," I began, but Lightman held up his hand.

"Now's not the time. Riley knows what he's doing. He has his orders. You have yours." Once we arrived in the area, the van pulled into an alley a block away. We'd have to move on foot from here to avoid being detected. I made sure my vest was tight and my gun was easily accessible. Since we weren't tactical, we'd be the last ones through the door, but we'd still be going in.

"Let's move," Lightman ordered, and the tactical teams sprang to motion.

"It's our turn." Petrocelli lifted a long gun and led the five of us to the warehouse.

We moved slowly, remaining in formation and keeping ourselves pressed against the buildings along the way. The assault team silently breached the side doors, flanking the suspects inside. We entered through the back, ensuring no one could escape. Snipers were covering the front. No matter what, the weapon would be contained in this building. Hazmat was on standby and the Feds had been notified. Hopefully, we wouldn't end up in decon showers or worse.

One question played through the back of my mind. *Where was Michael?* I hoped he was okay. I had no way of knowing what happened after he left my apartment. Since Stark came to the meet alone, I feared what he had done to my beloved. That word nearly froze me in my tracks. I wasn't sure how to think about Michael, but after seeing the condition he was in a few hours ago, all the fear, anger, and other negative thoughts I had evaporated. None of that mattered. I loved him.

Several shots rang out. We hadn't been spotted, and we definitely didn't open fire. Who was shooting?

I didn't have to be told to duck and cover. Subdue the hostiles and don't get shot. It always seemed simple enough in the academy, but the scene inside the warehouse was anything but.

"Spread out and take cover. Secure that case," Lightman barked, and we scattered like shrapnel.

Originally, they hadn't been firing at us, but now it was a free for all. Where was Stark? Who took the first shot?

Bullets flew in every direction. Muscle memory and autopilot took over. The two tactical teams had secured positions in the middle of the warehouse. Six cars were parked inside in various states of disarray. A few stacks of tires, workbenches, oil drums, and other metal canisters lined the walls and created a tiny maze in the middle.

I slid behind one of the cars. My Glock was nothing more than a peashooter compared to the weapons the syndicate had, but our assault team was doing a decent job subduing them.

"Shit. The syndicate and Jason's guys are waging war on one another," I said, but no one was around to hear my brilliant revelation. Could Stark have hired a team of mercenaries to take them all out? If only Michael had been able to ID the men from last night.

When something metal clinked against the ground, I squeezed my eyes shut and covered my ears to minimize the effects of the exploding flashbang. In the ringing silence that followed, I stood up, providing cover for the assault team and Petrocelli as they threw four different men to the ground and secured their weapons and bound their wrists and ankles.

"Sarconi, down," an officer yelled.

I dove to the ground as gunfire sprayed the area. Return fire ensued. I remained in a crouch, my gun poised in front of me. More suspects were apprehended. The man who had sprayed the area with bullets was down for the count.

A muffled "clear" rang out from the far corner where an officer had completed a check of an attached room. He stepped back into the center room, and bedlam broke out again.

There were more than seven hostiles. A lot more. Jason's team was at least ten, if I was interpreting the suits and fancy firearms correctly. But there were a few others too. Where was everyone coming from? We had eyes on the building. We would have seen incoming. How were they getting inside?

The assault team began closing ranks, and the rest of us dove for the nearest cover position. "Does anyone have eyes on the case?" Lightman yelled.

I spotted it abandoned near the center of the room. Where was Stark? Vargas and two of his guys had found cover near the case. They were firing on anything that moved. I wouldn't be able to get to it without getting a few holes punched in me.

"Hey, Dean," I said, when he slid into cover beside me, "feel like coming up with another distraction?"

He glared at me. "You didn't get enough yesterday?"

"Nope."

He spotted the case. "You stay here and provide cover fire. I'll get it."

"You just want to be a hero."

"And you have zero experience with WMDs. I'll handle this. Don't make me pull rank."

"No, sir."

Creeping around the car, I scurried to the next cover position behind a steel drum in the hopes of flanking the shooters. Gunfire tore through the air above my head. I ran from my position to the next disabled vehicle inside the warehouse. Taking cover behind the front wheel, I scanned the area to my left and right to see if anyone else was pinned down.

Petrocelli signaled to me, and I nodded. I'd open fire, and he'd run for the case. He held up his hand, counting us down. Once he hit one, I fired at them. From this angle, I didn't have a clear shot, unless they stuck their heads out. As long as they didn't do that, they couldn't fire on Petrocelli and he'd be able to get the case.

I fired, finding they had lost interest in him and had maneuvered around to return fire on me. He rushed the case, slammed the lid down, clicked it in place, and took off for the next cover position.

Realizing their mistake, Vargas and his men turned their gunfire back on Petrocelli. I couldn't get a bead on them. I'd have to reposition.

Petrocelli made it to cover, but he was trapped behind a shelf as two men fired in his direction. They were toying with him while more of the syndicate moved in to take possession of the chemical weapon.

I moved out of cover to fire on them, but someone grabbed me from behind and dragged me into a dark side room that I hadn't noticed. Before I could scream, a heavy hand clamped down on my mouth and nose. I moved to elbow my attacker, but he anticipated my move and easily blocked. I followed with an attempt to stomp down his calf to his instep, but he expertly maneuvered away from that too. Jerking forward, I hoped to reverse our momentum and knock him off balance or headbutt him, but instead, he moved in tandem with me.

"Don't scream. Don't make a sound. They will kill you. Do you understand?"

I nodded. My heart raced as I tried to come up with another attack plan. Slowly, he removed his hand from my mouth, and I spun, swinging. He deflected the punch with his forearm, and our eyes met.

"Michael?" I choked on his name.

He edged toward the barely opened door and looked

outside. "They had a laser sight on you. I saw the green dot. Hopefully, they think I'm with them, that I took care of you. Stay here."

"I can't. Petrocelli's pinned down. We can't let them take the weapon."

Before I could protest, Michael disappeared out the door. Was I hallucinating? Where did he come from? How had he gotten behind me? More shots rang out, cutting my musing short.

I pressed against the doorframe, spotting a sniper in the rafters. Keying my radio, I alerted the team. A moment later, the man who had tried to shoot me fell from his perch and landed with a bone-breaking thud. It was a good thing I didn't have breakfast this morning.

The men who had arrived in the SUVs were down for the count. Only Vargas remained, and he was retreating. The unidentified man who had been with him had vanished, as had Stark. Petrocelli was no longer pinned where he had been.

"Where's the chemical weapon?" Lightman asked. "The case is empty."

"It's empty?" I stared at Petrocelli who had saved the case but not the canister that had been inside.

"Search everyone. Be careful," Lightman instructed.

Sirens sounded outside the warehouse. Soon, a chorus of clears echoed inside. I scanned the room for signs of Michael. He was gone too.

"Are you okay?" Petrocelli asked. He and I were the only two who weren't hauling wounded or handcuffed men off the floor and toward the patrol cars. "A barrage of shots went off in your direction, but when I looked, you weren't there. What happened?"

"There's a room back there that isn't on the blueprints." I jerked my thumb toward it, shaken and confused.

Petrocelli opened the door. It wasn't so much a room as a large storage closet. It had a hidden side door that connected to another area. Aiming his gun and flicking on the flashlight, Petrocelli took lead as we followed the passageway from the closet around the side of the warehouse to a hidden exit. The path continued, running along the other side of the warehouse.

"That's how they snuck inside and surrounded us." He passed along the information over the radio.

I pointed to two men inside a vehicle almost a block away. "That's Stark."

Petrocelli radioed it in as we ran toward the vehicle. We were halfway there when Michael slipped into the back seat.

"Shit." I ran as hard and as fast as I could. The world blurring around me. I'd always been fast. I made it to the driver's side as Stark turned to the back seat with his gun aimed. "Drop it," I yelled. "Police."

The unknown man, the one presumably in charge of the syndicate, had the vial on his lap, his hands on the wheel. He wasn't moving, which was why Michael had been aiming at him, but now that I had my gun aimed at Stark, things were different.

Stark turned to look at me. He could see it in my eyes. If push came to shove, I'd shoot the son of a bitch.

Stark thought about grabbing for the vial, but he didn't want to die a horrific death in a sealed off car, and he didn't know me or Michael well enough to risk calling our bluff.

By the time Petrocelli caught up, Stark had tossed his weapon out the window and Michael had secured the vial.

Members of the tactical team ran up to us, long guns aimed. One of them carried a container to seal in hazardous materials. Michael carefully placed the vial inside before wincing and gripping his ribs.

"Can I go home now?" he asked.

THIRTY-FOUR

I stared at the mugshot on my screen. "Who is he?" I asked.

Petrocelli leaned over to get a better look. "Someone who wanted to cause a lot of death and destruction."

"Not so much destruction, just death." I rocked in my chair. *Aldis Kane.* He hadn't been on our radar. But he was a bank robber. He'd served time and was suspected of having been involved in several heists. The rumors and unrecovered funds on those jobs indicated he had quite a bit of mad money stashed away. No wonder he bought himself a gang. He could afford it. I found several statements he made after his arrest. He'd been pissed. He wanted to get back on top. "He had a target in mind."

"Search teams are tearing through his place now, but I'm sure you're right."

"Twenty says he had another robbery planned. Probably another bank." I pointed to the photo of the vial. It was a hybrid, some form of weaponized chlorine gas. I read the details and saw the pictures. It wasn't pretty. "He wanted to empty a place out so he could go in and steal something. He knows his way around security and is an expert safecracker. He could make it happen as long as everyone was dead or unable to follow him inside."

"You seem certain." Petrocelli gave me a cockeyed look. "Who's your source?"

"I'm just guessing."

"No one guesses like that."

"It's basic deduction. Maybe I'm wrong, but that's how it reads to me." I flipped to the photo of Stark. "They could have been hatching a plan together. Stark could use someone like Kane to assist him." I thought about the scene. "They escaped that warehouse together and left Vargas to fend for himself. Stark wasn't afraid to be alone with Kane. Guns weren't drawn until Riley showed up."

"Okay, so why was I almost shot a dozen times if they weren't fighting over it?"

"Jason." I turned to see where everyone else had gone. "Has he been arrested?"

"Yep."

"Good, go blame him for the firefight."

Petrocelli studied me. "When did you get so bossy? When this started, you were more go with the flow."

"I'm tired. It makes me bitchy. Deal with it."

He held up his palms. "Thanks for covering me."

"Yep." I went back to writing my report and reviewing our intel. I didn't have proof yet, but I knew I was right. Kane and Stark had a marriage of convenience. Each one had what the other wanted. Whatever target Kane planned to hit had something inside that Stark could sell. That's why we didn't find any cash at the scene. It wasn't a payday. It was the means to a payday.

Antonio Vargas, on the other hand, had been picked up a couple of blocks from the warehouse. He had a hole in his leg, which made escaping a little difficult. Despite being pissed, he was too afraid of Kane to turn on his boss, but Lightman was sure he could change that, either with threats or rewards.

The sunrise that morning wasn't beautiful as many people claimed. The sky turned from a dark blue to a dull gray before streaks of golden yellow replaced the gloom. I barely noticed, too caught up with work to look out the window.

At 8:15, my phone rang, and I nearly had a heart attack. It wasn't Michael. It was Jane passing along news that Madam Sinclair had been arrested for human trafficking. Penny and Delilah had provided statements we could use against Sinclair and Olivia Getting. The escort service was officially out of business.

I was glad Sinclair wasn't going to get away with this. She played a big part in what almost happened to those women. After all, she treated her newest escorts like property she could sell. No part of that was okay. It would never be okay. Hadn't we evolved as a species? Apparently not. Greed controlled everything.

A little before ten, my phone rang again. The name on the caller ID sent my heart hammering into my throat. My jaw clenched as I pressed answer.

"Where's Michael?" I asked Preston, barely able to hear over my pounding pulse. "Is he okay? When the ambulance showed up, his wound had started bleeding again. I was worried."

"He's fine. Lightman is driving him crazy with questions and debriefs, but he'll be discharged soon. He wanted me to tell you he's okay."

"Did he mention last night?"

"He just started going over those details when I stepped out. Michael always gets lucky." She laughed. "How fortunate you bumped into him when he needed some patching up." So that was the spin Michael was putting on things. Well, it was no wonder. He didn't want the entire department to know we were dating, even though they already knew. "They should be finishing up in another hour or two. He's still kinda banged up, so after checking in at the station, he'll be going home. Maybe you could give him a ride."

"Sure." I hesitated for a moment. "Thanks."

"No problem."

That gave me just enough time to finish my report. Even though I'd been part of everything, I wasn't invited to interrogate our suspects. Instead, I was told to go home. I'd been putting in a lot of overtime with the vice sting and working for gangs. And as Lt. Peterson pointed out, we had them dead to rights. No one was going anywhere.

By the time I clocked out, Michael had arrived at the station.

"Good morning, beautiful," he practically cooed.

"Michael?" I hissed.

He looked like he wanted to kiss me. Preston came up behind him and grabbed his elbow. "Not yet, lover boy. Go have a chat with Peterson and then Lexie will drive you home."

"Yeah." He smiled, a big goofy grin.

"What's wrong with him?" I asked as he walked away.

"I'd say it's a mix of pain meds and the endorphin rush from everything that's happened in the last few hours. He always gets giddy when he returns from working undercover, but this is next level. I'm pretty sure it's from the pain meds."

"Is he okay?"

"He has a cracked rib and a dozen stitches, but it's nothing serious."

"How often does this happen?"

"Michael getting cut?"

"No. The undercover work."

Preston looked at me like I should know the answer. "Not that often. Frank usually volunteers, but he busted Vargas before, so Michael stepped in."

I moved closer to her. "I think they're working together. Kane and Stark."

"Did Michael tell you that?"

"Shit. Am I not capable of having a thought or theory without someone feeding it to me?"

"I didn't mean that, Sarconi. But that's what Michael just got through telling us. He didn't piece it together until this morning when he met up with Stark again. Stark sent him to meet with Vargas's guys and make sure the warehouse was secure. Michael thought that was strange since the two were in the midst of a deal. The threat should have come from the other side, not from the outside."

"Yeah, that's what I thought too. Jason didn't become a threat until I stopped the party. So I don't think that was their only concern."

"No. They were concerned about police intervention and rival gangs interfering. After all, Vargas tried to buy guns from Ray. They wanted to arm the syndicate. News like that travels faster than wildfire."

"Do we know what the syndicate wanted to target? Kane

was a bank robber."

"Last I heard, it may have been a museum."

Before I could ask any other questions, Michael returned. He looked from me to Preston. "Are you talking about me?" he asked.

"No, the case." Preston gave me a look. "Good luck with him."

"Thanks." I led him to the parking lot. "I never thought I'd see you high."

"I'm not high. I'm exhausted." He chuckled. "And a little high." He poked at his cheek. "I can't feel my face."

"Please don't sing."

"What?"

"Never mind."

He opened the car door, climbed in, and grasped my face in both hands, kissing me despite his swollen lip. It felt like the first real kiss we shared since he began this assignment more than a month ago, even before he had to disappear without a trace. I melted into him, wanting to freeze this moment in time when we were both safe and ourselves. Well, mostly ourselves.

I pulled out of the parking lot and headed for his apartment. He reached over and took my free hand in his, kissing my knuckles, my fingers, and my palm. "These last three weeks have been torture." My breath hitched, and he realized what I thought. "Being away from you has been torture. This," he gestured to his face, "didn't hurt nearly as much as not seeing you."

~*~

I squinted at the clock. It was after seven. The sun had just set. Michael was still asleep. His head was nestled against my chest. He clutched my free hand. My other arm was pinned beneath him. He snored slightly, a result of his injuries.

I shut my eyes and listened to his breathing, feeling his warm exhales against the top of my breast. The peacefulness lulled me back to sleep, and I didn't wake again until Michael stirred.

"How are you feeling?" I asked.

He yawned and rolled onto his back. "A little achy," he admitted, "and definitely stiff." I caught the innuendo but pretended I didn't.

"Do you want heat or ice? Some pain relievers maybe?"

"You," he cooed.

"That's not an option."

"Then let's sleep until the morning, and we'll revisit this discussion tomorrow." He pulled my arm across his chest, and I tentatively laid my head on his shoulder, waiting for him to wince. Instead, he kissed my forehead and snuggled closer. "You're amazing," he whispered.

"Ditto."

I watched the rise and fall of his chest for the next few hours. I had slept so much that I couldn't sleep anymore. His bruises were purple now, no longer the red and blue they had been the night before. His cuts and scrapes had scabbed and the neat line of stitches looked okay beneath the bandage.

"Why are you smiling?" he asked groggily. It was ten a.m. He had slept for almost an entire day.

"Because you're back. Don't leave again."

"I wouldn't, but I have to hit the head." He climbed out of bed and went into the bathroom. By the time he returned, I had slipped back into my clothes from yesterday. "Where are you going?"

"To the store. I need to pick up some things. You haven't been home in weeks. We need food and first aid supplies."

He got back under the covers and made sad puppy dog eyes at me. "Fine."

"Is there anything you'd like?"

"Condoms."

"Anything more reasonable, like hot compresses or orange juice?"

"Some eggs and bacon for breakfast and something for sandwiches."

I leaned down and kissed him. "I'll be back soon." I took a moment to freshen up and brush my teeth and hair before leaving his apartment.

After I bought groceries, antiseptic, bandages, and a box

of condoms, I returned to his apartment and let myself in. He was still in bed. I scrambled the eggs, cooked the turkey bacon, made a couple pieces of toast, and brought a tray into the bedroom.

"Wow, I even get breakfast in bed?"

"Don't get used to it." I sat next to him, balancing my plate on the edge of his tray as we ate, famished from our lack of food intake the day before. I told him about the last three weeks working vice and everything he had missed while he was gone. "What's the deal with you and Preston?"

He wiped his mouth and put the tray on the floor. "We used to date."

"I know."

"She's a good cop. If you're ever in a bind, she will drop everything and be there. Keep that in mind, Detective."

"I will." I hoped he wasn't trying to derail my question. "Anyway..."

"Are you sure you want to hear this?"

I had to know. My trust issues demanded it. "Tell me everything."

"Everything. Jeez." He carefully rubbed his face. "We had a fling. It was casual, or at least she thought it was. I," he glanced out the window, "well, I found that part out when I walked in on her with a homicide detective."

"She cheated?" I hadn't expected the story to end like that. "On you?"

"I'm glad you hold me in such high regard, but she insisted it wasn't cheating. It was a miscommunication. After that, I was done. That all happened a few months before you and I hooked up, but Sam and I are still friends. She was willing to meet to pick up my intel and make it look like a tryst. Sam's always been protective of me. She feels like she has to make up for something. Maybe she does."

"Even now that we're dating?"

"I don't see why that would be relevant."

Maybe it wasn't. "Does she want to get back together?"

"No."

"She never asked?"

He shook his head. "We're friends, Lex. We work together. You don't have anything to worry about, I promise." He grabbed my chin and forced me to look at him. "I know how it looked and what you must have thought, but I won't do that to you. Not now. Not ever."

"You don't know that."

"Yes, I do." But no matter how serious he was, he knew I'd have to get there on my own. So instead, he teased, "Especially in a shitty motel like that. I was afraid I'd get herpes from sitting on the bedspread. Tell me you didn't sit on the bedspread."

"Michael, I'm serious."

"So am I." He shook his head. "I have no problem being partnered with her, but," he flipped me onto my back and hovered above me, "don't think for a single second I would ever entertain the thought of going back to her. It turns out," he looked around the room as if he might be overheard, "I'm an all or nothing guy. One night stands are fine, but I prefer to know what I'm coming home to every night. And I want that to be you."

"Wow, you'll say anything to get laid."

"Does that mean you bought condoms?"

"Yes, but," I gently rolled us over, so his back was on the bed, "you're in no condition to do the heavy lifting." I still had a million things I wanted to ask about his assignment and how he was, but his lopsided grin and sparkling blue eyes weren't willing to wait any longer. "Seriously, Michael," I said as I got off the bed, "are you okay?"

"As long as you're here."

THIRTY-FIVE

"I swear I wish we could stay here forever. No more work. No danger, no distractions," I said.

Michael's alarm had gone off, but neither of us made a move to get out of bed. He had to go to work, and I had gotten a call to check-in with vice concerning Stark's appearance at Sinclair's event. Michael and I had spent most of yesterday talking. He told me whatever he knew about Stark and the syndicate, and I filled him in on the disgusting things I'd encountered while being reassigned to vice. Today, the real world was knocking down the door again.

"We should take a couple of days and get the hell away from here." He kissed my cheek and got out of bed. "It's been a rough couple of months for us."

"You're telling me." I studied his greenish-purple bruises. "How many times have you gone through something like this?"

"Like what?" He looked down to see what I was staring at. "Getting the shit knocked out of me? I've lost track."

"That's terrible."

"It's not so bad. Don't tense up, curl into a ball to protect everything vital, and be a possum."

"What?"

"If all else fails, play dead. Or take a dive and stay down, although that's more of a boxing thing."

"You box?"

"Sometimes. Mostly with the guys from work. I was more

serious about it back in college." He shrugged. "We've sparred in the gym, remember? That's how I kept you from knocking me out in that warehouse. You really should mix up your moves. Although, I'm glad you didn't."

"How did I not know this?"

"Like I said, I have a ton of surprises up my sleeve." He gave me a sly smile. "Do you want to join me in the shower?"

"Another time, slugger. I need to go home and get ready. But tonight, let's revisit that idea of getting out of town for a few days, okay?"

"Great. I'll see you at your place."

~*~

Upon arriving at the station, I was instructed to meet everyone in the conference room for the official debrief. It had been a long three weeks. We'd made dozens of arrests, dismantled some of the gang-run prostitution rings, and taken down one of the premier escort services in the city, or so I thought. And that didn't include dismantling the syndicate, arresting an arms dealer, and getting a dangerous weapon off the streets.

"The man we arrested, known by numerous aliases including Jeff Stark, has once again been apprehended. The case against him is now airtight. In addition to that, we've arrested his associate and have strong leads that we've shared with government agencies to stop human trafficking and international arms deals," Lt. Peterson said. "The mayor is very proud of all of you."

My mouth must have dropped because Jane nudged me with her elbow, and I made the effort to close my mouth. The rest of the room posed a few questions that weren't answered, and the LT rerouted the debrief back to a more practical topic. Until further notice, we were coordinating our intel with the district attorney's office and stuck at the beck and call of the FBI and whatever other government agencies might want to ask us questions related to the string of arrests.

"You did good. Get back to work," Peterson declared, dismissing the room. As I followed the herd to the door, he grabbed my elbow. "Do you have a minute?"

"Sure." I sat in one of the chairs and stared across the table at him. My mind was running in a million different directions.

"Looks like you and your pals from vice had this under control," Peterson said. "How are you doing?"

"I'm fine. It's nice to know we made a difference."

"You sound surprised."

"When I used to work vice, the progress we made was questionable most of the time. Are you sure Stark's not going to get out of this again?"

"We won't let him. It turns out that theory of yours was pretty spot-on. The FBI has taken over the official investigation, but we're positive Kane was planning to use the chemical agent to gain access to the museum. They are supposed to be having an exhibit featuring some very expensive items. Stark already had a buyer lined up."

"They planned to combine forces and make a mint."

"Stark does it for the infamy. Kane has a touch of that, but he wanted to turn his syndicate into an empire. He wanted to give the Al Capones a run for their money."

"In that case, can we get him on tax evasion?"

The LT smiled. "Have you spoken to Preston or heard the scuttlebutt?"

"No, why?" I feared what he might say next. Was I going to have to work for a different unit now?

"If it wasn't for the weapons and Stark, we wouldn't have discovered the human trafficking element that was being supplied by Madam Sinclair's escort service. Even though you were reassigned to vice, you still found a way to work with gangs."

"I guess it's meant to be."

"I guess so." Peterson cocked an eyebrow. "Are you happy there?"

"With gangs?"

He nodded. "After all of this, RHD's expressed an interest. Even though we gave you your badge prematurely, this isn't official yet. You still have a choice."

"Unless Lightman changed his mind, I'll stick with gangs."

"You work exceptionally well with them. Best of luck, Sarconi."

"Thank you, sir."

After I left the LT's office, I detoured back to vice. Petrocelli was packing up the files from the conference room.

"Did you request I transfer to RHD?"

He glanced up. "Is that what you heard?"

"Don't do that."

"Do what?"

"Answer my question."

"Why would I want to work with you again? You're bossy, even if you did save my life."

"I didn't."

Petrocelli shrugged. "So you're heading back to gangs now? I mean you'll be back and forth with the arrests and cases, but your life is back on track."

"I sure hope so."

"And you have no interest in homicide?"

"I prefer to deal with the living."

"I can't fault you for that." He closed the lid on a box. "In that case, maybe you'd consider letting me take you out to make up for these last few weeks of hell."

"I told you I'm seeing someone."

"It's not a date. Just a thank you between coworkers." He slid closer to me.

Before I could say a word, someone knocked on the conference room door. Without waiting for an acknowledgement, the door opened.

"Sarconi, they need you downstairs." I didn't turn, but Michael's voice was unmistakable. He sounded cold and more businesslike than I'd ever heard before.

"Of course." I turned, catching a dead-eye glare on Michael's face. "Are we finished, Detective Petrocelli?"

He nodded, and I went toward the door, watching Michael glare daggers at the other detective. Maybe he hadn't completely shaken the undercover demeanor yet, or he might not be feeling so great. Then again, I wasn't even sure what he had walked in on, but I could only imagine what he must have thought. It was like me seeing him with

Preston, only without the excuse of an undercover assignment.

Just as I went out the door, Petrocelli said, "It's nice to see you again, Mike. We haven't hung out in forever. How long has it been? Six months? We need to get together. Maybe shoot some hoops."

The door slammed shut at my back, and despite the closed conference room, I could hear Michael's voice loud and clear. "I don't know what the hell you're thinking, but stay away from her. Lexie is not Sam. Do you understand?"

Holy shit, Dean Petrocelli had been Michael's best friend and the homicide detective Preston cheated with. My head was spinning by the time I made it to the stairwell.

When Michael caught up to me three minutes later, he pulled me into the corner and snuck a possessive kiss in one of the few blind spots in the stairwell, and that was it. There wasn't anything else to say. He knew I knew, and after the last few weeks, this wasn't the time to talk about it.

After running ragged the rest of the day, I caught up with Jane as I made a final stop at my temporary desk.

"Congratulations, Lex," she said. "You're really moving up in this world. From decoy officer to gangs detective overnight. Next, you're going to be vying for the sarge's spot."

"I'm not sure I want to be the next sarge." I glanced at him as he barked orders and shuffled through dozens of forms. "It's a thankless job."

"And this shit isn't?"

THIRTY-SIX

"Here ya go." I handed the officer the transfer orders. "In a few hours, he'll be someone else's headache."

"Great, one less asshole to contend with." The officer glanced at the paperwork. "Do you think the Feds will keep a tight leash on him?"

"They better."

I glanced down the corridor at our holding cells. Jeff Stark was being remanded into federal custody for further questioning. He stood in the corner, observing our conversation. Just as I turned to head back upstairs, he let out a bitter laugh and called to me.

"If it isn't our little working girl. You never did tell me what you enjoy. I guess I'll have to find out once I'm released."

"You're not getting out of this. But I'm sure your cellie won't have a problem making sure you do exactly what he likes."

The look on Stark's face was disconcerting. "I won't be inside that long. This was entrapment. I'll be out in a few days." His eyes flicked to my name tag and badge. "Don't worry, I'll be sure to look you up."

"Screw you." I went straight to the staircase, ignoring the lewd words and threats Stark screamed after me. "Shake it off, Sarconi," I whispered as I returned to vice to pass off the freshly signed paperwork. "Here," I tossed the sheets on Sergeant Hunter's desk, "is there anything else?"

"Not at the moment. The detectives are reviewing their reports with the ADA, so stay close in case they have any questions." The sarge looked at me. "Is everything okay?"

"Just the usual venom every asshole spews."

"Okay. Thanks for the assist. For the record, I miss having you around here."

"If I could work a desk, maybe I'd stay. But that's not the job." I continued out the door, annoyed with myself for the irrational fear Stark's words had triggered. Almost every guy we ever arrested said the same thing, but I couldn't help but think of the one who recently followed through on that threat. "Dammit."

Pacing the enclosed space of the break room, I dug into my pocket for some change and punched a few buttons, hoping a chocolate bar would sublimate my self-loathing and fear. The vending machine let out a whir but failed to release my snack selection. I was three kicks in when Petrocelli entered the room.

"Whoa, take it easy." He held up his palms and approached cautiously. "What's going on?"

"The stupid machine won't give me my candy." I slammed my shoulder into it, but it wouldn't budge.

"Take a breath and sit down." He waited until I was seated and docile before assessing the infernal vending machine. He reached into his pocket, pulled out a dollar, selected the bag of chips immediately above my chocolate bar, and let gravity work its magic. "See, it's not a big deal." He put the candy on the table in front of me and took a seat.

"Aren't you brilliant?"

"Lexie, what's wrong?" He watched as I got up to pace. "I promise today's the last day you'll be stuck on desk duty for vice. Once my colleague finishes up with the ADA, it'll be my turn. We'll call you in when we need you, and that's it. I'm not trying to jam you up or make your life miserable."

"It's not you." I stopped pacing and leaned against the counter. "I let Stark get under my skin. I forgot he was downstairs, and I took the transfer papers to the officer in lockup, and—"

"And that piece of shit said some nasty things. It happens."

"I know. I'm just pissed for letting it bother me. I'm a detective now, and I can't even keep my shit together over something stupid. What is wrong with me?"

"You're human. That's a good thing." He gave me a look. "Do you want a hug?"

"Maybe."

He gave me a quick hug and released me.

"Thanks."

"Sure." He popped open the bag of chips and offered them in my direction. "About the other day when we got interrupted, I didn't mean to put you on the spot. The offer for dinner was an invitation for you and your boyfriend. Like I said, I'd love to meet him."

I narrowed my eyes at Petrocelli, wondering what game he was playing now. He had to know I was seeing Michael. That was the only thing that would explain Michael's outburst. "I don't like to mix my private life and my work life."

"Does Michael Riley know that?" He crunched on a handful of chips while I busied myself with the candy wrapper. "He seems rather protective of you."

"Everyone in gangs is. I'm just that amazing."

"Yes, you are." Petrocelli picked up his bag of chips and went to the door. "I'll let you know when the ADA needs you."

~*~

"We're going away and celebrating," Michael purred in my ear. He had stopped at the liquor store and bought a bottle of champagne on his way to my apartment. "We have so much to celebrate. The busts we've made by stopping a major prostitution ring and putting an end to an arms deal which would have led to countless deaths."

"That was mostly you," I replied.

"It was us. We make a fantastic team, even when we aren't working together. But that's going to change soon enough since you're the newest gangs detective. Maybe partnering up wouldn't be such a bad idea. Didn't I say you were going to pass that test with flying colors?"

"Yes, but you'd say anything to get in my pants."

"The department owes me some time off after the last three weeks. And I have a nice chunk of overtime coming. I'm thinking maybe you could swing a three-day weekend. We'll drive to the coast and rent a beach house with a hot tub and fireplace. It's off season, so no one will be around to bother us."

"It sounds perfect. I have to talk to the prosecutor and figure out if there's a Friday or Monday they won't need me, and then I can put in my request after that."

"As soon as you know, let me know. I'll book a place and put in for my days off."

I cuddled against his chest, still afraid of hurting him, and sipped my champagne. "Are you sure you're feeling okay?"

"Lexie, I'm not that breakable." He took the glass from me and put it on the coffee table before pulling me onto his lap. "Everything's back to normal. I promise."

"I'm glad." I kissed him, silently hoping to never have a repeat of the other night, and then we made love on my living room floor.

Check out Killer Getaway (Lexie Sarconi #4) coming to Kindle, paperback, and audiobook.

ABOUT THE AUTHOR

G.K. Parks is the author of the Alexis Parker series. The first novel, *Likely Suspects,* tells the story of Alexis' first foray into the private sector.

G.K. Parks received a Bachelor of Arts in Political Science and History. After spending some time in law school, G.K. changed paths and earned a Master of Arts in Criminology/Criminal Justice. Now all that education is being put to use creating a fictional world based upon years of study and research.

Elisa Archer has always loved reading, writing, and romance. On most days you can find her hiding behind a computer screen, frantically typing away at her latest story. She's always been an avid reader and enjoys everything from technothrillers to steamy romance. In fact, there isn't a genre of book she doesn't like. Writing just seemed to be the natural progression of her passion for books.

You can find additional information by visiting our website at
www.gkparks.com

Sign up for the e-mail newsletter for the latest information on upcoming releases, sales, free promotions, and more.
www.gkparks.com/newsletter

www.ingramcontent.com/pod-product-compliance
Lightning Source LLC
Chambersburg PA
CBHW020756250626
47155CB00003B/1106